MEMOIRS OF A TIME TRAVELER

TIME AMAZON - BOOK 1

DOUG MOLITOR

THIRD STREET PRESS

Memoirs of a Time Traveler
Time Amazon — Book 1
by Doug Molitor

Third Street Press
Electronic publication date: December 2017

ISBN-13: 978-1-948142-14-4 (EBOOK)
ISBN-13: 978-1-948142-15-1 (PAPERBACK)

PRAISE FOR DOUG MOLITOR

"You couldn't ask for a finer guide to the future, or the past, than Doug Molitor. Having so thoroughly enjoyed his 'Memoirs of a Time Traveler,' the next book I read is, without a doubt, going to be his 'Memoirs of a Time Traveler' again."

LARRY GELBART, *M*A*S*H, TOOTSIE, A FUNNY THING HAPPENED ON THE WAY TO THE FORUM, CITY OF ANGELS*

"For Pete's sake, do not wait for the inevitable Major Motion Picture! See Doug Molitor's 'Memoirs of a Time Traveler' NOW, as it was meant to be seen: on that giant screen between your ears!"

RANDALL WILLIAM COOK, WRITER, DIRECTOR, AND OSCAR™-WINNING VISUAL EFFECTS ARTIST (*THE LORD OF THE RINGS*)

SUMMARY

MEMOIRS OF A TIME TRAVELER

In this journey through time, archaeologist David Preston comes into possession of a baseball supposedly signed by the legendary Ty Cobb in 1908, thanks to Ariyl Moro and her mysterious companion, Jon Ludlo. Except the ball tests out to be an impossible paradox. It was signed with a ballpoint pen (not invented until 1938) using ink that's several centuries older. But then, Ariyl and Ludlo aren't who they claim to be either.

Ariyl, a voluptuous 6-foot-3 beauty, turns out to be a tourist from a 22nd century paradise where time travel is the latest craze. Unbeknownst to her, however, her traveling companion, Ludlo, is a psychopath whose thefts are starting to alter history. In a world were even small changes in the timeline can cause catastrophic consequences, Ludlo's actions may completely destroy the future.

To stop Ludlo, David and Ariyl must solve a mystery involving Bronze Age swordsmen, modern-day Nazis, a steampunk world, Albert Einstein, some highly skeptical Founding Fathers, and a Golden Age Hollywood where the murder of a beloved movie star will spell doom for civilization.

SUMMARY

Sci-Fi Meets Romantic Comedy...With Sword-Swinging Adventure!

ALSO BY DOUG MOLITOR

Novels

Time Amazon Series

Memoirs of a Time Traveler

Confessions of a Time Traveler

Revelations of a Time Traveler

Chronicles of a Time Traveler

Full Moon Fever Series

Monster He Wrote

Pure Silver

Anthologies

Love and Other Distractions

Hell Comes to Hollywood II

To get information on new releases, sales or free books by Third Street Press authors, like Doug Molitor, sign up for our newsletter.

1

CHAVEZ RAVINE

"History, by appraising them of the past, will enable them to judge of the future." — Thomas Jefferson

ON THE DAY HE DIED, ANDY GRAISE AWOKE IN A LOUSY mood, never dreaming that the greatest afternoon of his life lay ahead. Even if I'd known what would happen, the only way to keep him from his fate would have been for me to kneecap him when I showed up at Dodger Stadium that morning. And what would that have saved him from? Not death. Just early death...but also, his incredible, epic last game.

Now that I've mentioned Andy Graise, baseball fans might assume that this narrative will be about him. Or about baseball. They couldn't be more wrong. Legendary and weird and tragic as Andy's last day was, it was only prologue for the events that swept me up next.

As for Thomas Jefferson, whom I quoted above, he had it backwards. Meeting an insane babe named Ariyl Moro convinced me that you have to know the future before you can be sure how the past will turn out. Now, I'm not saying you should flip to the last page of this book for the answer. I would never do that, nor advise anyone else to do it. But if that's you, see you in thirty chapters.

Despite our sharing 168 square feet for nine months, I never truly knew Andy Graise. I was too broke and he was too lazy to move out of the dorm, so we occupied the same three-dimensional coordinates from orientation till Andy left college, but our time-coordinates did not overlap. He would be out partying while I slept from midnight to six. He slept during class.

Andy was everybody's buddy except mine, the Dodgers' first-round draft pick, and engaged to my gorgeous cousin Lori, whom he met the day he moved out of my room. He chased her for another two years, but he finally won her over. They were to be married the following June. Andy had it made.

It took him just ten months, seven one-night stands that we knew of, and an estimated fifty thousand dollars' worth of Medellin marching powder up his nose, to toss his life in the toilet and flush till it overflowed.

A year after Lori broke up with Andy and moved back in with her parents in Pacifica, she called me and begged me to talk to him. Andy would not stop with the flowers and the gifts delivered to their home.

Despite his bad behavior, when he was on top of his game, full of charm, it was impossible to say no to Andy. But that was before his game started to fall apart.

Andy was a big guy of big appetites, and for a while I thought of him as another Babe Ruth, some unstoppable force of batting power and confidence and substance abuse. But if the Bambino had done as much cocaine as Andy, I doubt he'd have made it out of Boston. It was Boston, right?

Look, I admit I know nothing about pro sports, and care even less. I'm biased. I'm an amateur fencer, since there's no such thing as a pro fencer. Nobody sits on the couch drinking beer and watching us. We don't get the big bucks or TV endorsements. We fence because we love it.

Now, don't get me wrong, I'm not bitter. Baseball and basketball I'm good with. I even play them. Football, no thanks.

But watch pro sports? Life is too short to plant yourself in front of the tube, growing your gut as you observe hormone-mutated prima donnas like Andy killing themselves at an activity that was once, in the dawn of a long-forgotten era, a pure game played for fun.

But as I say, I'm not bitter. It's just that I'd rather crouch in the sand looking for broken dishware. And luckily, I found a career that allows me to do that.

Still, despite my determination to remain ignorant, I had become aware of the rumors that Andy would be cut from the team before summer. He was calling Lori daily, tearfully begging her to reconcile. She in turn pleaded with me, the dope who introduced them, to convince him to quit trying. Fool that I am, I thought maybe I could. Who knows why? When we roomed together I couldn't even convince him to stop puking in the trashcan.

But I have the kind of optimism that made me buy that 1988 Honda Civic that had driven the distance from the Earth to the Moon, and transported three other students through their entire college careers before the last one saw me coming.

So on a breezy Sunday morning in May 2011, under a sky full of scudding clouds, I beat the traffic to Dodger Stadium. It was my first visit to the ballpark. I swung off the Arroyo Seco Parkway, up the hill to Chavez Ravine, and into the vast parking lot. Happily, Andy had remembered to call in the parking pass for me.

I cruised past the oleanders and ice plants, getting directions from one Dodger employee after another, until finally by sheer random chance, I located Will Call. Of course, Andy had forgotten to get me a field pass so I could get in to see him before the game.

I tried reasoning with the hard-eyed security guard.

"Why on earth would I have gotten a parking pass, but not a field pass? It doesn't make any rational sense." He stared at me, unmoved. "Look, Andy was engaged to my cousin."

That changed everything. The guard searched me. Thoroughly.

Once convinced I had no weapons, and was just here to tell Andy to leave Lori alone, he made a command decision that my cause was just and escorted me onto the field.

Suddenly, a voice boomed from the dugout: "Hey, shoot that asshole, he's a terrorist!"

Andy bounded out into the sun, a big, blond, red-faced jock in Dodger blue.

"Hey, Andy," I said, forcing a chuckle, "That's only funny if he knows we were roommates." I looked at the guard with the big gun on his hip, and added, "Which we were."

"The hell we were," growled Andy. "He lived at the library." The guard narrowed his eyes at me. After a pause so pregnant it had to be octuplets, Andy guffawed, "Nah, he's cool, Juan."

Managing to contain his amusement, Juan nodded, "Thanks, Mr. Graise." Juan then muttered to me: "You better not be his dealer."

Before I could respond, Andy arrived and threw his arms around me in a bear hug. I caught a whiff of beer, pot and possibly Eau de Floozie. As an afterthought, Andy shook my hand. Then he wiped his nose. I wondered if he'd done that before he shook my hand.

"Thanks for coming, Dave. Hey, you want the backstage tour?"

I checked my watch. "Actually..." That was as far as I got before Andy clapped an arm around me and dragged me off.

Andy gave me a perfunctory walk-through, punctuated by friendly waves to vendors and groundskeepers who seemed, to my eye, to survey Andy with a mixture of tolerance and pity. We met none of his teammates, who always seemed to be walking away when I spotted them. Andy wiped his nose again. I asked if he had a cold. Andy snorted.

"Everything about me is cold these days. Can't get under the ball. And I haven't had a run all season. But I guess you know that."

"No. I don't follow baseball."

Andy cracked up. "Clueless as ever, Preston. That's what I love about you. But what the hell, I never came to watch you wave your sword around, did I?"

"Actually, it was a saber."

"Actually, I don't give a shit. You talk to Lori?"

"She's worried about you," I said. That was true.

"Then why'd she leave me? Does she know they're about to cut me?"

"You know that wasn't why she left."

"I need her back. I'm trying to get myself straight, but without her..."

"Andy, you have to do that without her." I maintained eye contact until I was sure he understood I was serious. Mission accomplished.

Andy nodded, miserable. I was actually feeling sorry for the big dope.

"Yeah," he began. "Shit. Look, when you talk to her, at least—"

"Mr. Graise!" A sharp voice cut into our conversation and we turned to its source. A fan approached. He was lean, taller than either of us, wearing a windbreaker and a Dodger cap. His angular features were perfectly symmetrical. He had jet-black hair and a sardonic, dangerous look, like a male model who was also the scariest pimp in Vegas. He was carrying a dust-caked leather bag that looked like it had been buried for a century.

An equally tall woman waited silently for the fan in the noonday shadows a few yards away. She wore wraparound shades, and was zipped up in a matching Dodger windbreaker, with her gold-blond hair peeking out from under her cap.

The fan put out his hand. "I'm a huge fan of yours."

"That right?" shot back Andy, in no mood to greet his public.

"Would you mind autographing this ball?" The fan pulled a brand new baseball from his pocket and held it out to Andy. Andy stared at the fan, his face darkening in rage. He shoved the man's chest hard. The stranger lost neither his composure nor his footing.

"Andy! Whoa!" I said, restraining him as best I could with a forty-pound disadvantage.

"Kiss my ass, you son of a bitch," Andy snarled at his public. "Who put you up to this?"

I expected Dodger staffers to swarm over to defuse the incident, but Andy was off everyone's radar at the moment. The stranger regarded Andy calmly.

"You ballplayers are a testy lot. I assure you, this is no joke."

"No? Then let me save you a few bucks, dickwad. Tomorrow that ball will be worth more without my signature." Andy turned to go, but the man reached into his soiled bag.

"What if I trade you this for it?" the fan called out. Andy glanced back. His pupils got very large, and for once, it wasn't drugs.

The stranger was holding out an antique baseball, made of horsehide. Andy put his nose up to the ball, staring at a faded ink signature. "Jesus Christ, Ty Cobb, 1908? Is this genuine?"

I peered closely at the ball. "It could be. I don't suppose you have any papers of provenance?" I asked.

Tall, dark and disturbing shook his head, but never looked at me. He was watching Andy, who never took his eye off that ball. I added, "It wouldn't be that hard to find a hundred-year-old baseball, and forge Cobb's name on it."

"Nunh-uh, Mr. History," said Andy. "This is Cobb's signature. That, I'd know anywhere." I believed him. If I learned anything from our months together, it was that Andy revered Ty Cobb. Andy turned to his fan.

"You got a deal, dude."

The fan handed Andy the Ty Cobb ball. Andy carefully conveyed it to me.

"Hold this till the game's over. You drop it, I'll kill you."

The stranger flashed his teeth, and handed Andy the brand-new ball.

"And would you mind dating it?" added the fan. Andy patted himself down for a pen, as did I. The stranger pointed at his female companion.

"Looks like we need your wonderful pen, after all." The woman frowned, but sauntered out into the dazzling sunlight to hand Andy a rusty-looking old ballpoint pen. She and I made eye contact...or would have, if not for her opaque wraparounds. She left the sun and retreated to the shadows of the stands. It only struck me later that she never looked at Andy once.

When I looked back, the stranger was now focusing on me, and apparently did not like what he saw.

"Have we met?" He said it as if he was sure we hadn't.

"I don't think so. But I suppose it's possible."

"No, actually, I don't think it is," he concluded.

"Well, then I guess we haven't." What was his deal?

The amazing Fan Guy and his lovely assistant vanished into the stands. I wished Andy luck and went to watch the game. I wasn't exactly in the Dugout Club, but Andy had gotten me a great seat just above it.

About an hour later the game got under way. I wished I hadn't agreed to babysit Andy's souvenir. I had stuff to do. But what the hell, I'd never seen a game. So I bought a beer and sat back.

In the top of the first inning, the Dodgers disposed of the Braves without allowing a man on base. The Braves took the field. Twice, Dodgers got thrown out at first. But then they loaded up the bases. I guessed I could get into baseball if it moved this fast every time, especially if I could get a seat like this again. But that seemed exceedingly unlikely. Then, somewhat to my surprise, Andy stepped up to the plate.

The spectator beside me in wife-beater and mullet shook his head in disgust, and turned to a fan on the other side of me.

"Aw, shit," groaned the Mullet. "Bases loaded and who do we get? Andy 'Cokehead' Graise. Game over, man."

His colleague cursed agreement. It seemed they would be talking past me a lot. They both looked like they'd gotten their tickets off someone at knifepoint, so I offered to swap seats with one of them. They politely demurred.

The pitch came over home plate. Andy let it by. Strike one.

"Hey, man, wake up! Do a line!" called the Mullet.

Another pitch. Andy swung and missed.

"Rehab!" shouted the Mullet.

The third pitch was faster than the first two. But a miracle occurred. Andy connected.

"Look at that! Run, Andy, run!" bellowed 'Cokehead' Graise's biggest fan.

The right fielder lost it in the sun and it went right into the outstretched hand of a kid in the cheap seats. Damn, a home run. If this had to be Andy's last game, at least he was going out in style.

Three-and-a-half hours later, my eyes were riveted on that diamond. I did not mind the sweat pouring off me, or the blended spoor of beer and body odor and sunblock and Dodger dogs. I was having yet another Budweiser. And I was now and forever a fan of nature's noblemen, the Los Angeles Dodgers, inducted into the brotherhood of America's pastime, the greatest sport ever, and I had a seat over the dugout for arguably the most historic game of the twenty-first century.

The stands were full of radios tuned to Vin Scully calling the game. He may have missed a play or two, but he was truly the Bard of Baseball. The Dodgers were, for the moment, behind. But Andy was way, way ahead. Vin's avuncular twang echoed across the multitudes.

"Eleven-ten, Braves. And Andy Graise—who's had a season of challenges filled with question marks, even a trade talk or two—has gone from zero to hero in one afternoon, as the Graise roller coaster keeps on zooming."

Andy came out of the dugout to a wall of cheers, as the Jumbotron replayed his second homer of that afternoon, then his third...then that amazing fourth. With each of Andy's entrances, the organist had grown more inventive: The theme from "Rocky," Queen's "We Are the Champions" (Andy had temporarily vaulted the team into the lead), and John Fogerty's "Centerfield" (which Andy's last homer had overflown.)

This time the organ played Andy six fast notes: The "Things Go Better With Coke" jingle. A joke that would have been wretched bad taste at one-thirty in the afternoon, now brought down the house. Even Andy laughed. He glanced up at me and grinned. He was the Golden Boy again. He seemed to glow with happiness and more...a sense of destiny. For some bizarre reason, I flashed on Greta Garbo in *Camille*, and the legend that women afflicted with consumption were at their most beautiful right before...

"Hey!" yelled the mullet-headed fan. He'd handed me a beer to pass to his comrade beside me, and in my reverie I'd automatically taken a sip.

His friend at my other shoulder regarded me with sleepy dead-shark eyes. I noticed what looked like a fresh bullet scar along his cheek.

"Sorry, I'll buy you another one," I said, reaching for my wallet.

"Forget it, man, you don't want to miss this," said the guy with the scar, with all the magnanimity a baseball fan witnessing an Historic Moment could muster.

I handed him his cup. I'd actually had one beer to toast each of Andy's homers, so I could be forgiven a little confusion.

Scully wove his web of colorful comments:

"Graise has hit four home runs today, a feat equaled by only fifteen men in the history of the leagues. Now, in the bottom of the ninth, he's back at bat for a chance to rewrite the record books, with the bases loaded with Dodgers, and the game on the line. Graise digs in at the plate. Forty-two thousand, six hundred fifty-one fans with one thought on their mind, the same one that is on the mind of Andrew Robert Graise."

"Please God, just one more." Was that me praying?

The pitch came in. Too low, I thought. Bound to be a ball. Unless Andy was sucker enough to swing at...

Andy nailed it.

It arced high, high over left field. A crowd more populous than Andy's hometown promptly went insane. His teammates mobbed him at the plate. Over the roar, I could just make out Vin making it official.

"Graise hits it a ton! Watch it now, watch it. Into the stands! Can you believe it? Andy Graise has just written his name above Lou Gehrig's, above Willie Mays' and Gil Hodges' and every other ballplayer who has ever played this marvelous game. Five home runs. And the Dodgers win!"

Inevitably, the organ played a joyous Dixieland riff on "Amazing Grace" as Andy trotted around the bases smiling and waving, looking for all the world like a newsreel of Babe Ruth. Except he was in color. And wiping his nose. But it still wasn't the drugs. Andy, being Andy, would have denied it, but I'm sure he was crying.

I found myself staring at the alleged Ty Cobb ball. Could a talisman from a superstar of a century ago have restored the magic touch to the hopped-up bum known as Andy Graise? Was it Fate that delivered this ball to him?

"Naah," I thought. Apparently out loud, since Mullet Guy turned and gave me a weird look.

A Dodger employee tapped me on the shoulder. She led me to the clubhouse. The press was waiting outside the locker room for the players to shower and dress. She said it would be an hour or more before Andy wrapped up his interviews. I settled into a chair to wait.

Five minutes later, someone nudged me and handed me a note—it was Andy's printed scrawl, telling me to go through the exit to the parking lot and meet him there. I couldn't believe he would do this. But when I stepped outside, there was Andy, in civilian clothes, dark glasses, and a ball cap pulled low over still-dripping hair.

I begged him not to blow off the press again. Just keep his word, do the one-on-ones, make nice, be humble, give them a quote. Then we'd go out to dinner, just the two of us...

"Hey, asswipe, if I'm having dinner, it'll be with someone who's serving make-up sex for dessert." He was determined to get to Lori while the heat of his historic accomplishment was too blistering for her to resist.

"Andy, use your head. For the first time in a year, you've got good will. The media are on your side. Don't blow this!"

"How 'bout you blow me? I'm going to Frisco. Lori's gotta take me back now."

"You're not going to get a flight," I warned.

"I'm taking my own plane, douchebag. I wanna get there while the mojo on that ball is still working. C'mon, hand it over." Andy was as amenable to reason as ever.

The turbaned driver of the Yellow Cab recognized Andy, and gave him a thumbs-up. I handed Andy his Ty Cobb ball. He gazed on it like a splinter of the True Cross. I decided to try once more.

"Andy, I'm glad for you, and I'm proud of you. But you have to know this won't change a thing with Lori."

"Oh, no?" said Andy. His pale blue eyes drilled into me. "Ty Cobb was a crazy, catcher-spiking asshole. But he was the greatest ballplayer in history and he always got what he wanted. And from now on, so am I." Andy stared at the ball for one more moment, as the manic smile faded from his face. He handed the ball back to me.

"You know what? You were holding it when I broke the record. I don't mess with success. Meet us at Burbank tomorrow and we'll fly you down for the Padres game."

Andy yanked open the cab door and barked to the Sikh cabbie, "Let's go, Osama. Bob Hope Airport. Make it in twenty minutes, your tip's a hundred bucks."

"Osama" gunned it while Andy was still closing the door. The cab left a pound of rubber on the asphalt as they raced off to Burbank.

Andy died two hours later.

2

WESTWOOD

The Collector's Card Shoppe was tucked away like an afterthought in a 1930s brick shopping arcade. Surely its neighbors, the jeweler catering to lovesick UCLA undergrads, or the tony French restaurant with its chocolate soufflé (please allow half an hour notice) had an easier time making the outrageous Westwood rent. A shop like this, I reasoned, must not move a lot of inventory in a year. Maybe once in a blue moon, it would hit pay dirt selling a Honus Wagner or some other rarity, but day to day, it must be a challenge to turn a profit. Which was why I worried I might be getting hosed.

Out on Lindbrook Drive, students strolled the streets, or circled in cars, trolling for a rare parking space. I listened to the ceaseless flow of traffic echoing through the concrete canyon of Wilshire Boulevard, rolling east to Beverly Hills, and west to the Pacific.

George Rath, a slow and deliberate man with a sunburned complexion and a gaudy Hawaiian shirt, was taking his time appraising the Ty Cobb ball. He kept staring at the signature, then turning to a thick book entitled *Celebrity Autographs*, now tapping keys and clicking his mouse, Googling patiently through web page after web page. Looking over his shoulder, even a non-graphologist could see the signature on the ball matched Cobb's known signatures. Moreover, the "1908" date was virtually identical to Cobb's handwritten numerals on a contract.

My suspicion, therefore, was that Rath was mind-gaming me, trying to make me doubt the authenticity of this treasure, before low-balling me on his offer. That was okay. I was all ready with my counter gambit. Rath lowered a set of magnifying lenses over his eyes and stared at the signature again. Then, without taking his eye off the ball, he addressed me.

"So you were friends with Andy Graise?"

"That would be stretching it. We were roomies."

"Poor guy flew right into Frisco Bay. You think it was suicide?"

"No way. He had everything to live for, at least he thought. He was descending into heavy fog at dusk. I think when the sun set, he just lost the horizon and went into a slow spiral. Like JFK Junior. If Andy had been a better pilot, he could have landed on instruments. But by the time he radioed for help, he was already too low."

"Man. He starts out the day a loser, that night he dies a legend. What a waste." On Rath's bulletin board festooned with baseball clippings, the fast-yellowing headline commemorated Andy's triumphant finish: "GRAISE'S PLANE LOST AFTER RECORD 5 HOMERS."

"Anyway," I said, playing the guilt card, "He was engaged to my cousin, and Andy managed to die in debt, without a dime of insurance. So I'm hoping to get a good price for the ball, maybe help her with her student loans."

"Not with this you won't. It's a fake." If this was Rath's opening position, it sure didn't leave much room for negotiation. He handed the ball back to me and hung up his magnifying lenses.

"You sure?" I asked. Rath nodded. "But Andy was convinced the signature was Ty Cobb's," I protested. "And if there's one thing he really knew, it was Cobb. He talked my ear off about him."

"The handwriting was fantastic. Hell of a forgery. Whoever did it was damn close, yet didn't copy from any source I can find. But the ink line was a dead giveaway. You need to see it magnified. Here." He moved a magnifying glass on a stand, with its own light source, over the ball so it jumped out at me in extreme close-up.

"See that thin white line between the two ink marks? Probably a piece of dust either on the ball or in the socket, blocking the ink from making a solid line."

"What does that mean?"

"That this was signed with a ballpoint pen. Which was invented in South America in 1938. Didn't hit the American market till after World War Two. If your forger had half a brain, he'd have used a newer ball, and sold this as an autograph Cobb signed in retirement. But he got greedy by dating the ball 1908, which can't be right. Not with a ballpoint. Sorry to be the one with the bad news." He handed me back the ball.

I thanked him for his time. As I put my hand to the door, Rath called out, "I don't suppose you have a ball Andy Graise signed, do you?" I shook my head.

"Too bad. That'd be worth some bucks."

Hell, yes, it would.

I wasn't going to phone Lori with any more bad news just yet. I had to get home and jump on eBay, to see if that cheap chiseler I met at Dodger Stadium was trying to peddle his treasure yet. He would be asking a lot for the ball Andy signed and dated on the very day he hit five homers, the last day of his life.

A week later, my neighbor Sven invited me to come over to his UCLA physics lab.

I'd met Sven Bergstrom as an undergrad here when he lectured on physics and radiocarbon dating. He was way past retirement age even then, but always drew an audience. The man made subatomic particles as fascinating as a Raymond Chandler mystery. He could go off on a tangent about the predicted mass of the Higgs boson and the ramifications it has for the fate of the universe. After his lecture I'd peppered him with questions, which gave him the idea I had the makings of a physicist. For months thereafter he pursued me with the friendly determination of the Lyndon LaRouche guy outside the post office. Finally, I convinced Sven my one and only love was archaeology, and he agreed to mind his own bosons.

But when I began my postgraduate career, Sven let me know about an upcoming vacancy in the West L.A. apartment house Sven had occupied since 1945. He and his beloved Naomi had a two-bedroom on the second floor, from which you could see the Pacific, though the way high-rises were shooting up, they expected to lose the view any day. I took in that vista many times, since with their two daughters grown and living far away, the Bergstroms more or less adopted me. They spent a lot of time trying to find me a girl. They clearly saw me as an obsessive Asperger type who couldn't possibly meet someone on my own. And by the time I met my girlfriend-to-be Moira Shea, it was too late to bring her by.

Naomi Bergstrom died the year after I graduated. Their daughters came from New York and Sweden for the funeral. They helped Sven settle Naomi's affairs...but he refused to budge from the apartment he and Naomi had shared for six decades. I promised the girls, who were twice my age, that I'd look after him. Sven mourned her for a year, and I was worried. It was all I could do to drag him out of his place for lunch.

Then one day, I sat on my couch, poring over a treatise on my specialty, the Minoan Empire. This seafaring civilization arose in the Mediterranean after Egypt's Old Kingdom, but fell around 1400 B.C.E., long before Greece was born. Scholars had thoroughly explored the Minoan ruins of Knossos on Crete, but as a specialist in languages, my angle was different: I would decipher their long-dead tongue.

As I sifted through maps of Minoan sites around the Greek Isles, I glimpsed Sven walking past my front door, dressed not in his usual slacks and Izod jersey, but in button-down shirt and tie and jacket. I called out a greeting, but he didn't hear me.

I didn't realize how much time I was spending with my nose pressed to my books until I heard Sven's car return at 5:30 P.M. When I asked Sven where he'd been, he said he'd gone back to work. I was pleasantly astonished to learn the University of California had such an enlightened policy about employing octogenarians. It gave me hope for my old age.

Well, to make a long story interminable, after my disappointment at the card shop, I knew exactly the right man to ask for a second opinion on the "Cobb" ball. Sven was happy to oblige.

When I entered the lab, a pretty teaching assistant named Cheryl Williams told me Sven would be right over.

"It's so great the University gave him his job back," I said.

"Oh, they didn't," she murmured. "I mean, he's in his eighties."

"But—he comes here every day. Are you saying you just...let him hang out here?"

"Why not? He's not doing any harm." She looked warmly over at Sven, visible a room away, in a white lab coat, pointing out something on another grad student's computer.

I shook my head, smiling. "And I thought all you physicists were cold and analytical."

"Aw, we love Sven. So does the department head. He told Sven he wouldn't insult him with a job offer...but asked if he'd volunteer as Advisor Emeritus."

"What's that?"

"You got me. Sven liked the sound of it. He just putters around, asks what we're working on, gives us advice. And he makes tea for everyone. I think he thinks he's in charge of the lab, but he's an easy boss. We run a test for him now and then. We even got him his own workspace and a computer."

"He's a lucky man."

"He tells these amazing stories. You know he started college at fourteen? He knew Einstein at Princeton. I think we're the lucky ones."

Just then, Sven bustled into the room. He spotted me.

"David! Did you meet Cheryl? She looks like that what-was-her-name...Moesha on TV, doesn't she?"

Cheryl and I shared an embarrassed look.

"She does," I conceded.

"Yeah, well, you're too late, she's married." Sven tugged me along as he walked the length of the lab. "And you've got that new girlfriend, Myra, right?"

"Moira."

"Right. When are you bringing her over for dinner so I can meet her?"

"I don't know if we'll have time, Sven. She's going to Washington this month to be on Congressman O'Hare's staff."

"You're going to be on opposite coasts? What kind of romance is that?" Sven stopped to inspect someone's open notebooks as he walked me through the lab.

"Well, I was going to take her out to L'Ermitage before she goes. Very romantic atmosphere."

"Bring her up to my place Friday. I'll make my special chili."

"I'm not sure she'd consider that a romantic atmosphere."

"You tell her love isn't about pricey salads served by snooty waiters. It's about being comfortable with someone." I tried to imagine convincing Moira of that over a bowl of chili. "Now come over here," he commanded. "You have some explaining to do."

I followed him over to his cluttered workspace, decorated with photos of Naomi, the girls, and the scientific giants he'd known. Sven sat down and fixed me with a look.

"You wouldn't be part of a hoax on an old man, would you?" he accused.

I shot a look at Cheryl, who got busy doing something else.

"I...I don't know what you're talking about, Sven." Sven set the brown horsehide ball in the center of his desk.

"Where did you get this ball, really?"

"I told you. A fan gave it to Andy. So is it a fake, or not?"

"Your baseball collector was right. Based on the striation in the ink line, and the impression left in the horsehide, this was definitely written with a ballpoint pen. But that's not the weird part." Sven indicated a chair. "You better sit down."

I obeyed. Sven had a funny grin, but not like he was joking.

"This ball is not just a phony. If I were to accept everything you told me, it's an impossibility."

"Why? What did the carbon-14 tell you?"

"Hundred years, give or take thirty. At least, at one-sigma—that's a level of probability. At two-sigma...well, suffice it to say, it's not ancient enough to date properly with carbon-14. However, the lead-210 test is a different story."

Sven held out the computer printout for my inspection. There were a slew of figures and Greek letters. I did recognize the words "alpha radiation" and "Polonium." My head started to hurt. I passed it back.

"You have a translation for a non-physicist?"

"The ball is printed with the manufacturer's name, A. J. Reach. That printing ink contained traces of lead. So did the writing ink in the signature, which wouldn't be surprising in an older ballpoint pen. Now, lead-210 is an isotope that has a half-life of twenty-two years, so based on its decay, with ninety-five percent assurance, I can tell you this ball is indeed a century old." He paused a moment. "But the ink in the signature tests out at two hundred and sixty years old." He waited for me to process that.

"But...if ballpoints were invented only seventy-five years ago, how could it have signed this baseball...with ink that's been around for two-hundred-and-sixty years? Isn't that impossible?"

Sven gave me a what-did-I-just-say? nod.

"No mistake. We ran the test three times. Sorry we chewed up part of your ball, but it's not like you can sell it." Sven looked pleased with himself. "Quite a mystery, huh? The weird thing is, I can't even find any evidence that they made ink of this variety in 1750. But someone went to the trouble of putting it in a ballpoint pen, to sign that ball. That is a dumb forger. Now don't you wish you'd stuck with physics, instead of digging up old trash and dealing with shifty antique peddlers?"

"I love archaeology, Sven. I have no regrets. Look, obviously everyone is wrong about the ballpoint pen. Somebody invented one a hundred years ago but forgot to patent it."

"And just happened to have some hundred-and-sixty-year-old ink to fill it with?" smiled Sven.

"An *eccentric* inventor."

It sounded kind of thin even to me, but it beat trying to think of another explanation. I reached for the baseball.

"Wait, wait, what's your hurry?" said Sven. "One of the kids here noticed something else you might find interesting." He swiveled in his office chair and tapped a few keys on his computer. On his screen was a black-and-white photograph of the ball, and some faint marks I'd overlooked before.

"We found more ink on the ball. Just traces, largely hidden by the darkness of the horsehide. So we scanned in a photo and by adjusting the colors, we brought them out." As Sven clicked the mouse, successive images of the ball appeared in starker and starker contrast, and letters became more and more apparent. Sven pointed at the screen.

"You said this fan of Andy's had the old ball in a leather bag. If you ask me, he had a piece of paper in there too, on which he'd written in the same ink. It got a little moist, and it came off on the ball. Of course, the letters are reversed. Oops, forgot a step." Sven clicked the mouse again, and the letters flipped left-for-right.

I stared at the screen. The letters were sketchy, a few were illegible, but the brain is a marvelous computer and my mind easily filled in the gaps. The lettering, in crabbed, tiny script, read "SANTORINI DOLPH NS 10-06-__13." The first two digits of the year simply weren't there.

"Now, I know you're no sports fan, David," Sven began. "But I am. And I'm afraid there's no player on the Miami Dolphins named Santorini. Never has been. There was an *Al* Santorini, but he played baseball, for the Padres and the Cards."

"And if that's a birthday," I put in, "Either Mr. Santorini is ninety-eight...or else he won't be born for another one-and-a-half years."

"Right. So all we've managed to do is to make your mystery a bit more mysterious."

Yes, I thought. Except...

Santorini. I knew the name well, and not from watching baseball. I'd been researching the Greek Isles for months, and trying to justify to myself squandering my savings on a field trip. Crescent-shaped Santorini, remnant of an ancient volcanic caldera, always fascinated me. It was a central part of the Minoan Empire, with several major ruins...but what the hell did "Dolphins" refer to?

"What?" pressed Sven, reading my expression.

"Ehh, it's nothing. You'd laugh," I said. I didn't want to admit that I had needed a kick in the ass like this to book a trip I should have already taken. I got up to go.

"Thanks for running the tests."

"Anytime, neighbor." Sven tossed me the ball—a good throw for a man in his eighties. I caught it, bending a finger in the process. Pretty sad for a man of twenty-three.

It would be a year-and-a-half more, before I realized what that baseball was really telling me.

3

SANTORINI, 10-06-13

As I gazed at the broken column of the long-lost Temple of the Dolphins protruding from the hard-packed sand, my sat phone rang. It was Sven, a hemisphere away in West L.A. I told him of my find. I said I'd give my right arm to see the Temple in all its original glory. Who knew that within twenty minutes someone would take me up on the offer?

It was the kind of hyperbole you might have indulged in if you'd been living in a dank Mediterranean sea cave, digging and sifting sixteen hours a day, five months straight, crunching gritty black sand in everything you ate, wore or used...and then finally, oh my God, finally, you uncovered the base of a shattered wooden column, miraculously preserved from shipworms by a hard-packed, oxygen-deprived layer of silt...and realized that in a trench a few yards away, six feet down, what you'd thought was a random sharp stone was in fact the corner of a step on which no human being has set foot in thirty-six centuries.

It was exaltation, piled on top of relief, underlaid with a layer of "Well, it's about goddamn time." And several strata below that, lay a tiny seed of worry about the mysterious writing on that bogus baseball.

By the time of my first visit to Santorini in June 2011, I had learned there was a sea cave on the south end of the island called the Cave of the Dolphins. It had gotten its name centuries ago, from the broken crockery (actually, Minoan potsherds) depicting dolphins, that had been found in the sand there.

It had taken me a year to get funding and permission to dig in this cave for a temple I had only the barest educated guess was there, in the hope I would find inscribed therein, a certain word in Linear-A, the alphabet of the dead Minoan language, to prove "Atlantis" was the actual name of that empire.

And I kept telling myself it was all a bizarre, self-fulfilling coincidence that today, the day we finally found a column of that temple, was October 6th, 2013. 10-06-13.

That's when Sven rang my sat phone, and I uttered the hidebound cliché about giving my right arm to see the Temple intact. Come to think of it, hidebound cliché is...well, you know. Hey, I was excited.

"I'm proud of you, Dafid," said Sven. He was seven decades away from his native Sweden but still slipped into his childhood accent whenever he spoke on a phone.

"Thanks! This connection is lousy!" I shouted. "I can barely hear you!"

"Quit yelling, I hear you yust fine," came Sven's muffled reply. "Relax, I'm vatering your plants." I could clearly hear the squeak of the faucet as he shut off the kitchen tap. I realized immediately what was going on: Sven had clamped my cordless headset between his ear and his shoulder while wandering around my apartment, and the mouthpiece had slid down under his jaw. I'd seen him do that a couple of times with his own phone.

A loud whistle on his end interrupted us.

"Sven, is that a teakettle? I thought we agreed you wouldn't cook in my place." In my mind's eye, I pictured the burner left on when he departed, my plants and my Ansel Adams prints soon reduced to ash, my fencing trophies melted into puddles of pot metal.

"Who's cooking? I'm making a cup of tea." The whistling stopped and I could hear him pour the water into a mug. "Holy jumping cats, look at this view. I can see Catalina Island. How did you ever talk me into switching apartments?"

"It was your idea. You got tired of climbing stairs, remember?" He still came up on good days to enjoy his former view.

"Right, right. Goddamn arthritis. If anyone offers it to you, tell 'em no. Say, did I tell you a young lady called here a while ago? She was in a real hurry to get hold of you. I know you don't give out your phone number so I told her your email address."

I went to my laptop and re-read the email that had arrived before his call. "Yeah, I got it. She's here on Santorini. According to her, she's my new assistant. I can't reach anyone at the university to confirm it. Why would they send her without checking with me? All I can figure is her father must be a huge donor."

"Did she send a photo? Is she pretty?"

"Pretty illiterate. Her email is nothing but typos. I don't even think she spelled her own name right. It looks like Ar...Ar-yi..."

"Um, it's Ariyl?" said a chirpy voice behind me, pronouncing her name like the character in *The Tempest.* Is that pedantic? Okay, like the Little Mermaid in the cartoon.

I whirled to squint into the orange glare of the setting sun. The owner of the Valley-girl voice seemed no more than nineteen, with a striking, perfectly symmetrical face. She could have been on the cover of Cosmo, except there was something odd about her super-model looks I couldn't quite quantify.

"Professor Preston, I'm Ariyl Moro? I emailed you?" She had that schoolgirl habit of making statements sound like questions. From her voice you'd expect a mere slip of girl; but this was a very big girl. I'm just a shade under six feet; she was several shades over it.

She had long, straight, lustrous honey-blond hair, held back from her face by a thin white headband. She'll make a great assistant, I thought. Looking after that hair will occupy her for an hour every morning.

She was dressed in a thoroughly impractical wrap-around print skirt—something she picked up in town, I guessed—that didn't match the rest of her white linen outfit: A light jacket with padded shoulders, over some kind of low-cut tank top that began wasp-waisted at her silver-linked belt but mushroomed outward most distractingly. If you're a film buff, think Sophia Loren, or Anita Ekberg. Or Christina Hendricks, the redhead on *Mad Men*. Nestled in the valley of her décolletage was a donut-shaped crystal pendant—possibly the world's most garish cubic zirconium.

It occurred to me I'd been staring at that pendant, and its zaftig setting, longer than was strictly polite. I forced my gaze up to meet hers and put out my hand. "Uh...hi. David Preston."

Ariyl took my hand in hers. Instead of shaking it, she fondled it. "Ooh, are these calluses?"

As I tried to frame an answer, I let her continue running her fingers over my palm. Now she took my other hand, and inspected the wristwatch Dad had given me.

"What's this?"

"It's a Panerai. You have an eye for antiques. They were made by Rolex for the Italian frogmen in World War Two, though this particular one was actually used by a German unit."

"No, I mean, what's it used for?"

"It...it tells the time," I said with a chuckle. I found myself staring into her eyes, wondering what was so strange about them.

Halfway around the world in West Los Angeles, my teakettle started up again, breaking the spell. Sven must have set it back on the burner.

I'd forgotten all about him. I reclaimed my left hand from Ariyl and put the phone to my ear.

"Sven...I have to go."

"Is that her? How does she look?"

"You wouldn't believe me. Goodbye. And don't forget to turn off my stove!"

"What do you think I am, senile?" Sven groused. I convinced myself I'd heard the teakettle stop whistling just before Sven hung up.

I finally got my right hand back from Ariyl Moro.

"Sorry, I didn't hear a car arrive. Or a boat."

"'Cause I landed down the beach. And you were shouting pretty loud."

"Oh, that was my neighbor in West L.A., Sven Bergstrom. Old professor of mine, and he...it's a long story. Look, I'm not sure how much you heard, but I hope you didn't take it the wrong way."

"I'm sure you meant illiterate in the nicest sense. I admit I can't type." At this point, she carelessly cast aside the top-of-the-line iPad she'd been carrying. I cringed as it landed face down in the sand.

"But if you're worried about my language skills..." she began. She went to the broken pieces of pottery on the folding table. Their glazed patterns were similar to the murals at Knossos, of bare-chested girls and boys vaulting over bulls. She picked up the potsherd labeled 27 and peered at its angular markings, then translated them:

"It says, 'temple of the dolphins'."

After a moment, a sand flea flew in my open mouth. I choked for a spell until I could locate it with my tongue and spit it out.

"Am I right?" she asked.

"You're way beyond right. There are maybe five people in the world who could translate this first word as 'temple.' As for 'dolphins'...well, that was my guess. Though I think it also refers to their sea-god. Poseidon would be the Greek equivalent; but the Minoan word for him was forgotten when Troy fell."

"Ooh, sorry. Did he hit his head?"

"Who?"

"Your friend Troy who fell."

I stared at her. My Achilles' heel (sorry) has always been that I'm slow to pick up on someone else's joke. So, playing it safe, I forced a chuckle.

"Heh. Troy hit his head when he fell. Good one."

But Ariyl didn't return my smile. In the back of my mind, a dim suspicion was being unearthed.

What was with her accent? She didn't actually say, "'Cause I landed down the beach." It was slurred and run together, like, "Zi lanadown abeach." "Did he hit his head?" was more like, "De hitiz hud?" "Head" pronounced "hud" gnawed at me.

Vowels shift over centuries. In Shakespeare's day, "a wound" rhymed with "a sound." And they're still shifting. Only that morning on the radio I had heard a BBC reporter say "treeps ah messing ite in the raid," which I finally translated as "troops are massing out on the road." That's how distinctive Ariyl's accent was, albeit Californian rather than Brit. It was as if Val-Speak had actually mutated into a new dialect.

"Have you seen many inscriptions in Linear-A?" I asked.

She turned her gaze to the excavation of the temple step. "No, mainly in Athens."

"Linear-A isn't a city," I began, trying not to sound irritated. "It's a language that's not related to English, Greek, Sanskrit, Hebrew, Arabic or any other Indo-European or Afro-Asian language. It predates most of them." She nodded knowingly, though I'd have bet money she knew none of this. "And yet, somehow you read it like a native."

"Does that surprise you?"

"Yeah, kind of, because it was a language so unknown, so completely dead, it could only be described by the shape of its alphabet. How can you read it and not know what it's called?"

"Well, I've always had a deep interest in Atlantis."

Now the blood began pounding in my eardrums like an angry neighbor on the wall of a late-night party.

"Atlantis?" I repeated. She looked away.

"Well, whatever you call it."

"I, and everyone else who knows about it, call this culture the Minoan Empire. The language you just read is Linear-A Minoan. How could you not know that?"

She shrugged, with a badly assumed air of nonchalance. "We call it Atlantis where I come from."

"And where the hell would that be?"

"You're saying nobody but you believes in the lost continent of Atlantis?"

"It wasn't a continent, just a large island. Plato was working from Egyptian records and misread some hieroglyphs. He got the size wrong by a factor of ten. He also said it was nine thousand years before the time of Solon, when it was actually more like nine hundred, give or take. But yeah, we know the Minoans were the most advanced people of that era, that a volcanic eruption crippled their civilization...and that they were the source of the Atlantis myth. But I go one step further. I say that their society literally called itself 'Atlantis'. So far, no reputable scholar agrees."

"So you're a disreputable scholar?" she smiled.

"At the moment, yeah. That's what I get for following a tip from a baseball. Of course, I was already toying with the idea of digging on Santorini. When I heard of this place called the Cave of the Dolphins...well, let's just say my Spidey sense was tingling. And now *you* are making it zap me like a Taser."

"What's a Spidey sense?"

"Something that's forcing me to choose between two unpleasant hypotheses: Either you're an airhead who's just going to waste my time, or else you're extremely sophisticated and sly, and trying to horn in on my theory before I can publish." Then came the dawn. "The university didn't send you."

She shook her head.

"I figured you wouldn't tell me much unless I had a convincing reason to be here. But now that I see what you've uncovered, we can help each other out."

"Or, I could just help you out," I said, gently taking her elbow to escort her to the cave mouth. She didn't take the hint, so I pulled more firmly.

Now, I work out. When I can't get to the gym, I do forty pushups every morning. And I'm not a small man. But I couldn't budge her. I might as well have tried to drag the Venus de Milo across the sand. She sure didn't look that heavy. I could have used my excavation crew at this point. But by now they were back in town on their third round of ouzo...though probably their first one outside of the jeep.

Ariyl ignored my straining at her arm, and locked eyes with me. *That's* what was odd about her eyes: Her irises were purple. Not just Liz-Taylor-kinda-violet, but actually purple. And trust me, they weren't contacts.

"What if I could find you something that proves your theory about Atlantis?"

"Wouldn't that be wonderful?" I remarked, glancing at the costly equipment all over the cave. "I wouldn't need all this stuff."

She gave me a tolerant look.

"Show me the temple, and I'll show you the proof." I wanted to explain that at this point, the temple tour would be exceedingly brief, just a few steps. Still, in the five minutes I had known Ariyl Moro, she'd already surprised me half a dozen times. Chalk it up to my exhaustion, or simple boredom, but I was fascinated to see what she'd do next.

I led her to the trench, six yards long and two wide, where we'd spent the day clearing sand from three steps. It would be weeks before they were anything more than a collection of staggered stone corners poking out of the hard packed sand.

"The Temple of the Dolphins," I announced. "What's left of it."

Ariyl dropped into the five-foot deep pit, landing as easily as if she'd stepped off a curb. She scanned the steps, then announced, "Right...here. This is the bottom one." The next instant, she was digging barehanded into the hard-packed sand beneath it.

"What the hell are you doing?" I exclaimed, envisioning those flawless fingernails crumbling irreplaceable potsherds. "Stop, you're going to damage..."

I never finished the sentence. From beside the bottom step, Ariyl had scooped around a foot-long chunk of something encrusted in sand. I jumped down beside her. She held a hunk of sand covered in a thin layer of decomposed tan spider web that a few millennia ago, might have been a leather sack.

"Let me!" I breathed. As I felt the chunk of sand, it broke loose of the stone step. Normally, I'd have worked on it in the pit, but whatever damage there was, was already done. I carefully carried the hunk out of the pit, and set it on the table. Time stood still as I worked. I can't tell you how long it took to remove the sand...but in the end, there lay a statue of the legendary half-man, half-bull, the Minotaur. It was magnificent, styled in the Minoan fashion, not so stiff as an Egyptian sculpture, nor as realistic as a Hellenic one. Its elongated horns echoed those on the bulls in the murals at Knossos.

Oh, and did I mention it was solid gold?

I stared at it for a small eternity, until a loud wave crash outside the cave made me jump. I was so intent on the Minotaur that I didn't even notice how Ariyl got out of the pit. I had the vague, peripheral impression she'd simply hopped out, but of course that was impossible.

Suddenly, she snatched it off the table and held it up so the day's last sunrays illuminated the markings on its base.

"Careful!" I gasped.

"Minotaur of Atlantis," she translated.

My mouth went dry. "What are you talking about? Let me see that!"

She passed me the statue so casually that I was unprepared for its weight and nearly dropped it.

"Careful," she said.

"How do you know this word is 'Atlantis'?" I demanded.

But the hell of it was, I already knew she was right. That spring I'd published my paper theorizing that the Minoan language was the ancestor of Euskara, Spain's mysterious Basque tongue, which stubbornly resisted the Indo-European linguistic invasion for millennia, clinging to survival in the remote, rugged valleys of the Pyrenees. Using Nancy Dexter's language algorithm (developed to trace back changes in Greek over three millennia) on Basque word-roots, I had worked up a system of vowels and consonants that could correspond to the Linear-A alphabet.

If I was right, those final letters on the Minotaur would have been pronounced "Aht-lahn-tees"—meaning that the name itself predated Plato and Solon, predated ancient Greece itself, and was spoken in the legendary land of King Minos.

"Oh my God, oh my God," somebody kept repeating. As it turned out, it was me. I was starting to hyperventilate. "This is it. This is proof. You found it. I don't know how to thank you." I'd clearly misjudged this girl. She was my muse, my guardian angel, my goddess of vindication.

"Don't mention it."

"I'll do more than mention, it!" I sputtered. "I'll *publish* it! I'll dedicate the book to you! If it wins me the Gold Medal for Archaeological Achievement, I'll grab a hacksaw and give you half. But how the hell...? I mean, that had to be a lucky guess! How on God's green earth could you have known that Minotaur was there?"

"'Cause I was there when it was buried."

I told you about me and other people's jokes. Long pause.

"Very funny."

"I'm not joking."

"I just excavated this pit. No one's touched that sand since 1600 B.C.E."

"True. Anyhoo, the Minotaur belongs to me. You mind?" She put out her hand. When I didn't respond, she rested her other hand on her hip, and cocked her head with an air of impatience.

"Yes, I do mind," I said. She had to be kidding. "And so would the Greek government. They own whatever I dig up here. And believe me, these days they're in no position to be generous."

Ariyl looked hurt.

"You don't understand. It was given to me as a present. You can take a picture of it, but I want it back."

I actually laughed this time. She sighed with mild disappointment.

"Oh, don't make me get unpleasant."

"What are you, on crack? This is a priceless find. I'm not handing it over to you."

She rolled her eyes.

"God, you are so rude!"

She put her hand out and grasped my belt buckle. Did she really think she could seduce me out of this treasure?

She did not. Instead, as easily as you or I might raise a carry-on bag, she lifted me over her head.

As I said, I'm not a small man. I weigh exactly 174 pounds, yet I was now in mid-air, staring down at Ariyl while she held me with one hand. I grabbed her fist and tried to pry her fingers from my belt, but she had me in the proverbial grip of steel. I now had a particularly good angle on her prodigious cleavage, but I couldn't enjoy it.

My attention focused on the arm that held me aloft: Her elbow wasn't even locked, and I could see the white linen of her jacket was straining to contain the bulge of her flexed biceps. And I saw that what I'd assumed were her jacket's shoulder pads, weren't pads. They were shoulders.

I once saw a female bodybuilder contest on ESPN. Ariyl could have won first prize without taking off her coat. I was certain her arms had not been that big in repose. But now, she was pumped.

"Put me down!" I demanded.

"Put you down?" she simpered. "Okay...those glasses make you look like a geek." She giggled, infuriating me. "I'll take that, thank you," she added primly.

I was gripping the Minotaur with all my might, but she yanked it from my fingers as if confiscating a baby's rattle.

"Hey!" I roared. I was helpless in the grip of this 'roid-raging lady weightlifter, but for some reason, it hadn't yet occurred to me to be terrified. So I reached down and punched her in the jaw as hard as I could. Pain shot through my fist. Okay, now I knew what it felt like to *sock* the Venus de Milo.

She laughed out loud. Now, at last, I was scared. Forget steroids or crack, this babe must be on angel dust.

"It's been real, Professor," she smirked. She drew me close for a sarcastic Hollywood air-kiss, trilled, "Ta-ta!" and then flung me aside. I flew backward, limbs flailing, a dozen feet.

The sand pounded me on the back, knocking the wind out of me. For the longest moment I couldn't inhale, but as my shock faded, a new wave of fury washed over me. I forced myself onto my elbow. I saw Ariyl turn toward the pit, holding the key to my life's work. Instinctively, I yanked off my glasses, stuffed them into my shirt pocket, and tensed to spring. She touched her fingers to the crystal at her throat, which seemed to give off a glow. By now I was up and moving, launching a flying tackle.

I hit her just below the hips, expecting to knock her flying. Instead, it was like I'd sacked a Naugahyde sofa. My impact did tear off the flimsy outer skirt, revealing a white miniskirt and long, muscular legs. I might not have had any effect, except that she was perched at the edge of the pit, so my weight was just enough to overbalance her.

She teetered, and yelled something fast and slurred at her crystal that sounded like, "Return (something-something) beezy(?)" as we both fell in.

That's when things went beyond weird. We didn't hit the ground. It was like we were falling in slow-mo. There was a burst of energy and color around us as the walls of the pit raced away in all directions. It was like looking at everything through the wrong end of the binoculars. The world went utterly still. Even the sea was silent. Around us it was dark, but not entirely black. Somehow, I could still make out the distant walls of the cave and the steps, flickering like an underexposed silent film. It was hard to tell in the jittery light, but it seemed the rocks in the cave were gradually growing larger. Like they were dis-eroding, if that's even a word. Meanwhile, the pit of my stomach felt like I was somersaulting blindfolded. I thought I was going to puke.

Suddenly the cave walls vanished in blinding light, and the roar of the ocean returned, louder than ever. Ariyl belly-flopped to the ground. She broke my fall, as I landed on her firm backside.

"Get off," growled Ariyl, annoyed but apparently uninjured. Before I could comply, a powerful twitch of her posterior bucked me off. I landed on my back in the dust, and blinked up into the noonday sun. Which was odd, because seconds earlier, we had been inside a cave, at dusk.

4

THERA

I TURNED OVER ON MY STOMACH, DESPERATE TO ORIENT myself with a familiar sight. As I would have expected, we had landed beside the temple's bottom step, but inexplicably, that step...all the steps...were now completely cleared of sand, and I could see they were twenty meters long. Stranger still, the walls of the pit were gone. The steps sat completely above ground.

"What the *hell*...?" I gasped. I again squinted up into the brightness overhead. Had a cave-in brought down the roof? If so, where was the debris? Also, there was that troubling detail about the sun being in the wrong part of the sky.

I turned to look at Ariyl as she got to her feet, and was astonished to see she was changing her clothes. I don't mean she was taking off the old ones and putting on new ones. I mean in a twinkling, her clothes changed *while she wore them.* Her modern white sandals shriveled into primitive leather ones, her skirt grew to full-ankle-length, her jacket shrank into a vest and took on a blue Minoan pattern, and her top now sank toward her belt. It wasn't just the temple steps that were now fully exposed. Ariyl's considerable endowments were revealed in the charming Minoan topless style that later *fashionistas* have never quite dared to emulate.

As she stood up, I noticed that she slipped the Minotaur inside her vest. But the priceless object I had been so determined to regain now faded into triviality. Even the spectacular Ariyl couldn't claim my attention for long, not in these inexplicable new surroundings.

"Where are we?" I stammered, getting to my feet. The brilliant sunshine stung my eyes, and the air was uncomfortably warm.

"You've been digging around it all day," said Ariyl. "Don't you recognize the Temple of the Dolphins?"

My eyes moved up the steps. I saw not the one broken stub we'd unearthed earlier, but an entire colonnade, the short wooden columns painted an exuberant orange, supporting stone upper walls with murals in hues of aqua, rust and ochre.

"You're crazy. That was destroyed more than three thousand years ago!" Her suggestion was absurd, insane...and yet, the fabled temple certainly would have looked a *lot* like the building before us. My head swam. A curious detachment came over me, as if I were observing a digital reconstruction of an ancient world on a particularly absorbing History Channel show.

The temple's columns were textbook Minoan—painted wood. The lintels were decorated with circular patterns. Definitely not Egyptian, though showing some of Egypt's influence. On its walls were murals that duplicated some of the potsherds I had found, with dolphins leaping over waves. The closest thing I'd ever seen to this structure was the ruined palace at Knossos on Crete. But the building before me was no ruin. It was intact. In fact, it was practically in mint condition.

Surf crashed in the distance behind us. I turned, disoriented. The temple steps I excavated had faced south, toward the Mediterranean, and judging from the angle of the sun, they still did. But the sea cave on Santorini had been in a narrow promontory so that the cave itself faced the sea to the west. We now stood on a knoll overlooking a long stretch of rocky seacoast to the south, close by a rushing stream that emptied into the sea.

I could see no sign of the cave. Or for that matter, of the island of Santorini as I knew it. Instead, where the sea and smaller islands west of Santorini should have been, rose a steep peak some six miles away, wreathed in clouds.

I became aware of an angry babble of voices from the village of dazzling whitewashed adobe that crowded the temple on all sides. I saw no women or children, no merchants or tradesmen. The place had the look of a freshly-sacked city, with fires in several buildings. Bronze-armored men, with helmets in the Minoan style, were everywhere. A knot of them were gathering to gape at Ariyl and me, but mainly Ariyl. Their eyes grew wide, their hands gripped sword handles. They were dark, squat, burly, and seemed to take a dim view of our presence.

I wondered if we might be in trouble.

A soldier taller than any of the others, nearly my height and a lot thicker, burst through the crowd. We'll call him Stretch. His steely glare demanded an explanation.

Ariyl supplied it. Pointing at me, she declared, "*Sashoko genko lydushatu berdu!*"

And now, one of us was definitely in trouble.

Roughly translated? She told Stretch and his pals that I'd called their sea god a dirty pig. Judging from the snarls, the outraged faces glaring at me, and the swords yanked from sheaths, her pronunciation was flawless.

"No!" I exclaimed in my best reconstructed Minoan. "She is, uh..." It was then I realized I had no idea what their word was for 'liar'.

"Not good! Not good!" was the closest I could come.

Strong hands gripped my right arm. I shook it free a second before a bronze blade flashed downward to amputate it. I pivoted away and lost only a few inches of my shirt and a shred of epidermis to its keen edge. I grabbed the swordsman's wrist, brought my knee up hard and broke his grip on the sword. I snatched it up and slashed at him, forcing him to flee. Then I turned to face the others.

I must admit I am not bad with a sword. My senior year, I took the silver medal at the California state championship. I like the saber. I'm less capable with a foil. This sword was shorter than either of those weapons, and its ergonomic design left everything to be desired. But the moves all came back to me in a flash, and served me well against these opponents, whose one tactic consisted of running at me, hacking and screaming. I managed to sidestep and trip the first. He stumbled and fell in the dust. Then I parried Stretch's thrust, and with one of my own, forced him to retreat.

With a particularly vigorous parry, I actually knocked my third foe's sword from his hand. Before I could congratulate myself on my skill, a hard blow to the back of my skull introduced me to the dirt.

I rolled over and saw my first attacker, who sooner than I'd hoped, had recovered from my tripping him. He was glaring down at me. Stumblebum, as I will refer to him, had apparently clubbed me with his fist and the end of his sword handle. Two of his comrades clutched my arms and yanked me to my feet. I thrashed, to no avail. Opponent number three, a sorehead who hadn't taken kindly to being disarmed, retrieved his sword and marched toward me, with clear homicidal intent.

Ariyl stepped into his path, commanding him, "*Ey sasulil, brutik gwanadu.*" Which meant, "Don't kill him, he's gone mad."

I didn't take offense. I half suspected I had. In any case, it stopped Sorehead in his tracks. That, and the fact he was staring up at a purple-eyed giantess.

"Okay, Ariyl, you win," I panted. "Keep the Minotaur. Just tell them to let me go, it was all a mistake."

"First, I have to drop this off at home," said Ariyl, adjusting her vest, "So be a good boy and I'll check in on you later." She patted my cheek and waltzed off toward a collection of abandoned market stalls.

It suddenly hit me that she was hiding the Minotaur from these soldiers. I started to accuse her, but before I could, their tall leader barked something, an arm went across my windpipe, and his men dragged me up the temple steps. I yanked my neck loose enough to yell.

"No!" I bellowed after her, "Ariyl, you can't leave me here! Ariyl!" Stumblebum took exception to my show of disrespect and gave another whack to my cranium with his sword-butt.

Woozy, I looked back at Ariyl, but where she had been a moment before, there was just a fleeting, colorful shimmer, as if the sunbaked road were the reflection in a breeze-rippled pond. The ripples diminished, leaving only what passed for your everyday, normal Minoan Main Street, sixteen hundred years before Christ.

5

BENEATH THE TEMPLE, 1628 B.C.

BETWEEN MY THROBBING SKULL AND MY EMOTIONAL upheaval, the rest of the day zoomed by in a blur. They dragged me into the temple, down some stairs, through a stout wooden door, and into a room underneath the main floor. It may have been designed as a storeroom or a hiding place, but today it would serve as my Bronze Age Bellevue.

My Minoan turned out to be rustier than I thought. All my reasoned arguments, dire threats and heartfelt pleas were ignored, aside from eliciting a few hearty chuckles from the soldiers. I did get what I assume was the special "madman" treatment: They carried in a brazier of coals, an anvil and tools to forge manacles for me. They passed narrow ingots of bronze through some big, clunky bronze chains. Sorehead heated the ingots, then hammered them into a circle, then banged them closed around my wrists and ankles. They were kind enough to put strips of wool between the hot metal and my skin, but I still got some swell second-degree burns in the process.

Afterward they brought out primitive U-shaped spikes. I knew what would come next. It was only my desperate pantomime that got them to permit me to relieve myself on the far wall first—and if you think that's easy when being held at spear point, you try it. Then they dragged me back to the other wall and drove the spikes with my chains deep into chinks in the stones.

There were gaps a foot-and-a-half square at either end of the room that admitted light and breeze. If these Minoans weren't much for freedom of speech, they were sophisticated when it came to air circulation.

Standing where I was chained, I could get a decent view of what I assumed was the ruler's or viceroy's two-story palace, nearly as elaborate as the temple. Beyond it loomed the distant mountain peak. One thing I did know: There was no such peak anywhere near Santorini. So where in God's name was I?

After my captors abandoned me, I had a number of quiet hours to work out a few theories that could possibly explain where I was, and why I was seeing all the things I was seeing.

Scenario one: This was all an incredibly elaborate hoax. Perhaps some savvy reality-TV producer, knowing how networks loathe paying for anything that resembles a script, had contrived to bring back *Scare Tactics* or *Punk'd*, with me as the guest star/unsuspecting victim. And with a budget of about fifty million dollars. Judging from the extent of this village of real adobe and stone, and all the armored extras milling about, I didn't think they could have done it any cheaper. But wouldn't that expense undercut the whole idea of reality TV—of saving money by making stars out of suckers off the street, instead of paying union actors?

Another objection to this theory was that every extra I heard was speaking the ancient Minoan tongue that I had only recently reconstructed for an obscure scientific journal. So it seemed the odds that I would any second get a surprise visit from Tracy Morgan were vanishingly small. Call it a thousand-to-one.

The second scenario, one I resisted for as long as I could, was that I was in the midst of a psychotic break. Possibly through overwork, or maybe because someone—Ariyl?—had slipped me a hallucinogenic mickey. My having gone insane was certainly a depressing prospect, but upon reflection, it had the virtue of explaining every bizarre event I'd experienced since a crazed supermodel had sashayed into my dig and bounced me around like a beach ball.

One bright spot in this diagnosis was the knowledge that LSD wears off, and psychosis is treatable. I could only hope that while my mind was out wandering, that world-class doctors were deciding upon the best course of treatment for it. Of course, that depended on where I was when I flipped out.

If my breakdown had happened months ago back in Los Angeles, I was probably at UCLA Medical Center, an excellent hospital in the world capital of mental illness; but sadly, it would mean that I had only fantasized that I'd found the Temple of the Dolphins.

On the other hand, maybe it was the overwork and stress connected with my discovery that finally pushed me over the edge this afternoon. That would mean my great discovery was real, and my crew would probably find me soon, gibbering on the floor of the sea cave like a lunatic. I felt sure they'd look after me. But I was concerned about the quality of care a psychotic foreigner like me might receive in Athens during an economic crisis. Much less in tiny Fira, Santorini's capital, population twenty-five hundred.

There was a third scenario: That Ariyl had magically whisked us thirty-six centuries back in time. This was an extremely disturbing notion, not least because it meant that my ride had gone and left me stranded. But this scenario relied on the existence of time travel, which I knew was not merely impossible but illogical, so I felt safe assigning it odds of a million-to-one.

My best proof of that impossibility were these bronze chains restraining my singed wrists. I suddenly realized that they were anachronisms. The earliest known chain was forged in 225 B.C., a millennium after the Minoan Empire fell. Of course, it was possible chains had been devised earlier by the Minoans, and no examples had yet been unearthed. Bronze does corrode, and they *were* a clever people...but, no. I'd already used the "earlier invention" hypothesis on the ballpoint pen. I had to be imagining these chains.

So my odds-on favorite became scenario two, temporary insanity. As there was nothing I could do to alleviate it, other than remind myself that my perceptions were not real, I might as well observe the fantasy before me. I had to admit, my fevered brain was putting on quite a show. Three-plus years of post-graduate research definitely provided a wealth of raw material. But certain things I observed in my hallucination surprised me.

All day long, the armored Minoans were coming and going from the palace. From what I could overhear, there had been an attack from the sea, which accounted for the burning buildings and the absence of civilians. The townsfolk had been carried off, enslaved by the sea raiders—probably distant ancestors of Homer's Greeks—who had also looted the other buildings. However, the Minoan shaman had foreseen the raiders, and had hidden his temple's treasures in the hills.

Alas, even as the Minoans were retrieving the relics, their main object of veneration had been stolen just hours ago: The golden Minotaur. Some darkly swore I must be the thief. But they hadn't found it on me. I knew who had really stolen it, but it was too late to withdraw the insanity plea Ariyl had entered on my behalf. Meanwhile, my captors debated whether the gods would be angered if they tortured a madman to see if he would talk.

The rest of the relics, the Minoans replaced in the temple. I overheard Stretch telling his men that even if the people were gone, the temple was the only place for these holy objects. Well, if your women and children must be carted off in chains, at least it would be a comfort to have a carved fetish to which you could pray for divine retribution.

This part of my fantasy—an invasion of the Minoan Empire—actually made sense. If there had been a war with cities put to the torch, it would explain the deep layer of ash found not just at my dig in Santorini, but around other Minoan sites of this period. As far as I could recall, I had never read such a war hypothesis, let alone formulated it myself. But if Robert Louis Stevenson could dream up *The*

Strange Case of Dr. Jekyll and Mr. Hyde during a catnap, then why couldn't my subconscious assemble an important theory while I was in wackyland?

Sorehead, my jailer, fed me around sundown, a kind of mutton-porridge swill that wasn't too bad compared to, I don't know, warm mud. I realized I hadn't lost my glasses—they were in my breast pocket. I belatedly recalled putting them there. But the chain between my manacled hands which ran through the U-shaped spike, was just short enough that I couldn't reach them. So I was fairly blind at close range. Naomi Bergstrom always said those black frames spoiled my looks and told me to get contacts, but I never got around to it. Now I could kick myself, except that my leg chain was too short for that.

So I stared at the bowl Sorehead had brought my dinner in. It had a very familiar, if slightly blurry pattern. If I could've gotten my glasses out of my pocket, I'd have been certain, but I was fairly sure it was the source of potsherd number 27.

The chains that held me to the wall allowed me to sit, as long as I kept my arms slightly raised and my knees somewhat bent. It was as comfortable as flying no-frills coach to New Zealand beside a circus fat lady. I found I could actually doze in this position for minutes on end.

I was in the middle of a dream about Moira when I awoke. This bothered me for several reasons.

First was the lonely ache it raised in me. Moira and I had an understanding that we were to be married as soon as our schedules permitted, but I hadn't seen her since I'd left for the Greek Isles. We hadn't talked on the phone for a month, not since she flew back to D.C. to work with Congressman O'Hare. She hadn't replied to an email in well over a week. Either she was busy, or trying to signal me that she was upset about something.

In my dream she'd been right there, nestled in my arms. I swore I could inhale the scent of her soft, auburn hair against my nostrils. But when I opened my eyes she was gone. There was just me in that dank, chilly, predawn dungeon, and the only smell was a sulfurous stench from one of the many fires in the sacked village. My heart sank. I'd never felt more alone.

Another reason to feel perturbed then occurred to me: Is it possible to dream while you're in a psychotic state? I mean, let's say you hallucinate that you're watching Santa Claus in a battle with Satan: As I understand it you're not supposed to drift off during their showdown and have a dream about your old flame. Not during the same breakdown. You'd think that if such a thing happened, at least a few patients cured of psychosis would have reported this *Inception*-style, multi-level unreality. Then again, maybe they were all just too crazy to notice.

A third reason to worry, the one that made me really uneasy, was that an instant before I awoke, Moira had yelled something to me in Linear-A Minoan. Even in the dream, I was perfectly aware that Moira hasn't a shred of knowledge of, nor interest in, that language—it must have been a voice intruding on my sleep from the real world.

No, not the real world, I reminded myself, just another fantasy in my temporarily impaired brain. But the Minoan phrase, I was positive, meant, "To the ships!"

I got to my feet, joints aching from sitting all night in the pose of a discarded marionette. I was chained underneath the window facing east, but I could tell from the pink light radiating from it that the rosy-fingered dawn, as Homer would describe it centuries later, had arrived.

What had awakened me was the frenzy of activity outside. Minoans poured out of buildings, pulling on their armor, roused from sleep themselves. By what, I had no idea: There were no trumpets, no drums, no flights of arrows.

"To the ships," Stretch called over and over, but his tone was not a call to battle. It was an evacuation order, given in a voice at the edge of panic. They were also shouts of concern about someone named "Turu," whom I assumed was the invader who had raided the town.

"Brave sirs! Remember me?" I called out in my best Minoan.

As a convicted mad blasphemer, I wasn't eager to take a sea cruise with these pious and intolerant gentlemen, but I tried to make it clear how unfair it would be to leave me chained to a wall to starve to death. Or be slain by raiders. This time, I didn't even get a chuckle out of them. The city cleared out in fifteen minutes and they set sail.

Afterward, I heard two or three voices outside. From what I could gather, they were deserters, planning to loot what they could. They, too, ignored my calls.

So I was on my own for breakfast. I looked around to see if anyone had collected my bowl from last night. If I doubted my sanity, I was quite certain of my empty stomach, and the prospect of any leftover swill sticking to it was more appealing than it had been last night.

Alas, the bowl was not on the low wooden bench where I'd set it. That must have been some dream I'd had, one with plenty of thrashing, for the bowl was now on the floor, in several pieces. And yes, one of them was definitely potsherd 27.

That made my neck hairs rise. Wrack my memory as I might, I couldn't recall a single detail of my research, or of my excavation of this site, that put the lie to my current sense that this was the unruined Temple of the Dolphins.

Every gateway to my mind led to the same perception. The Minoan sights and sounds, the humid early morning cool, the mephitic odor, the swill's gamy aftertaste that I couldn't lose...this was a full five-senses experience. Actually seven, if you counted my hunger and the pressure in my bladder. The scene wasn't pleasant, but it seemed absolutely, undeniably real.

At least until Ariyl materialized.

There was a rush of wind, a flash of color, the room rippled in front of me—and there she was, appearing right out of thick air.

Okay, it was definitely scenario two. I had flipped out.

Ariyl was still carrying the Minotaur, but she had changed. I don't just mean her clothes. These were back to the white miniskirt, jacket, tank top, silver belt and narrow cord headband she wore when I met her. But they were a bit disarrayed. So was she.

She was not the smug princess who had bid me farewell yesterday. My first instinct was that she'd just had a bad scare, and was doing her best not to show it. But I'm better at reading pottery than people, so I didn't ask her what was wrong. Besides, hallucination or not, I was pissed at her.

"Professor, I need your help," she began, politely.

"Oh, please, no formalities. Call me David. What can I do for you? That doesn't involve using my hands, I mean."

"I'm sorry...David. I made a huge mistake. I'm going to tell you the truth about me."

"Sure, why not? It'll pass the time until my nurse brings me my anti-psychotics."

"What do you mean?" she asked, bewildered.

"That you're not really here, and neither am I."

"You think this is all some delusion?"

"No. A delusion is when I think I'm Napoleon. A hallucination is when I know I'm David Preston, but think I'm seeing things from three thousand years ago."

"You *are*," she insisted.

"Says my imaginary amazon."

"Look, if I was a hallucination, wouldn't you believe in me? You wouldn't think you were hallucinating. Right?"

I tried to find a flaw in that argument.

"Okay, fine, then I'm having the world's longest nightmare."

Ariyl pinched my arm. I yelped.

"Either you're awake, David, or else you're in a dream where you can get hurt."

I remembered the burns on my wrists and ankles, still tender from the hot manacles. Her logic was compelling.

"All right, no more pinching," I said. "I'm listening. Explain."

"First off, I'm a tourist."

"That much, I guessed. From where?"

"L.A. In the year 2109 A.D."

I took a long beat, looking at her. "You're a *time* tourist. From the future."

"But you can't tell anyone."

"Yeah," I agreed, "I better not, they might lock me up."

Ariyl's eyes flashed, which made them practically magenta. "Damn it, before I get you out of those chains, you have to believe I'm not some jacko."

"Jacko? What's that, some kind of future slang?"

"Jacko means crazy person. You know, a wacko-jacko?

"Ohhh," I nodded. "I know who Wacko Jacko was."

"He was a person?"

"Apparently, he's like Charles Boycott and General Joe Hooker... a once-famous man reduced to an infamous noun."

"Glad we cleared that up," Ariyl commented dryly. "Can you stop blabbing and listen, before it's too late?"

6

L.A., 2109 A.D.

ARIYL STARTED PACING, TRYING TO FIGURE OUT WHERE to start. "Back when I was a baby, like before the turn of the century..."

"The twenty-second century?" I interjected.

"I guess. Twenty-second, twenty-first, I'm not real good with dates or numbers or stuff. Anyway, something happened we call the Change. Life became completely different from what you know. We totally got rid of war and disease and famine and pollution and crime."

"That would be twenty-second, or later," I nodded. "Definitely not my time."

"Yeah. I hear L.A. was, like, one of the last places to get fixed up."

"How is it in your era?" I was curious how creative she could get.

"Beautiful. New. Oh, we still have some of the old places. I love them. Union Station, the Library...and that Bradbury Building? And most of City Hall."

"*Most* of City Hall? What happened to the rest?"

"You don't want to know," she said evasively. "Sometimes I go to the ruins of the Disney Concert Hall and wonder what it looked like before the disaster."

"Probably much the same." Then it hit me. "Wait, *what?* What disaster?"

"Let's focus on the good news. The town's all spiffed up again."

"Look, don't sugar-coat on my account. I've got a fair notion of what the future will look like, and it's not pretty. I'm expecting an L.A. out of *Blade Runner*."

She frowned. "What's that, one of those old flat-flix?"

"If by 'old flat-flix' you mean classic films, yes. The special effects might look a bit creaky to your sophisticated eye, but they were made by artists who understood human nature. And who would tell you no society has ever, or will ever, eliminate war or crime."

"Well, we did. Nobody kills or steals. They don't need to, not since N-Tec brought the Change."

"What is this N...?"

"N-Tec. Short for NanoTec? It's like this computer that's all over the world?"

She explained it was a global system that anyone could access anywhere. It programmed zillions of tiny "bots" that she said could "turn air into ice cream or diamonds or anything."

My first impulse was to laugh, but then I recalled Sven reading a scientific paper to me (well, *at* me) about nanotechnology: The possibility of building robots so small they could shift individual electrons and protons around, transmuting elements, turning one substance into another. Lead into gold was just the beginning. And they would be programmed to build duplicates of themselves too, so they could increase exponentially to any number that the task required. Theoretically there was no limit to what they could fabricate, nor how much of it.

"You say nobody steals," I pressed, "but what about people who can't afford this N-Tec?"

"What do you mean, afford?"

"To be able to pay. To have money. You do have money in the future, don't you?"

"You know, sometimes they talk about that in the vidz, but I never get what it means," marveled Ariyl. "Why would people be so fixated about having pieces of paper?"

"Well, what do *you* give somebody if you want them to do something for you?"

"You mean, sex?"

I stared at her, but decided that was a whole other discussion I better not get into. "Never mind."

"No, really, what's the deal with money?"

"You said N-Tec banished disease and crime and famine? Well, back in my day, money did that for you."

"How about war?"

"It generally kept you out of that, too. Very few rich people fought in wars." I wasn't getting through to her at all. "Look, your nanobots must run on power. Who pays for that? Where does it come from?"

Ariyl gave a helpless shrug.

"The sun, I think. Or maybe seawater? I think."

"You mean, solar power and hydrogen fusion?"

She nodded, without certainty.

"Well, if you perfect that kind of technology, that *would* mean unlimited energy. Okay, let's say everyone's rich, so no crime. And the only reason left to fight a war is religion."

"I think that was World War Three," she said, rubbing her chin. "But N-Tec won't let that happen anymore."

"It outlawed weapons?"

"Religion."

"You're kidding!"

She laughed. "Yeah. You can believe in whatever you like, but if you try to make anything deadlier than a penknife, N-Tec knows, and disassembles it. So nobody bothers trying."

"Not exactly paradise for the N.R.A. Or Al Qaeda," I remarked. "But it does sound peaceful."

"And yet...you still don't believe me."

I shook my head.

"Though I must admit for a loony fantasy, it's remarkably logical. Tell me more about this utopia of yours. What do you do all day, if you don't have to work?"

"We travel, y'know? It's nice and all. Paris, Yosemite, Angkor, Rio... been there, done that. I mean, you can only climb Everest so many times."

"You've climbed Mount Everest?"

"Not since I was twelve," she chuckled. "And after awhile, even bouncing around on the Moon gets kinda old."

I was glad they weren't neglecting space travel, even though she made it sound like they were renting out the Sea of Tranquility for kids' birthdays.

"Does anyone live on other planets?"

"Not really. They say we might have kind of a population problem coming. So if you wanted to have children, you might have to agree to live off-world. But since the Change, the birth rate has pretty much plunged. I don't know anyone with kids. Most people just want to have fun. But everything is really getting boring? People have been getting kinda rowdy? Fights break out over nothing?"

"I see. So what does society do for the rich tourist who's been everywhere?" I asked rhetorically. "Invent time travel!"

"You don't have to say it like that."

"Like what?"

"Like I'm jacko. I told you, N-Tec can build anything. It designs things nobody human could ever figure out." She paused, rueful. "Well, almost nobody."

"Okay, let's cut to the chase," I said. "If you're from the future, prove it. Pull out your particle-beam and cut me loose."

"I don't have whatever that is. N-Tec won't let you bring anything back in time that might alter history. I have nothing except the Time

Crystal...and my clothes. And even those will self-destruct if they're off me too long."

"Time Crystal?" I stared at her doughnut-shaped zirconium. What a letdown. I imagined a time machine would be huge and high tech and cost a billion bucks...not resemble a bauble from a Vegas gift shop.

"How does it work?"

"Yeah, like I listened to the lecture!" she snorted. "It has its own nanobots. Something about making an exotic matter wormhole whip around at light-speed? Who cares, it gets me around."

"It's handy," I agreed. "And I like your programmable nano-dress. Care to show me that little Minoan number again?"

"Dream on, ogle-boy. I reset the default. And that's not really N-Tec, just SmartFab."

"Which is...?"

"Short for SmartFabrix. You guys'll have something like that in twenty years. Or maybe fifty."

"I can't wait."

There was a distant rumble. It didn't smell like rain, and we were indoors. But Ariyl glanced out the window in a way that made me nervous. And there was something else I knew from my studies, something I wasn't allowing myself to worry about at the moment, since I still didn't believe we were where and when Ariyl said we were. It was just too absurd. Yet with all her chit-chat about Tomorrowland, I still hadn't found the hole in her story.

"If N-Tec doesn't want you altering history," I pressed, "why did it send you back in time?"

"The real question," she fumed to herself, "is why did they send Ludlo?"

"Who's that?"

"Jon Ludlo. He's...well, I guess you'd call him an art collector. He collects everything from antique weapons to baseballs."

"Baseballs?" The truth smacked me hard. "Damn it! I *knew* I saw you before. That was Ludlo who gave Andy the fake Ty Cobb ball, wasn't it?"

"Yeah, at Dodger Stadium," she admitted. "A couple years back... for you. For me, a few hours ago."

I lunged at her, but those bronze chains did exactly what they were designed for. Ariyl didn't flinch, but for the first time since I'd met her, she actually looked ashamed. Good. I wanted to grab her and shake her.

"God damn you! You knew he was going to die that day!" She avoided my glare. "You could've warned him!"

"No, we couldn't. N-Tec would've caught it. It totally monitors us, and erases any change to the past. And our trip would be over."

"So you thought what the hell, he's gonna die anyway, let's get a souvenir?"

"It wasn't my idea, David! I didn't even think we *could* carry stuff through time like that. But once Ludlo snuck that pen back to 1908, he decided he could do something bigger."

"So you're saying, he figured a way around N-Tec's monitoring?"

"I dunno," she responded, lamely. "I still think that was an accident."

"Yeah?" I said, dubious. "How dumb is this guy?"

"Not dumb at all. He knows, like, everything. He's the only genius I know."

"So what is this Ludlo, your boyfriend?"

"Not anymore, we're just friends. Well, it's complicated. And not really any of your business. Let's just say, we were taking this trip as pals."

"Wait a minute. There are more of you future-tourists gadding about through history?"

"No, just me and him at the moment," Ariyl answered. "There are only two Crystals. The Time Travel Agency can only send us back in pairs. Anyway, this morning was our turn. Ludlo told me to meet him at the Hollywood Canal."

"The Hollywood What?"

"I hear it used to be some kinda road," she began. "But no one uses roads anymore, and Downtown really needed some water, so we flooded the—what did you call them—freeways? And made them into canals. Anyhoo, Ludlo was early, as usual. And maybe I was a little late. We had to get to the Travel Agency, which is in the old train station, so we grabbed a couple floaters..."

"Those are levitation vehicles?"

"Duh," she confirmed. "Look, I need to get through this story, okay? Could you please like not interrupt?"

More thunder rumbled, closer. But the sky was clear.

7

THE TIME TRAVEL AGENCY

Ariyl sped up, nervous: "We got to the Agency only a few minutes before we were supposed to make the trip. Sumi —she's the Agency lady—was all hoarked off at us. 'There are only two Crystals. You could have thrown off our schedule!' Y'know, lighten up. She doesn't have to work there. There's only seventy million bored people in the world who'd be happy to have her job. Or any job."

I almost asked how the Earth's population had been reduced from seven billion to one percent of that in just a century, but figured I wouldn't like her answer.

"We're waiting in the lobby, and I'm up for it. We saw the couple ahead of us turn their SmartFab to velvet brocade—I really love that look—and then they put on the Time Crystals and jumped back to the Renaissance. I'm all, 'I can't believe we're going to Atlantis!' And Ludlo's like, 'Ariyl, you've been playing too many bad vidz. The real name of the island was Thera, and it was part of the Minoan Empire.' He's kinda like you about that detail stuff."

"I like him already."

"Then I get kinda worried it might be depressing? And he's

laughs, like, 'Ariyl, you've only seen virtual reality. This will *be* reality. Back in time, before N-Tec, they had real life. Real death.'

"And I'm, 'Shyeah, and real starvation and poverty and crime...'

"Then he gets this weird look and asks me, 'What makes something precious?' Before I can answer, he goes, 'It's when people want what you have. Imagine being the only one to own the mask of Tutankhamen. Shakespeare's first draft of *Hamlet*. Or the Holy Grill.'"

"Holy Grail," I corrected. "From the Last Supper, not the Last Barbecue."

"Whatever! So I remind Ludlo we can't bring souvenirs back with us, and he's all, 'Yeah, thanks to good old NanoTec.' He's always ragging on N-Tec. I, like, point out without N-Tec we wouldn't have time travel, or anything else. He goes, 'And things would have value again. Life would have meaning.' I say, 'Life *has* meaning!' And he goes..."

At this point, Ariyl laid her hand on my cheek with great tenderness and leaned close, "...and says, 'Does it, Ariyl?'"

Ariyl waited, clearly expecting me to share her scorn. I felt blood rush to my face. "I mean, euu, right?" she prompted. I gave a belated nod.

"So I have to, like, remind him I don't feel that way anymore. And Ludlo looks all bitter, and goes, 'that's because we live in a world where my talents mean nothing. In a simpler time, I could offer you so much.' Then he reaches up, pulls down the Lisa Mona—they have all this awesome crusty art on the walls—and he's, 'Look. Beautiful as the minute Leonardo laid down his brush. The most valuable artwork in history. But now we can reproduce it down to the last atom.'"

She paused, amused. "Did I mention he talks like that all the time? Anyway, then he punches his fist right through her funny smile."

"My God...not the original Mona Lisa, right?"

"That's what *I* asked. And he cops a 'tude!

"'Who even knows?" he yells. 'When you can make a million

identical copies, *nothing* is real. That's what I loathe about N-Tec!' And now Sumi the travel agent is really giving us the stink-eye."

"They'll do that when you start busting up the office décor," I remarked.

"It's no biggie where I come from. The bots fix stuff in half a sec. But now she's standing right there going, 'Mr. Ludlo, you're aware we will screen out anyone we feel lacks the discipline required for time travel?'

"And Ludlo tells her he's kidding. And Sumi turns to me.

"So I say, 'Do you know who his grandfather was? Plus my dad's on the City Council. You think he'd let me hang with some utter jacko?' And she thinks that over, and says, 'No. I'm sure he wouldn't.'"

Ariyl shook her head, remorseful.

"That's what I told her. God damn, I am such a stupid idiot! This is all my fault!"

"I still don't get it. What is all your fault?"

"I gave that sonofabitch cred."

"You vouched for him."

Ariyl nodded, miserable.

"Sumi goes back to her station and I tell Jon to stop slamming N-Tec. I mean, I'd already spent hours convincing the Psych-Board he didn't mean any of the crap he spews. And Ludlo just grins and goes, 'Of course I don't mean it. I use our big, digital nanny all the time.'

"Then he has N-Tec show his last data search. But what kinda creeps me is when I see N-Tec display all these dates and places in midair? See, we agreed he was only going to 1908, 2011, and Atlantis. But here are all these other dates and places, and he starts writing them down. On paper, with a pen? The antique pen I gave him for his birthday? And I'm, 'What's with the pen, are you an artist now?' He says a century ago, people actually recorded data with them.

"Just as he finishes, that couple returned from the Renaissance and you can tell they partied like it was 1599. 'Cause it's been three days for them.

"Some tech puts the Crystals in the charging thing, while Sumi comes over and does the whole talk we've heard kajillion times in the training sessions. You know..."

And here Ariyl slipped into a deft imitation of what sounded like a flight attendant spiel:

"'Your trip will last seventy-two hours from your standpoint, but you will return to the present only five minutes after you leave. Your Time Crystal contains a translator programmed with every known language.'"

"So *that's* how you speak Minoan? A translator chip?"

"What'd you think," she snorted, amused, "I *learned* it?"

"I've learned nine, not counting English. It can be done. Jesus. *Now* I know how a brilliant linguist could send such a bonehead résumé."

"Oh, excuse me, Professor Genius. You figured out a dead language. But I use it to get *you* chained up, and *I'm* the bonehead?"

"I am not blind to the irony."

"Anyway, when Sumi says, 'Your Crystal will be your link to NanoTec, which will monitor your every move'...I look at Ludlo, and he looks *pissed*...but also, like he's about to bust out laughing? And they give us these shiny disks with funny little designs..."

"Coins! So they did give you period money, to buy food or admission to places?"

"I guess. Ludlo took charge of those."

"A gentleman always pays," I muttered. Ariyl either missed my sarcasm, or ignored it.

"Then she puts the Crystals on us and she tells us any action which could alter history will result in the immediate erasing of our trip, and permanent loss of time travel privileges."

Aha! The inevitable hole in her story.

"Ariyl, just being back in time would mean you're already

altering history the second you arrive. Every molecule you exhale would..."

"No, no, the trainers told us all this stuff about the Certainty Principle."

"You mean Uncertainty Principle?"

"And probability waves and how history has what they call inertia? Time's kinda in a rut, and it's hard to shove it out, as long as you just, y'know, observe and don't leave stuff behind or tell people the future or kill them or anything. Now let me finish."

"But..."

"Don't make me pinch you again."

I almost pointed out she was telling *me* enough about the future to change it, but I kept my mouth shut. Hey, maybe I was destined to remain tight-lipped...or not be believed. Or was fated never to leave the 17th century B.C.E.

And that was assuming I was even here. I still leaned toward the out-of-my-skull theory. But now, the odds I gave against time travel were down to ten-to-one, if only because I still hadn't tripped her up on a thing.

"So just before we leave, Ludlo takes out his paper and scans it *again*. And I'm like, 'Why do you have that? You can get the data anytime from N-Tec.' And he gets that same funny look and says, 'You never know.'

"Then we put on our Crystals and we set our clothes. He was making a stop in 1908, to meet Ty Cobb. After that, he jumped to Chavez Ravine the same year, and buried the ball by a big rock. His idea was to have this old, valuable souvenir we could trade for something better. All this time, I have to wait for him in the hot sun at Dodger Stadium in 2001. No, wait, it was 2011, right?" I nodded.

(Yet another strange thing about Ariyl—she didn't say "two thousand one" the way most people do. She said "twenty-oh-one.")

"My first trip back in time," she fumed, "And I spend half an hour of it watching cars roll into a parking lot! Finally Ludlo shows up, and we dig up his sack with the ball."

"Why didn't you go with him to see Ty Cobb?"

"Jon just said it was a guy-thing. And I'm not real big on sports, anyway. But now I think, it was really 'cause he didn't want me knowing he was going to get an autograph."

"Sounds that way. Where did the baseball come from?"

"That was Cobb's. Ludlo told me he was after an autograph on paper, but saw the ball and decided that was cooler. Then after your friend Andy signed the other ball for Ludlo, we both jumped back here...the Temple of the Dolphins, May 10th, 1628 B.C." Then she saw the skeptical look on my face. "What?"

"If you were really from the future, you'd know that historians dropped the whole 'Before Christ' and 'Anno Domini' thing. In a hundred years even laymen will say Common Era—C.E. and B.C.E."

She gave me a blank look, then shrugged.

"Naah, we don't. I guess that never caught on. Maybe they sound too much alike?" Annoyingly, she had a point.

"Let me ask you something," I snapped. "Why was I so lucky? Why would you pick me to rob?"

"I didn't rob you! You wouldn't have found anything, if not for us," insisted Ariyl.

"What's that supposed to mean?"

For a moment she was silent, looking out the east-facing window. "The last time I saw Ludlo was an hour ago—or I guess to you, yesterday afternoon—right out there. Okay, we're just taking in the sights, and I kind of lose him for a while? The Time Crystals are supposed to be linked, but I couldn't contact him. Next thing I see, he's coming out of the Temple of the Dolphins with this leather bag under his cloak. And inside it is..."

"Let me guess. The golden Minotaur."

"Like I said, it was my gift. From Ludlo. I tell him I can't take it with me, but he's like, it's perfect and if I don't take it, it'll just be destroyed. He says if taking it was gonna affect history, N-Tec would've already yanked us home and erased our trip, right?

"He goes, 'It's unique, Ariyl, you'll be the only one to have it. Just drop it off home then we'll meet here at dawn.' Which would be like now, this morning? And as he finishes telling me all this, the priest-dude –"

"Shaman."

"I didn't get his name. He comes skidding out of the temple screaming that the golden Minotaur's been kyped! I'm like, 'Great gift, Ludlo.' Warriors are swarming all over, going through all the other priests' garments. It's too obvious Ludlo and me are gonna be next, and I'm not really up for a body-search by ancient barbarians? But we're not supposed to beat anybody up, either? That's when Ludlo sticks the Minotaur in his leather bag and scoops a hole in the sand and buries it. We walk on a little way and the soldiers show up. I show them I don't have anything on me."

"I've seen how you do that."

"And so does Ludlo. The soldiers go off scouring the countryside. People were so easy to trick in olden times! But we go back to the steps and now there's a bunch of soldiers sitting right on top of where Ludlo buried it! Ludlo says no prob, and tells me the date you were going to find the temple steps. All I have to do is find you and dig the Minotaur up, just like Ludlo did the baseball. I'm still real nervous but he just jumps downtime leaving me behind. Then wouldn't you know it..."

"You forgot the date he told you?"

"What are you, psychic? Yeah, all I remembered was 2013. So I jump ahead to New York in 2014 and get a salesman to show me how to work one of those old ePads."

"iPads."

"We search for the exact day you dug up the temple, he helps me whip up a résumé thing, then I jump back in time a year to meet you."

"So by next year, I'm all over the Internet?" I was intrigued. Time travel was now eight-to-five, and heading for even money.

"Yeah, there's something called Google that has you mentioned in three different places."

"Three hits?" I sighed. "A regular superstar. I don't suppose I had my book out yet?"

"No book," she reported. "But one was your old high school trying to find you. Somebody asked if you were ducking your ten-year reunion."

"Yep. If I don't have my book out in three years, I'll definitely be a no-show."

"So I jump back to Santorini on the day you found the temple, call your apartment, your neighbor Sven gives me your email address, and I contact you at your dig. You know the rest."

"No, no, don't stop there. Let's see...then you barged in, snagged your buried treasure, manhandled me, dragged me three-and-a-half millennia back in time, then skipped home leaving me here holding the bag."

"David, the way you put it makes me sound awful."

"Does it now? Can you put it a better way?"

"Well, when you tackled me, I *was* a little pissed. I thought it would serve you right to actually get stuck in the time period you were so obsessed with. I wasn't going to leave you there long. A quick trip home, then I was coming right back for you. But..."

"But what?"

"When I got home, um, home wasn't there anymore."

8

BAD PART OF TOWN, 2109 A.D.

There was a quiver in Ariyl's voice. Was this acting, or was she genuinely fighting panic?

"What do you mean, not there? Your house was gone?"

"My house? Try my city!" She forced herself to take a deep breath. "I tell the Time Crystal to take me to my house, okay? Which is right on the Hollywood Canal, on the same morning that Ludlo and I left?

"Instead, I wind up in a desert. The canal is dry and at the bottom of it there's broken up concrete and weeds and totally toasted antique cars. No grass, no trees. All the new buildings are gone, and the old ones are all smashed in, burned out and barely holding each other up. But I know this has to be L.A., cause I can still see a tiny part of City Hall. Only it looks like the piñata at the end of the party. I'm guessing they had three mega-disasters in a row, minimum, and nobody cleaned up after any of them.

"I'm like, this is a mistake. I don't know that much history, so I have no idea when all this crap went down, but this is *so* not my time. I keep going 'L.A., June 4th, 2109 A.D.' But I'm not going anywhere. I try to access N-Tec, and tell it to bring me home. I get nada. I yell for Jon, for my mom and dad...Nothing. It's like the whole city's dead. All I can hear is the damn wind.

"But someone heard me, 'cause out of this trashed storefront come two guys. And I'm using the term 'guy' loosely. They're somewhere between mid-twenties and dead, in these crappy, ripped-up leather clothes that are so last-Halloween. And truly serious hygiene issues. But I'm relieved. I go, 'Am I glad to see you!'

"The big one gives me a grin with teeth like rocks in pond scum, and goes, 'It's mutual, baby.'

"I look down and thank God, the SmartFab has gone back to my street clothes. I don't know what he would have tried if I'd been all Minoan-topless. That's when I tell the Crystal to disable the clothing change. Speaking of which, it's getting hot in here."

It was. Minutes ago, the sun had made its entrance through the east window, burnishing Ariyl's golden tresses and banishing the predawn chill. The air had become surprisingly warm. Ariyl touched her shoulder, murmured something, and the jacket shrank into a sheer white tank-top, revealing her voluptuous, powerful physique, with her flawless skin now glistening with sweat. I didn't need any further distractions, so I looked away as Ariyl continued:

"Then I notice the little, even-dumber one is carrying, what do you call it, a machete?" she continued. "And the taller guy's got this big assault-gun thingy. Now I'm *sure* I'm in the wrong time period, cause N-Tec wouldn't allow that.

"So I'm kinda backing away and asking them what year it is, and they don't seem to know. I go, 'Well, it's not 2109, right?' And the little dude is like, 'I think it might be. Lessee, Mama said I was born in 2080, right after the big plague.' And he's counting on his fingers. And I'm starting to freak?

"The big guy goes, 'Ehh, shaddap, nobody gives a shit about numbers anymore.' Then he gives me that moss-eating grin again and says, 'Come with us, babe, we found some genu-ine dried food.' Like I could eat after seeing him smile. And I'm all, 'Nooo, thanks, I already have plans for lunch.'

"That's when Mr. Green Teeth grabs my arm. Major euu. I tell him let go, and he's, 'I said come on!' and I'm, 'I said let go!' He doesn't. I'm getting ticked, so I slap him. Not even that hard. He flies into Little Dude and they hit the ground together."

I could imagine. I was fortunate that Ariyl kept her temper when I laid my hand on her arm back in the cave. I realized a smack from a two-by-four would be a love-tap compared to what that lovely hand could deliver.

"How many of those green teeth did you knock out?"

"I dunno. He did spit one out while he's calling me a bitch and cocking his gun. God, I hate guns. In the vidz, whoever has his gun out first mows down the other guy who wasn't ready. What's heroic about that? Or are you supposed to be a hero 'cause your aim's better, which means you've had more practice killing people?"

"All good points, Ariyl, but about this guy who's ready to blow you away...?"

"Oh, right. Lucky for me his gun's rusty. I hear it jam. Little Dude starts to nag him about single shots and not wasting a bunch of bullets on me. I barely have time to say, 'Previous destination!' before he unjams it. I swear I saw the flash just as I jumped out of time. And then I showed up here in front of you."

"Except you didn't come back to your previous destination. If you had, you'd be outside, at noon yesterday."

Ariyl shook her head.

"No, the Crystal won't let us revisit the same time and place. Otherwise, you could run into your past self. So if you say 'previous destination' the Crystal makes you lose some hours. And you appear somewhere else in the area, not the exact spot where you left."

"N-Tec thinks of everything."

"Can we focus up here?" Ariyl snapped. "I got a real problem. I knew Ludlo hated N-Tec, but I never dreamed he'd do anything like this!"

"Do what?"

"Change history, *duh!* Somehow he erased the world I was born into."

Rats. It looked like Time Travel was fading fast and My Mental Breakdown was moving into first place.

"Sorry, Ariyl. Sincerely, it's an awesome story and I wish I could believe in it. And in you. Especially in you. But your story is illogical."

"Stop saying that! It's perfectly logical. I'm telling you the truth!"

"You can't be. If your world was erased, then you were never born. So how could you still be here?"

"I don't know! Same reason Ludlo could erase history, I guess. All I know is, N-Tec is supposed to be there in 2109 to cancel out any changes to history. But when I go to 2109, N-Tec's gone."

"And you think Ludlo did that?"

"Who else? He just loved the idea of taking stuff from history. I have to think something he took, kinda kept N-Tec from being invented, or something. I was still hoping I'd find him waiting for me here this morning, and everything would be okay...but he's never late. Like, ever. So now I know something's wrong."

God, it was hot, and it was still early. This day was going to be a scorcher. I was dripping sweat, and imaginary or not, these manacles were uncomfortable.

"Okay, let's say I believe all this. What do you want from me?"

"You know history," Ariyl replied. "I don't. I need you to help me find Jon Ludlo, so I can tell him to undo whatever he did."

"Has it struck you it might be something *you* did? Stealing a historic object like the Minotaur must change something."

"Not this one. In a few hours, it would've been vaporized."

"Well, then I guess it's..."

Belated realization socked me in the stomach.

"What do you mean, vaporized?"

"That's why we were meeting on Thera today. To watch the volcano wipe out the island."

9

SHOWTIME

"WHAT?!"

"The idea was to jump downtime at the last second," she enthused. "Major thrill."

Now I knew. I knew where that sulfurous stench was coming from. I knew it wasn't me kicking in my sleep that broke the bowl this morning. It was the same thing that awoke the Minoans and me: a heavy foreshock.

"When?" I demanded. "What time?"

"I'm not sure. Sometime after dawn."

"*Sometime?*" I yelled, my voice starting to crack. "It's past dawn now! How can you not know the time?"

"Ludlo knew. If I could still access N-Tec, I could tell you to the second." At that moment, the room undulated. The distant thunder rose in volume to a gut-gripping rumble, as the walls began to shake.

"I guess it's now," she added.

I'd been through the 1994 Northridge earthquake when I was a kid in Santa Monica. It was 6.7 on the Richter Scale, and Santa Monica was on an alluvial plain, which shook like Jell-O. I'd lain in bed, terror washing over me, as I wondered how strong it would get, and when it would end. But then it had subsided.

This quake was just as bad...for the first five seconds. The next five seconds it was twice as bad. Then four times, then eight, then sixteen...The stone floor bumped my buttocks as I was thrown up and down.

Ariyl managed to stay on her feet. She looked scared, but not to death. It was more akin to the manic exhilaration of a kid on the wildest ride at Magic Mountain.

Dust rained down and I saw daylight flicker between the temple's shifting stones. Adrenaline shot through me. My Mental Breakdown hit the rail and Time Travel won the race.

"Oh, my God!" I bellowed above the cacophony. "You were telling the truth!"

Ariyl gave me a superior look as she rode the bucking floor.

"Is that an apology I hear, for calling me loony?"

Out the west window, I saw the peak of Thera flame like artillery, blasting into the atmosphere orange plumes of lava and flaming stones that had to be the size of Airstream trailers. The jumping adobe houses across the roadway split along fracture lines and one by one, collapsed.

This was the fabled event of which I'd read so much, but that I'd told myself not to worry about since time travel couldn't possibly be real: the eruption which would obliterate Minoan civilization. Little Santorini, site of my dig, was but the eastern rim of the crater, all that would be left after this much larger volcanic island called Thera finished blowing itself to bits.

The worst eruption in recorded history, Krakatoa in 1883, was equal to a 300-megaton hydrogen bomb; Thera was estimated to be four times more powerful. At some point, maybe an hour from now, maybe any minute, the volcanic cone would explode, sending out a blistering pyroclastic cloud that would instantly cremate anyone it touched.

I realized now that terrifying foreshocks must have gone on here for months. That was why the inhabitants had fled, why human remains had not been found in the ruined cities.

"Turu will destroy us!" the Minoan warriors had cried as they'd abandoned the city. At least I would die knowing that Turu was the Minoan word for the volcano Thera.

I threw myself against my bonds in a painful frenzy, thinking I might break them with sheer panic. "I've got to get these freaking chains off!" I may have said something stronger than "freaking." Now, thirty seconds after the flash from the eruption, its deafening boom reached us.

"Hold still," instructed Ariyl. She set down the Minotaur, seized the chain that bound my wrists with both her fists, and strained. Her biceps and triceps at rest appeared merely athletic, but flexing, they bulged like Serena Williams' mighty arm smashing home the game point at Wimbledon. With a dainty grunt more appropriate to opening a pickle jar, Ariyl broke the chain.

"Jeez Louise!" was all I could think of to say.

The first earthquake had subsided, which is to say the ground was only swaying like the worst part of Northridge. I looked out the west window again. Glowing molten rock was cascading down Thera's mountainside, torching olive groves into walls of flame that spread to either side and raced ahead of the lava flow.

Fiery stones launched from the initial eruption began landing in and around the city. The first we only heard, but it must have been huge; it rocketed down into the sea, accompanied by a resounding boom and hiss. A second, no doubt smaller, set a thatched roof across the road aflame. The third thudded off the wall above the west window, sending a shower of embers onto Ariyl's back. She shook it off.

After that I lost count of the rain of fire, until a blazing boulder the size of a school bus landed on the Minoan palace across the street, reducing it to a pile of stone blocks. My ears rang from the deafening impact. Blast-furnace heat and smoke radiated through the window from the inferno of ruins, and a blizzard of ash began to fall.

"Hurry!" I coughed.

Ariyl, having trouble with my leg chains, which were thicker, gave me a stare: "You want to try it?"

I shook my head. She braced her feet against the wall and again flexed her rippling thighs for all they were worth, which was considerable. I could see the weakest link distend. Ariyl relaxed for a second, then with her next flex, burst it apart, one of its hot shards whacking me in the forehead.

I staggered away from the wall a free man. I began to thank her, but before I could get a word out, another super-temblor hit. The entire temple swayed five feet sideways, knocking both Ariyl and me to the floor.

I looked out the window, and saw the entire mountain of Thera vanish in a rapidly expanding cloud. White-hot death raced toward us at the speed of a jet plane. In thirty seconds, our smothered, cooked bodies would be encased in Pompeian ash.

Above us I heard the wooden columns snapping with unimaginable violence and the stone above them collapsing onto the stairway. The floor went in two directions at once as a crack tore through the stones right between my legs. I tumbled to one side as a chasm opened up, a yard wide and deeper than I could see. The floor on the far side of the chasm dropped a foot and tilted downward toward the crack.

To my horror, I saw the spot where Ariyl had set the golden Minotaur was on the sloping floor beyond the gap. That priceless relic was sliding toward the chasm.

"No!" I howled, and dove for it. The Minotaur toppled over the edge. My arm extended into the crack. Had those gleaming horns been a centimeter shorter, the statuette would have fallen into the depths. Instead, it stuck three feet down, wriggling its way lower between the shuddering halves of the floor. If I could just stretch my fingers another inch, I'd have it. Maybe I could somehow dislocate my shoulder?

"Leave it!" shouted Ariyl. "Take my hand!"

"Like hell I will!" I snapped. "I spent three years of my life looking..."

I heard another horrific crack, this one from above. I looked up at the fitted blocks of stone that comprised the ceiling. Beneath the crack was Ariyl, one hand on her Crystal, the other reaching down to me. She could not see the huge section of stone over her head that had just broken away from the rest and was sagging towards her.

"Look out!" I cried, diving at her.

She called out something I couldn't hear over the deafening cataclysm. At least this time I had sense enough to tackle her at the knees, where I had a little more leverage. She toppled sideways. I heard the ceiling cave in on us, landing with a hideous thud as darkness and silence closed in.

10

THE OCEAN BLUE

Abruptly, I felt cold and damp and sandy. I opened my eyes, and gasped. I coughed up ash, but the air I inhaled was now cool and clean. It was daylight outside, but I was back in the sea cave, several yards further inland. I was in a low spot I had avoided excavating because of the chance we'd hit water. It was just where the back of the dungeon under the temple would have been. As I turned, I recalled the big stone block that was now...

Oh, my God, it was on top of Ariyl's leg! She was unconscious. By some miracle her leg wasn't crushed. Well, she did have formidable thighs.

"Ariyl? Ariyl!" I cried. "Are you all right?"

I strained to lift the stone off her, but it must have weighed five hundred pounds. I couldn't budge it. I shook Ariyl's shoulder.

"Ariyl, can you hear me? Ariyl!"

Ariyl sat up, blinking in the light. "Yeah, I broke my leg, not my eardrum." With that, she put her hands under the stone and flipped it off her. It crunched deep into the sand. The sharp end of the broken block had torn her thigh open, down to the muscle. Blood poured down her leg. I winced.

"We have to stop that bleeding. This is going to hurt."

"Go ahead."

"Hang onto something."

"I'm fine."

I whipped my belt out of my belt loops, and wrapped it around her thigh. Then I pushed the lacerated muscle and skin back together.

I was nervous, but I'd already had to fix someone's compound fracture, on a dig in Central Mexico.

"Ooch," said Ariyl.

"That's some threshold of pain you have. Last time I had to do that, I made a two hundred pound Marine scream like a baby."

"I see why you're not a doctor," she commented.

I had to let go of the skin to thread the belt through the buckle... and at that moment, I saw into the briefly opened wound. The muscle tissue was *knitting itself together*. The severed blood vessels were growing back, as if reaching out to each other. I didn't believe my eyes. I blinked, but the image didn't change. Then I cinched the belt as tight as I could, and looped the end around the buckle a couple of times till I could fit the prong into a hole. By then the blood flow had slowed to a trickle. At the same time, the tear in her skin began closing up.

I sat back on the sand, and stared at Ariyl Moro. It's not that she wasn't quite normal. It was that she wasn't quite human.

"What?" she asked me.

"Lady, you are scary. You snap chains with your bare hands, you heal from a lacerated leg in about a minute. Is this N-Tec doing this?"

"I told you, N-Tec's broken. Nah, this is just standard gene-splicing. We've had bodies like this since...I dunno. Sometime after my parents were born? Oh, here, let me," she added, helpfully peeling my bronze manacles apart.

"Can you heal from anything? I mean, what if that stone crushed your head? Or you got incinerated by the volcano?"

"Oh, then I'd be dead. For a while."

"What do you mean, a while?"

"Well, till N-Tec activates my clone."

"You're telling me you have a spare body, just waiting around in case you do something fatal?"

"Everybody does. A body that's never lived, kept in cold storage. Nothing in its brain. And no wisecracks, thank you."

"But it's not you."

"Not at first. But there's an implant in my brain that signals my memories to N-Tec every hour for backup. If I get killed again, they download the latest memory into my clone's brain, and I'm good to go."

"Again? You've already had this done?"

Ariyl nodded, embarrassed.

"Once. I was kinda goofing around on Everest and fell into a crevasse. I actually remember falling. I guess I was uploading memory at the time. It took them weeks to find my original body. My parents were furious at me."

"So...you people have immortality!"

"Yeah. Otherwise, I'd never fly."

Ariyl got to her feet. Her wound was closed now, with barely a scar. I couldn't tell one hyper-developed leg from the other now, though she did limp for her first couple of steps. She brought up her left foot so she could grab it, and experimentally flexed her thigh. The sculpted muscle swelled and with a sharp pop, snapped my belt in half.

"Oops, *sorry*," she giggled, sheepish. "Forgot that was there."

I swallowed hard. "That's all right. It was cheap and worn-out." I was being chivalrous. It was a fifty-dollar, top grade leather belt, practically new. Well, I didn't need it; my pants weren't exactly loose.

"Look, if N-Tec's gone," I suggested, "You need to be less reckless. You haven't got a backup anymore."

"Yeah," she agreed. "Least till we find Ludlo and get things back on track."

"What do you mean 'we'?"

"Like I said, I don't know history. I need you to guide me."

My eyes would have widened in astonishment if they weren't already bugged-out at that belt-busting stunt.

"Right. And people in hell need ice water."

"I just saved your life!" she exclaimed.

"After you got me chained to an island that was about to blow up!"

"You tried to take my statue!"

"Your *stolen* statue!"

"David, my entire world is gone!"

"Any era that produced a head-case like you deserves to be erased! And now that I'm back in my own time, it's my turn to say, Ta-ta!"

I turned and marched up the sand toward the table where I had left my sat phone. I didn't care who I had to call or how much I had to pay, but I was going to get a boat over here and get away from this nutjob before she could do anything else to me.

But my sat phone was not there. Neither was my laptop. Nor, for that matter, was the table I left them on. Also gone were my camp stove, my tent, and every bit of my equipment. Had thieves totally cleaned out the camp in the time we'd been gone? Of course, I didn't know how long we'd been gone. It could've been weeks. The weather was no longer warm, but chilly and foggy. Well, if I had to, I would hike back to town.

I walked out of the cave. Fortunately, a ship was sailing close by the shore. Unfortunately, it was a Spanish galley, drawn by oars. I might have thought it was Roman or Greek, except that it had a big red Maltese cross on the mainsail, and its captain was dressed in doublet and hose. His crew was also in costume. It occurred to me they might be cruising over to the local Renaissance Faire, but somehow, I doubted it. I took a deep, cleansing breath.

"Ariyl," I said, without turning around, without raising my voice, "What date did you bring us to?"

"Um, I couldn't remember your year. I knew it was October 6th. But then I blanked. I said the first thing that came in my head."

"Which was?"

"1492?"

"Mm-hm. I thought you didn't know any history."

"Well, duh, I know the year America started."

"Okay, you're right."

"About...?"

"You not knowing history. America started in 1776. That's three centuries from now, but still not close enough to do me any good." I looked at the galley again. It being 1492, you might expect a caravel, the kind of ship in which Columbus was even now approaching the New World... but those were designed for ocean faring, not for Mediterranean hops. Galleys had been in use since ancient times, and would still be part of the Armada for another century. Eighty years from now, one of the slaves at those oars might be Cervantes, dreaming of the day he could chuck his day job and write that novel about the man who tilts at windmills.

"I could've just said 'previous destination'," Ariyl told me as I reentered the cave. "But the skeeves with the rusty gun might've still been hanging around."

I stood on the site of my excavation. Or where it should have been. No pit. Nothing but smooth sand and one little potsherd poking out. The cave looked like I had never been there...and of course, I would not be, for another five centuries.

"Ariyl, I am not digging this all up again. So bring me back to October 6th, 2013, the same moment we left. Please."

"I can't. I told you, even if I say the same time, the Crystal skips a few hours..."

"As close as you can. Please." I thought I was doing a splendid job of keeping my temper, but then, I really had no alternative.

"Okay, one day later. And you'll help me track down Ludlo?"

I stood on principle. "I refuse to even discuss this until you return me to where you kidnapped me."

"I didn't kidnap you, you grabbed my ass."

"I can see where you might have experienced it that way. Once we're back to 2013, we can have that discussion."

"Discussion is good," purred Ariyl, with a knowing smile. She sauntered up close, until I was staring into those violet eyes. She was exhaling into my nostrils. She smelled sweet and minty, with a hint of some exotic liqueur. She slipped her arms around me and tenderly embraced me. Gradually, she pulled me in close, squeezing me against her impossibly lush body. As Groucho Marx put it, if she held me any closer I'd be behind her. How could someone so powerful feel so soft?

"I can be very persuasive," she whispered in my ear.

"I'm sure you can," I stammered, "One way or the other." Her amorous bear hug now had my feet dangling an inch above the sand. She chuckled softly, her breath warming me.

"In some of the old vidz, I see men initiate sex. Is that what you're used to?" I nodded. "That's so funny. Where I come from, it's almost always the woman."

"I got that impression," I replied, as dryly I could. This future of hers was looking stranger by the second.

Then Ariyl gave me a long, long, long kiss, a kiss to make my toes curl and my clothes shrink. Finally, she let me up for air. I was dizzy with desire for her. I needed to make her stop while I still had any wits left.

"Look, I find you very attractive," I panted.

"I can tell."

"But let's get me home, first."

Ariyl heaved a deep sigh, which I experienced all the way in to my spine and back out again. Then she let me back down on terra firma.

"Okay, where's home?" she asked, brightening. "The Crystal can take us anyplace. Or did you mean back to this cave?"

"Yeah, I meant...no, no, come to think of it, home would be good. I live in L.A."

"I thought you said West L.A."

"Well, that's just what they call the neighborhood," I riffed. "Take us to Union Station. It's actually just a few blocks west of there."

"Are you kidding? I'd love to see downtown in 2013! I've always wanted to know what L.A. looked like before the Big One."

"The Big One?" I asked. "What Big One?" Ariyl ignored me, took my hand in hers, and put her other hand to her Crystal.

"Destination: L.A. Union Station, noon, October 7th, 2013 A.D." Her Crystal glowed and the world went away again.

11

UNION STATION, 2013 A.D.

THIS TIME, THE DARK, SPED-UP MOVIE WASN'T OF ONE location. I saw what looked like a cruise missile's view of the Earth spinning eastward under us, clouds pixilated crazy-fast as we crossed ocean, what might have been Spain, an awful lot more ocean (the Atlantic?), then what could have been Florida-Louisiana-Texas-New Mexico-Arizona, and then it stopped and all around us was what looked like a desert at midnight. In a moment, wooden structures rose up everywhere in wild jump-cuts. Amid these flickering shadows I had the vague impression of upturned eaves and Chinese signage. Of course, I recalled...Union Station was built on the site of Los Angeles' original Chinatown. Suddenly the wooden structures were gone and the imposing Mission Deco architecture of America's last big train depot magically sprang up around us.

Then color returned, with daylight streaming in through tall windows. Sound arrived in the form of traffic outside, footsteps echoing off the polished tiles, and P.A. announcements about train departures.

I staggered, again motion-sick, but managed to master it. We had emerged in an alcove of Union Station's cavernous interior.

"Wait. What Big One?" I repeated.

But Ariyl had already whipped open the big bronze-and-glass door and stepped outside. Her top had again become a white linen jacket.

I followed her into the noonday heat. Almost immediately my eyes watered and my lungs hurt. The pollution was a second-stage alert, at least.

The city was always bragging how they'd cleaned up the air in the 1990s, but these days I guess the Clean Air Act is an endangered species. I couldn't even make out the Cathedral of Our Lady of the Angels, a quarter of a mile across the Hollywood Freeway. It was just a brown shape in the haze. It actually looked better this way. On a clear day it was a modernist nightmare, more like the box a cathedral came in.

A man with a Skid Row tan passed us by, wearing a filthy coat. He carried on an animated conversation without benefit of companion or cell phone as he schlepped two trash bags full of cans. But he forgot his imaginary friend when he caught sight of Ariyl. His jaw gaped. He wasn't that far gone.

"Is that a homeless guy?" gushed Ariyl. The man saw a cop car in the distance, and took off at a run. I was impressed. He didn't look like he had that kind of stamina.

"Ariyl, you mentioned something about a Big One...?"

"And look! Graffiti!" She practically swooned at the colorful defacement of the depot's exterior. I shook my head, but in truth, I'd seen it a lot worse. They must have had a recent cleanup.

Ariyl marveled at the spray-paint: "Aw, man, this is much better than the samples we have in the Art Museum!"

"You mean, the *earthquake* Big One?" I pressed.

"Oh, yeah. It was bad. They recreated it for *In Old L.A.* I cry every time I play that vid." Then she scanned the horizon: "Where's Disney Hall?"

I stepped into her field of vision. "Ariyl, when does this happen?"

"What happen?"

"The quake! The Big One!"

"Oh. Uh...2014."

"2014?! Next year? My God!"

"Or was it 2040? Or 2041. Something like that."

"It would be nice if you could remember," I said, keeping the edge out of my voice. Ariyl rolled her eyes.

"Jeez, nobody learns history anymore. N-Tec tells you." She inhaled, and wrinkled her nose. "Is this smog? Eeu, it's gross!" she giggled.

I had to get away from this lunatic, and talk to someone normal. I looked around, and saw a Yellow Cab waiting at the curb. I edged toward it, trying not to make a sudden move or any sound that would disturb her sightseeing.

I climbed in, shut the door as softly as I could, and whispered urgently: "West L.A., and step on it!"

"Yes sir!" answered the driver. He was over sixty, African-American. Only what he actually said was a raspy "Yassuh," just like Eddie "Rochester" Anderson on the old Jack Benny show. (My dad, the old-time radio freak, played me those tapes so many times that if a gunman ever says, "Your money or your life," I will automatically pause, and say "I'm thinking it over!")

This driver was old enough to have seen Benny and Rochester, live. He did a great impression, I had to give him that.

The cab started up.

"Oh, wow, look at the trash!" cooed Ariyl, pointing to a brimming refuse bin. The cabbie shoved his car in gear and swung away from the curb. Ariyl turned at the sound.

"David?" she cried in disbelief. "David!"

I looked away, feeling a pang of guilt as we accelerated.

"1151 North Bundy," I told the driver.

We crossed Alameda and rolled uphill past Olvera Street. I settled back into the vinyl seat. She'll be fine, I told myself. Whatever goes down a hundred years from now is between her and another guy who hasn't been born yet. They'll hash it out. Changing history is illogical and impossible and she probably just set her whatzit wrong.

The cab driver glanced up at his rear view mirror, and slowed a bit. "Say, Boss, you forget your lady friend?"

No, he wasn't joking. That sounded like a genuine old-time deep South accent.

Wait, what did he mean, *lady friend?*

I whirled around, and saw Ariyl's face. Six feet away, she was running alongside the taxi. The cabbie was doing 30 miles per hour. So was she. Those long, long legs were pumping faster than any pair of gams I'd ever seen. She was reaching for my car door with a look of determination. If she got hold of the door, I knew she'd tear it off.

"No!" I yelled, "Go! Punch it! She's crazy!"

"Crazy, maybe, but she sure is fast," drawled the cabbie, flooring it. There was a loud backfire. "Woman should be in the Olympics!"

The damned taxi needed a tune-up, but at the last second we accelerated out of Ariyl's reach. I admit it, I lied to Ariyl about the distance to my apartment. West L.A. is more like ten miles west of downtown.

I heard Ariyl shouting, but I put her out of my mind. The cabbie kept up a line of chat, good-naturedly informing me of my luck in getting into his cab, and what skill it would take for him to skirt all the new road work. There was construction everywhere, but he navigated masterfully. He took side streets I'd never been on, and I'm an L.A. native. Figuring I was in capable hands, I stopped paying attention.

I needed to plot my next move. Should I buy a plane ticket and go back to my excavation? Of course, as soon as possible! Leaving the find of the decade unattended was out of the question, with or without that golden Minotaur. But how would I reenter Greece without my passport, which was still in my tent on Santorini? Enough money would get me a replacement, pronto. Still, what if Greece's computer system caught that I had entered their country five months earlier...but never left? That would take some explaining.

And if I overcame that hurdle and got back to my dig...what was to prevent Ariyl from showing up there again? She didn't seem like the type to take a hint.

The more I thought about it, the more hopeless it all seemed. I was starting to understand all those fools I saw hijack the nightly news with a freeway chase, trying to escape police cars and copters in a mad dash to nowhere. It might be pointless, but somehow, putting distance between me and Ariyl Moro seemed the only solution. I'd figure out the rest later.

First, things first—I had to get home.

12

WEST L.A.

ONE MINUTE, WE WERE DOWNTOWN AND I WAS resting my eyes. The next thing I knew, the cab driver announced we were at 1151 North Bundy. I must have fallen asleep. The fare came to thirty-five dollars, even. I gave him two twenties, leaving me exactly three bucks in my wallet. He stared at the forty bucks then gave me a suspicious glare, before U-turning and heading back to Wilshire.

Was fifteen percent such a cheap tip? I didn't expect a hug, but all of a sudden *I* was Jack Benny?

Whatever. I was too sore and bone-weary to care. I now realized I'd left all my keys in my tent on Santorini. At the front door, I caught a break and I slipped in as another resident left. I keep a spare apartment key hidden under the carpet upstairs—but close to a neighbor's door, to fool any burglar who found it.

I was almost home free.

The old building was not exactly up to code. It was built in 1939, and had no elevator...but it had handsome paneled oak doors, oak wainscoting and a thick oak banister rail. The flight of stairs had never felt so steep. But padding up those familiar steps with their dusty ancient carpeting made the whole misadventure with Ariyl retreat into unreality. I was starting to think maybe, just maybe, someone really had slipped me a mickey, and I had just imagined the rest, up until I came to in the cab.

I never got around to needing my spare key. When I arrived in the second-floor hallway, I found my door ajar.

Uh-oh.

I'd asked and asked Sven to be sure and lock up when he left. I pushed on the door. It swung in. No one was inside. All was silent, unless you count a few birds outside, the omnipresent hum of the L.A. traffic and *Lohengrin* on a stereo way down the hall.

I entered carefully, and looked around. Whatever burglars might have gotten in, had been and gone. But my stuff—all of it—was gone. Every stick of furniture, every picture, every trophy, even the new blinds. The only thing still there was the view.

And yet, I had the sickening realization that this wasn't a burglary.

There was new, or rather, old-but-different furniture and curtains. On the walls were a reproduction of Mercator's 1587 map of the world, a photograph of Gothenburg, Sweden, and the periodic table.

I finally got my glasses out of my pocket and put them on for a closer look. At least these pictures were familiar, and that really made my heart sink. I'd seen them a hundred times.

They were Sven's. They belonged in his ground floor apartment. Sometime in the months I'd been gone, he'd moved back up. In a hurry, since most of his favorite photos weren't up yet. But he'd had time to make a fair mess of the place, with piled newspapers, several unwashed teacups and overflowing waste baskets.

In the last year, I'd suspected Sven's memory was ebbing. Sven confided in me that he had half a dozen sets of his house keys, because of how often he misplaced them. But this—taking back his old place, and lying about it to me on the phone—this was beyond forgetful. It was irrational.

"Aw, Sven," I groaned to myself.

"Yes?" said a voice behind me. I whirled, and there stood Sven in the door, his thick wooden cane in one hand and a bag of groceries in the other.

"Hey, neighbor!" I drawled jovially, trying to stay upbeat. "Ah, I know this is kind of sudden, I just called you yesterday from Greece, and now here I am..."

"Would you mind explaining what you're doing in my apartment?"

"I was going to ask you the same thing, Sven," I began. "Where are my plants, and my trophies, and my furniture?"

"In your apartment?" suggested Sven.

"This is my apartment, 212," I said, helpfully pointing to the number on the door.

"212 is my apartment," he said slowly.

"When did you move back in?"

"When did I move out?"

"Nine months ago. We switched. Oh, no, Sven. Is your memory going?"

"It must be, because I don't remember you at all."

Oh, God. Full-blown Alzheimer's.

"It's me, David Preston! The archaeologist. Your neighbor, your former student?"

Sven set down his bag and his hand went to the telephone. He had a strained, upbeat tone to his voice.

"Don't take this the wrong way, but I've never seen you in my life. Maybe you should talk to a doctor?"

I gently took the receiver from his hand and hung it up.

"Your name is Sven Bergstrom. You were born in Gothenburg, Sweden, in 1926. You were a boy genius who went to Princeton. You got that scar on your left hand from a fishhook when you were six."

"That's right!" marveled Sven. He seemed less suspicious, but more troubled. "I'm told I've been a bit forgetful lately. You do look vaguely familiar," he added, without conviction. "What class were you in?"

"Physics, six years ago."

"Well, uh...David, is it? Why don't you sit down? I'll make us some tea." I sat in the armchair, as Sven closed the door and locked it. Better late than never.

"Thanks. I could use something to settle my nerves. Uh, can I use the bathroom?"

"Sure, make yourself at home," said Sven, setting his teakettle atop my stove burner.

As I washed my hands, I checked in the medicine chest. Even my toothbrush was gone, but I definitely recognized the ancient rust stains I'd been meaning to paint over. Not that I'd had any doubt, but this was absolutely the same apartment Sven had traded to me nine months back.

In the kitchen, I heard the teakettle's whistle start up, then die down.

I emerged to find Sven setting my cup of tea on his dining table. He started to go back for his cup, leaning on his cane quite a bit. His arthritis had gotten worse, too.

"Let me get that," I said, hurrying into the kitchen.

Sven sat back down. "Thanks."

I handed him his cup. He took his usual two lumps, and as usual, took forever stirring them till they completely dissolved.

"So...I don't suppose my class came in too handy for archaeology."

"Not until today," I said, squeezing lemon into my tea while working up the nerve to ask my question.

"Sven...do you believe time travel is possible?"

"In theory? Of course it is."

I bumped my teacup, sloshing it.

"You're kidding!"

"Don't be so astonished. It's basic quantum theory. Many physics equations move backward as well as forward in time. Kip

Thorne at M.I.T. even proposed a design for a wormhole time machine."

"Caltech. He's at Caltech," I reminded Sven gently. Even an archaeologist knows a giant like Thorne.

"Is he?" Sven looked even more confused. "Anyway, it's certainly doable, although the level of technology we'd need is several centuries off."

"Or maybe just one," I muttered.

"I didn't catch that," said Sven. I shook my head.

"Okay, what about changing history, though? Isn't that a logical impossibility?"

"No. Remember the problem of Schrödinger's cat?"

"Right, the cat in the box," I nodded. I recited the concept, even if I never found it convincing. "If the uranium atom decays, the cat dies. If not, it lives. But quantum theory only says there's a fifty-fifty chance the atom has decayed, so until we open the box and look, the cat is both dead and alive."

"Exactly. And not just cats with uranium atoms. Any event creates two potential universes. One where the event happened, one where it didn't. So if you invent a time machine, and go back in time, you're not changing your past, you're just opening up the cat's box and picking one future or the other. By the way, I don't recommend opening a cat's box. That's why I only ever had dogs."

"So, if someone went back in time and, say, eliminated the inventor of time travel before he invented it?"

"Then your traveler would literally branch off from history as he once knew it, and move into a new history where time travel isn't invented. At least, not how it originally was."

"But how could his time machine still work?"

"Well," Sven pondered, "Is this a time-car or a time-tunnel?"

"I don't even understand the question."

"Is the means of time travel some wormhole generator in the future—a kind of time tunnel that leads back to ancient Rome? Or is it self-contained and self-powered...like H.G. Wells' time machine?"

"She said it was self-contained."

"Who said?"

"Nobody. But say it's self-contained."

"Then it has to still work."

"Wouldn't it just...you know...vanish when your traveler prevents it from being invented?"

"No more than he would. If your time traveler continues to exist back in time, obviously his time machine from his original timeline must continue to exist too, regardless of what will be invented in the *new* timeline."

Sven could see I wasn't getting it. "Look, a plane would still fly if you took it back to 1903 and strafed the Wright Brothers, right?"

"But then who invented that airplane?"

"Someone in a universe you can't get to and as far as you're concerned, no longer exists. It's lost time."

Okay, not only was time travel possible, but so was Ludlo changing Ariyl's world. I must have looked as miserable as I felt. Sven noticed.

"What, did I lose you a bet?"

"Kind of," I sighed, raising my specs to rub my weary eyes. "I was hoping you'd tell me I was out of my mind."

"The day is young," he shrugged.

"Can I ask one more question?"

"Shoot."

"Say there were two time travelers...both back in time when the first traveler changed history. Could the second time traveler undo whatever the first one did?"

Sven set down his cup with a sharp clink, and regarded me as he would an escaped lunatic.

"Young man, is this a hypothetical or do you have a personal reason for asking?"

"Me? No, no." I sipped my tea, nonchalant as all hell. "I'm asking for a friend." The locked door clicked—someone had just tried the knob.

CRASH!

Ariyl didn't bother to knock. She just smashed down the oak door, right off its hinges. She strode across the wreckage, mad as a soaked cat, and made for me.

I would have said something like "I can explain," but I was busy choking on my tea. So I did the next best thing. I backed away, grabbed Sven's fireplace poker and brandished it as a warning. I certainly didn't intend to hit her, just spook her.

No matter—her hand darted out so fast I couldn't react in time, and she tore it from my grip.

Then, never taking her eyes off me, she slowly bent the half-inch steel rod until it looped back on itself. The metal gave one last squeal as she wrenched it into a curlicue. Then she let it drop with a clank on the brick hearth.

I dashed for the door, but in an instant those beautifully manicured fingers seized my shirtfront and tightened into iron fists. She raised me into the air—again, nice and slow so I couldn't fail to notice how easy it was for her. My feet kicked helplessly.

Whatever punishment she had a mind to dish out, there wasn't a thing I could do physically to stop her. I'd better say the right thing, and fast.

"Ariyl, if you'll let me explain..."

That was not the right thing. She shook me like a dusty throw rug. My glasses flew off my head, landing God knows where.

"Explain what, you bastard? Explain why you ditched me?"

She waited for my teeth to stop rattling, perhaps expecting me to beg for mercy. But now I was mad, and not about to give her the satisfaction.

"Lost in downtown L.A.? Well, boo-hoo!" I snapped. "You left me on a live volcano, babe!"

"At least I came back! And the volcano didn't stink as bad as your smog! If I didn't need your mind, I'd beat your brains out!"

"Is this your girlfriend?" Sven inquired.

"No!" we yelled in unison.

Sven looked doubtful.

I glared down at Ariyl, and went for broke.

"Listen, crazy girl. I'm home now, and I'm not going on a hunt for your ex-boyfriend. Period. End of discussion. Now, if you still want to beat me up, go ahead!"

Ariyl glared at me for a long moment. Then she set me down on the floor, sank into Sven's armchair, and started to sob.

If it was an act, she deserved an Oscar. Tears streamed down her face.

I looked at Sven. I don't know which of us looked more amazed. I was determined to tough it out.

"What did you do to her?" demanded Sven.

"Oh, for the love of God!" I exclaimed.

She kept sobbing. I shook my head. "You know, a woman's tears work a little better on a guy she hasn't tossed around like a rag doll."

"You don't get it," she wailed. "Everybody I ever knew is gone. They were never born! And it's all my fault!"

Sven muttered near my ear, "Did you two meet in the bughouse?"

I had no answer. I waited for her to get hold of herself.

Outside all seemed normal: The sun was still October-hot, the breeze from the Pacific kept the smog east of Robertson Boulevard, and the city hummed with traffic and the usual distant sirens.

But Ariyl just kept sobbing in the armchair, and I felt terrible. Don't ask me why! A falling stone probably brained me during the earthquake on Thera.

For whatever reason, I put my hand on her arm. It felt rather soft when it wasn't dangling me in mid-air.

"Ariyl," I said soothingly. "It's not that bad."

"What the hell am I going to do?" she wept. "How am I going to find Ludlo?"

"You'll do fine," I assured her. "Hey, you've been in his century less than an hour, and look how fast you tracked me down." I took a paper napkin from Sven's table and gave it to her.

She mopped her eyes and sniffed.

"That was easy. Stuff I learned from vidz. I found Sven Bergstrom's address in the phone book. Then this cab driver pulled up and I asked him to take me here. But he gave me major 'tude, started hassling me about taking the phonebook out of the payphone."

"Aren't those bolted to the booth?" asked Sven.

"I guess I broke it a bit. And get this, then he slaps these incredibly tacky bracelets on me." Ariyl held up her wrists to display shiny chrome handcuffs.

"I told him I don't accept jewelry from strangers."

Sven touched the broken chain dangling from one of the cuffs. She had snapped it in two.

"Then I got mad. I put my fists on my hips like I meant business and went, 'Are you going to drive me, or not?'" Ariyl shook her head. "Well, he went for his gun, so I had to take it away and teach him some manners."

"His *gun*?" I repeated, my mouth going dry.

"Then I took his cab. Lucky for me, the phonebook had a map that showed the freeway to West L.A. I got off on Bundy. The signs are really simple, just like in the vidz. Man, any moron could drive in this town."

"Many do," said Sven.

I had a horrible premonition.

I went to the kitchen window, and looked down at the parking lot of our building.

Idling there, door wide open, was an unoccupied LAPD cruiser.

"Ariyl, in your vidz, do the cabbies drive black and white taxis and carry guns?"

"Yeah. Sometimes," she said, a bit defensive.

"Well, this guy was not a cabbie. He was a cop. You stole a cop car."

"Okay, so the vidz don't get all the historical details right," she conceded, meekly.

Those sirens weren't so distant anymore. They were about ten blocks away, coming west on Wilshire, racing toward us.

Down in the parking lot the cruiser's police-band crackled to life with a female dispatcher's voice: "One Mary Queen Six, what is your location?"

A male voice responded. "Get off this channel! Maintain radio silence."

Oh, crap. That could only mean One Mary Queen Six was the stolen unit, and they knew it, and they were closing in on it.

Looking east, I saw three cruisers shoot through the red light at Federal, sirens wailing, zooming toward us. Sven saw them too.

"What have you two done?" gasped Sven.

"This is going to get ugly," I told Ariyl. "You have to leave, right now!"

The three cop cars screeched to a halt out front, sirens cutting out but radios blaring, blocking the street between our lot and the little postal annex across Bundy.

I expected them to cordon off the building and address us by megaphone, but I underestimated their zeal.

Six cops leapt out with guns drawn and dashed into the building: Two headed for the back stairway as four rushed to the front.

I could tell the one in the lead, with a lot of bruises on his face, was loaded for bear. No doubt the "cabbie" Ariyl had chastised. I heard him kick in the lobby door. The next instant boots pounded up the stairs. "Move, move, move!" yelled the lead officer.

"Ariyl," I whispered, "Use your Crystal, quick!"

"Ohhh, no," she replied, shedding her jacket. "When I leave, you're coming with me. Wait here." She leapt over Sven's flattened door into the hallway.

"No!" I yelled.

Cursing myself with every step, I ran after her. I couldn't let this idiot get herself killed. But the hallway was empty—she'd vanished. I arrived at the head of the stairs just as the first cop rounded the landing. I put up my hands.

"Officer, it's cool –"

He aimed at me. Instinct took over and I dove back into Sven's apartment as I heard a gunshot that made my ears ring. I felt something hot smack my pants leg—flying plaster from the slug which just missed me.

I scrambled into Sven's kitchen, where he was scrunched in an alcove between his refrigerator and the window. I cowered alongside him.

I couldn't see the front door from our hiding place, but I was certain that's where the cop was heading.

"Stop!" I hollered. "We surrender!"

Sven clamped his gnarled hand to my mouth as, in answer, gunfire pocked the living room wall.

"You ever hear of police brutality?" hissed Sven. "Shut up and lie low, or we're dead!"

"Who trained these guys," I whispered back, "The Gestapo?"

We heard the cop stumble as he ran in across Sven's fallen door. I heard a sickening snap, which I knew meant the thug had crunched the frames of my glasses. In another second, he'd be in the kitchen, shooting first and asking questions never.

I snatched Sven's heavy wooden cane from him and leapt out from behind the fridge just as the cop charged in. I parried his gun to one side—it went off, shattering Sven's window.

I brought the cane down hard on the cop's wrist. He swore in pain and dropped the gun. I jabbed him in the solar plexus—with a rubber-tipped cane, I couldn't exactly run him through—and as he stood gasping for air, I opened the freezer door in his face as hard as I could. I caught him right on the nose and he went down, unconscious.

For a second I was scared I'd killed him. But he was still breathing.

Then I saw the red armband on his arm—with white circle and a black swastika.

"Jesus Christ!" I exclaimed, "This guy *is* a Nazi!"

Sven urgently pressed his finger to his lips. "Of course!" he hissed. "They can't get on the force without joining the Party!"

I stared at Sven.

Then I looked out the kitchen window at the little postal annex across the street.

On a pole, snapping in the stiff breeze, was Old Glory with its familiar colors: The thirteen red and white stripes and a blue field. My vision is just fine at long range, so I could see that instead of fifty stars, there was one white swastika.

And it occurred to me I'd glimpsed red armbands on every single damn cop who'd dashed into the apartment house. We were in deep *Scheisse.*

13

2013 U.C.E.

"I WISH THINGS HAD GONE DIFFERENTLY BACK IN '46," lamented Sven as he tried to tug me toward the bedroom, "But what are you going to do? They won the war."

"What do you mean, Germany won the war? How could they?"

"Don't you kids learn history? Hitler built the atom bomb." His voice dropped to a mutter: "Let me tell you, we tried to get our government to do it, but they didn't listen till it was too late."

Thud. Another cop leaped in the doorway, aiming his pistol at us. Then the next second, he had nothing in his hand. Ariyl was behind him, holding his weapon. She tossed it away, grabbed him under his armpits and hefted him off the ground.

"Finished already? Here's another!" Then she threw the cop, two hundred pounds if he was an ounce, across the room. Though I turned aside, his forearm still caught me in my diaphragm and knocked me against the wall. He kept on going, landing on Sven's dining table, snapping its legs off as it collapsed.

But the cop was more resilient than I was. Before I could get to my feet, he leapt onto me with his nightstick out and tried to crack my skull. I clutched it with both hands and we fought for it. He was on top and pressed down with all his considerable weight and garlic-laden breath, until the nightstick was across my throat.

I could see Sven's cane, which I'd dropped just inches away, but if I let go to grab it, my windpipe would be crushed. If the garlic didn't finish me first.

I yelled to Ariyl for help, but through the empty doorframe, I could see she was busy. Two more cops reached the hallway from the front staircase. Ariyl darted into view at incredible speed, and with each hand clutched their wrists and forced their pistols aside. They each fired once, but the bullets hit a wall and a light fixture. She squeezed until the cops screamed and dropped their guns.

Ariyl flung her arms wide apart, smacking the men against opposite walls so hard the lights flickered. Then, as if cracking a pair of whips, she flipped the cops head over heels. I felt the floor bounce as their backs slammed down in unison.

The room darkened as my oxygen supply dwindled. The last thing on earth I expected to see was Sven, pouring the teakettle on Garlic Gus's neck. And if he'd done it two seconds later, it *would* have been the last thing I saw.

Gus howled and dropped his billy club to clutch his scalded neck. I grabbed Sven's cane and whacked Gus across the temple, which banished his burning neck pain for at least an hour. He fell on top of me like a load of tires. I managed to shove his unconscious carcass off me.

"Thanks, Sven!" I gasped, still trying to inhale.

"You're welcome," he replied, "Now get the hell out of my apartment!"

I got to my feet. I heard the siren of yet another cop car blurt as it skidded to a halt outside.

In the hallway lay two dazed cops.

Ariyl was stripped to tank top and miniskirt, her muscles pumped from all this exercise. She held a third cop by his necktie and bitch-slapped him unconscious, then dropped him.

One of the cops she had flipped got to his hands and knees,

groggy. Him, she lifted by his collar and the seat of his pants, swung him back as if he were a bowling ball, and pitched him down the corridor, where he landed on the hall table, reducing it to kindling.

"Look out! " I cried, too late. Nazi Cop #4 sneaked up from behind and cracked her hard across the back of her skull with a foot-long black flashlight. I expected her to collapse in a pool of her own blood. Wrong again.

"Ow," she complained, massaging her head. The cop gaped at his bent flashlight. A microsecond later she had it in her hands. The steel made a high-pitched squeak and D-cells flew as she broke it in half. Before he could flee, she had him by the collar.

"You want police brutality?" she growled through clenched teeth. "Here." She uncorked an uppercut that propelled him airborne through a neighbor's front door. He lay in the apartment amid splintered oak, moaning and bleeding.

Yet another cop charged around the corner and ran smack into Ariyl. She slapped his gun away, grabbed him by his shirt and his thigh, and hoisted him over her head. He let out a terrified cry. She turned around as two more cops emerged from the front staircase. One took aim but the other knocked his hand down.

"No, she's got Beck!"

"Take him!" said Ariyl, tossing him at his comrades. All three officers tumbled back down the stairs to the landing, where they lay in a heap.

I turned and saw another cop had revived enough to retrieve his gun and aim at her. Luckily I had Sven's cane. As I smacked the gun from his hand, it discharged. Ariyl turned, startled.

"I got your back," I told her.

"Oh, that's so cute," she smiled, and dropkicked the cop down the stairwell.

That's when I felt the floor thud as another cop came charging up behind me. A guy with a face that would scare his own children, six-foot-four, heavier than Garlic Gus—and all muscle.

I turned to meet his charge, and all I got for my trouble was a punch to the jaw. A moment later, the floor had my back.

The Big Cop was about to stomp my face when Ariyl grabbed his foot with one hand as her other yanked away his gun.

"Okay, now you pissed me off." She gripped Big Cop's leg like a baseball bat and swung him until he connected with the wall, cratering the plaster. But she wasn't done.

Ariyl scooped up the dazed man in her arms, then literally punted his ass through the big hall window. There was a tremendous crash of glass and I heard his thick bulk thunk on a car roof below.

I ran to look down, and was astonished to see the Big Cop roll off the dented top and land on his feet. Miraculously, he had only a few cuts. He rushed to his squad car. This was one tough cop. But not a smart one. He should have fled for his life. Instead, he yanked out his riot gun.

Ariyl swore, pushed past me and leaped out the broken window to the sidewalk below. Fearing the worst, I dashed down the stairs four at a time.

Before I reached the bottom, I heard a shotgun blast outside.

I burst out of the lobby into the street.

Ariyl held the riot gun. "I *really* hate these things," she commented as she bent it double over her thigh, the gunsmoke curling from its barrel.

Meanwhile, Big Cop dove into his car and clutched his radio mic.

"Five Adam King Three, I need backup—!" Then he saw Ariyl striding toward him. He dropped the mic, slammed his door and grabbed his shift lever.

"Ariyl..." I began, but she grasped his bumper and with one herculean heave, dead-lifted the rear end of his car a foot off the ground.

I swallowed hard.

"What?" she asked between clenched teeth.

"Uh...lift with your legs, not your back."

The cop gunned his engine. His wheels spun uselessly. Straining, red-faced, Ariyl staggered back with the cruiser a couple of steps. With a last loud grunt, she heaved the rear chassis onto a fire hydrant. The tires still raced, hopeless, inches above the pavement.

Ariyl, breathing hard from her exertion but now in a fine temper, marched to the front of the car and slammed her fist down on the hood, caving it in four inches. Her blow cracked the radiator—steam jetted out from under the buckled hood and there was a brief screech as the fan hit the crumpled steel—the engine shuddered and died. She turned back to the cop behind the wheel.

"Ariyl, no," I pleaded.

"Ohhh, yes. I'm gonna teach him not to pick on a little guy," she growled.

"It's fine, I'm five-eleven-and-a-half!"

The cop was hollering into his mic.

"Eight officers down! Female suspect on drugs, superhuman strength! We can't stop her!"

"'Sright, you can't," purred Ariyl as she seized his door, wrenched it off and carelessly cast it across the road. With a taunting smile, she crooked an inviting finger at him, but he scrambled to the passenger side, brandishing his nightstick.

"Leave me alone, you crazy fucking bitch!" he snarled.

Well, that just made her a little bit madder. She snatched at his arm, but all she got was his swastika armband. She reached in again, dragging him out by his tie.

"I don't like your language," she commented. He struck her savagely with his nightstick, but she took it away from him.

"If you can't kill me with a gun, you really think this'll help?"

She snapped his billy club in her fingers like a breadstick, then threw Big Cop over her knee, and spanked him. His furious curses quickly gave way to cries of pain.

"Goddamn it, Ariyl, that's enough!" I exclaimed. What was wrong with her? Yeah, he almost stomped my face in. But this wasn't fighting anymore. She was playing with the poor bastard like a toy.

Ariyl looked surprised at my outburst.

"Fine," she said, exasperated. With a backhand smack, she knocked Big Cop back into his dry-docked car. He bounced off the seat and came to rest on the steering wheel, dazed. The horn blared on and on, painfully loud.

"God, that's annoying," said Ariyl. She slammed her fist on the car hood again, crumpling it in two more spots until she silenced the horn. Now all was quiet, except for the groans from the battered cops...and some neighbor lady screaming hysterically.

"Whoa!" Ariyl exhaled. Then she grinned. "I had no idea time travel could be such a blast!" She looked me up and down. "And you didn't do so bad, History Boy. You're not too strong, but you sure can handle a cane. Any other hidden talents?"

"I don't want to brag."

"One Adam King Five, what's your location?" demanded the radio dispatcher.

I looked back, and winced...because Big Cop had foolishly regained consciousness. Didn't he know enough to play dead? "Bundy and Wilshire!" he gasped into his mic, "Send...!" But he never got out another syllable, because in an eye-blink Ariyl reached in, wrapped her arms around him and dragged him out. His feet kicked uselessly in the air as she bear-hugged the breath out of him.

"Ariyl, don't!"

"Please repeat," asked the dispatcher.

"Unnnnnnhhh," was the Big Cop's reply, exhaling in Ariyl's crushing embrace. Without loosening her arms, Ariyl reached her hand to take the mic from his and craned her head to speak into it.

"Sorry, it's his naptime," she said. Then she closed her fist, pulverizing the mic. She calmly continued to empty his lungs, until at last he went limp.

She let him drop. At last, she met my gaze, then rolled her eyes.

"Jeez, don't look at me like that. I just squoze him till he blacked out. I'm no killer."

A shot from upstairs exploded the strobe right beside Ariyl's cheek.

"At least not yet," she muttered, as she dashed back in the building.

I heard another gunshot, a slap, and then a man yelling for help. Ariyl reappeared at the broken window, holding the last cop by his belt buckle. She cocked her arm and hurled her human javelin across the lot into a dumpster. That ended his screaming. After that he just moaned a lot.

I ran inside and up the steps. As I arrived in the hallway, Sven poked his head out of his apartment. He gaped at the broken lawmen left strewn about the hallway in the wake of Hurricane Ariyl.

"Are they...?" began Sven.

"They'll be fine," Ariyl assured him, stepping over her victims as she reentered Sven's place.

"Sure," I said, following her in. "A few months in the ICU, the rest of their lives on disability, they're fine."

"Why are you so worried about these assholes?" she snorted, grabbing the two limp gendarmes off Sven's floor by their Sam Browne belts and flinging them into the hallway. She flopped herself down on the couch. "They're Nazis."

"Don't remind me!" I winced. "It all makes sense now! The ultra-clean streets. The graffiti painted out as soon as it appears." I paused. "Actually, those I don't mind. But these killer cops! No wonder the homeless run when they see police cars...I don't suppose they end up in treatment centers?" Sven shook his head sadly.

"No, this is definitely a police state. Oh, we still get to vote for mayor and senator and president, but the Party picks all the candidates."

Ariyl noticed her wrists, still sporting what looked like S & M jewelry. She worked a finger under one of her handcuffs, and began twisting the chromed steel apart. Off it came. She went to work on the other.

"Even I know the Nazis were scum," said Ariyl, "And I don't know squat about history." She glanced at Sven's fallen door. "Do you want me to stand that up?"

"Leave it," said Sven. "It'll be down again soon enough."

I thought back to the cabbie.

"So that's why the old man kept calling me 'Boss'—in Nazi America, there wouldn't have been a civil rights era. Poor guy probably didn't dare accuse a white man of handing him funny money, which I bet my forty bucks were to him. Sven, who's on the twenty-dollar bill now? Hitler?"

"No, always our current president," said Sven. He pulled a twenty from his wallet, and handed it to me. I retrieved my glasses, which at least had their lenses intact, but had snapped across the bridge of the nose. Sven helpfully passed me a roll of adhesive tape, with which I effected a most ineffectual repair.

Harry Potter without the magic, I now peered at what my dad used to call a double-sawbuck. It was dated 2004, but the design was entirely retro, like the silver certificates of the 1940s, only with swastikas rampant. The eagle didn't clutch an olive branch; both its talons bristled with arrows. And the president in 2004 was...well, let's just say some things never change. Whether your country is a river or a sewer, some folk always float to the top.

"Looks like this is 2013, U.C.E," quipped Ariyl.

"U.C.E.?" asked Sven, mystified.

"Un-Common Era," I translated. "Very droll." I squeezed my throbbing forehead. "What the hell happened to World War Two?"

"You really don't know?" asked Sven.

"All I know is, Hitler shot himself in a bunker in Berlin the last day of April, 1945, a week before Germany surrendered. He never got the bomb."

"First of all," insisted Sven, "Hitler died of a stroke at Berchtesgaden in January '46, on the night of their victory. After he died, things weren't quite as bad. I mean, the end of the war was horrible. Hitler atom-bombed Boston and Stalingrad with those damned V-2s, but when Dönitz took over as Führer he agreed to spare the rest of our cities if we surrendered. The Japanese demanded the West

Coast, but after the Germans obliterated Kyoto, Hirohito realized the partnership was over."

"My God," was all I could say.

"And I take it all this is not supposed to happen?" said Ariyl. I nodded impatiently.

"And, yes, the Nazis hung Einstein and Truman and Eisenhower," continued Sven. "But they knew America would be easier to govern if they didn't try to change us too much. They even let the Jews alone, as long as they signed away their property," and here Sven's voice dropped to a murmur, "which I understand was better than what happened in Europe."

"You have no idea," I said. This sad old man who'd lived six decades in a colony of the Third Reich, reading only censored history —how could I begin to convey to him the vast, unspeakable nightmare of the Holocaust? I didn't try.

"This is crazy, Sven. America invented the atom bomb!" Sven shook his head, wistful. I persevered. "I'm telling you, in 1939, Albert Einstein wrote a letter to President Roosevelt, saying we had to develop it!"

"Oh, sure, Professor Einstein wrote FDR," agreed the old man. "He told me that himself, the night we surrendered. Right before he was arrested. What I'll never know is why Roosevelt didn't respond."

"That's impossible. Unless..." suddenly, everything was clear. "Unless Roosevelt didn't get the letter."

"You're saying a letter to the president got lost?" asked Sven, raising an eyebrow. "How could that happen?"

Ariyl and I looked at each other and spoke at the same moment: "Ludlo."

"It's just the kind of thing he'd collect," she admitted. "But could one little letter change a whole war?"

"Not by its mere absence. But I think it *could* have," I continued, thinking out loud, "if someone showed it to Hitler, and he committed the kind of resources that FDR did to the Manhattan Project."

"No way," said Ariyl, shaking her head. "Ludlo would never help the Nazis."

"No? Then you explain why we just had to fight off a squad of Gestapo." Then I got a sick feeling in my stomach. "We beat up Nazi cops. Oh, God. We are so dead." In the distance, but getting closer, I heard more approaching sirens.

"Well, maybe *you* are," said Ariyl, patting my knee as she rose. "But as promised, I did bring you home." She picked up her white jacket and put it on, then put her hand to the Time Crystal. I jumped up.

"Ariyl, you can't leave history like this, with the Nazis in power!"

"Ohhh. I guess it's different when it's your world that's screwed up."

Sven was staring at us now, comprehension dawning in his eyes.

"It wasn't a hypothetical at all, was it? The time travelers are you two."

"Not me," I corrected. "She's from the twenty-second century. And so is the other guy, Ludlo. I just hitched a ride. In the history where I grew up, the Nazis were defeated. I swear to God, Sven...we won World War Two."

Sven slowly shook his head.

"You know, ever since we lost, the last sixty years...most of my life...it all seemed like a bad dream I needed to wake up from." His eyes misted over.

I looked again at the pictures on his wall, and now I knew why his favorite photos weren't up.

Sven cleared his throat.

"To answer your earlier question, David...logically, yes, I think you can prevent whatever another time traveler did, and restore the original timeline. If we're lucky, it's a kind of closed time-loop: You must succeed because you already have, and this Nazi victory is merely a temporary fluctuation from the most probable outcome of history. A mutation, if you will. A maladapted universe doomed to die out." He paused, then added, ominously, "But you have to stop this Ludlo fella before he does it again. Or worse."

"If he's in our past, hasn't he already done it?" I wondered.

Ariyl shook her head.

"Ludlo told me our Crystals are linked. If it's been an hour for me since I last saw him, it's an hour for him, even if we're in different eras. So whatever he's done in the last couple hours hasn't generated one of those wave-thingies..."

"Probability wave!" Sven sat up, agitated. "You're right. You have no time to waste. He must have been up to something for the last hour. If he's in an era prior to this one, you're in danger! He could kill your ancestors, anything! You have to get behind him in time, before he erases *this* history...with you *in* it!"

The sirens outside cut out. The reinforcements were here. I grabbed Ariyl's arm.

"We can't leave Sven here. They'll kill him for helping us."

"But the Crystal can't bring three people through time! It's low on power just dragging you and me."

"Forget me!" ordered Sven. "Don't you get it? If you succeed, I'm already as dead as Schrödinger's cat, and this whole rotten world dead with me. Good riddance." He paused, then quietly asked, "David, you obviously knew me in your timeline...was I married?"

"Were you ever," I smiled. "Naomi. She was...she is beautiful. You have two wonderful daughters. And grandkids. Their pictures hung right over there."

"I knew it," smiled Sven. I gave him back his cane. "Good luck," he said, and turned to hobble into the other room, and lay down on his bed. He looked like he needed a good long rest.

Downstairs heavy boots thumped into the lobby.

I turned to Ariyl with my hand out: "Okay, I help you find Ludlo, you help me fix history."

"Deal!" said Ariyl. I managed not to whimper as her hand squeezed my hand like a soft vise. She put her hand to the Crystal. "Destination, Temple of the Dolphins, six P.M., October 6th, uh..."

She was blanking on the date, *now?* Shouts erupted from the LAPD phalanx thundering up the stairs.

"1492!" I yelled.

"1492 A.D.!"

Her Crystal glowed again, but not as brightly as before. It flickered.

Ariyl smacked it. "Come on, come on!" The glow brightened.

The first cop through the door opened fire, just as he and the entire room went away. In fluttery coal mine shadows, the world spun westward beneath us, this time in a dizzying blur. I thought Ariyl was going to break my fingers. Perhaps because we were returning to our previous stop, we were back in the sea cave in what seemed like a second.

Ariyl let go of my hand, and swooned into my arms. It's a good thing I work out because a weaker man couldn't have held her up. I smiled at what I assumed was a mock faint. But she didn't smile back. Then I saw the bullet hole in her chest.

14

THE CAVE OF THE DOLPHINS, 1492 A.D.

"OH, GOD! ARIYL!" I YELLED. BLOOD PUMPED FROM HER wound. Her stare was glassy and she panted in shallow breaths. She kept murmuring, "Don't let me die, don't let me die." I lowered her to a sitting position. When I moved my right arm from behind her, my shirt was soaked in blood. She was also bleeding from the exit wound in her back. I pressed my right hand to the back wound, and my left to the front. Her blood was gushing through the cracks between my fingers. I moved my left forearm over her chest wound and grasped her Time Crystal, my fingers sticky with her blood.

"Ariyl, how do I work this?" I shouted. All she could do was whimper in pain. I gave it a try.

"Destination: Good Samaritan Hospital emergency room, Los Angeles, October 1st, 2013 A.D.!" No glow. I tried again with another hospital, another city, another date. Not so much as a glimmer.

Either it would only work for her, or it was out of power. I had no time to mess with it. We were all alone, miles from a surgeon, a nurse or a midwife, and centuries before the first trauma unit. Even if Ariyl healed as fast as she did from her lacerated leg, at this rate she'd bleed out before her wounds closed up.

I yanked her jacket off her, ran one sleeve over her shoulder and tied it tight to the other, behind her back, while her heart pumped big spurts of blood. Then I pressed the knot into her back wound and used the heel of my other palm on the fabric in front. I had to hold it as long as I could, praying that if or when that remarkable body of hers knit its wounds back together, she would still have enough blood in her veins to survive.

It was sunset when we appeared in the sea cave. It was nearly dark when I dared peel back the makeshift bandage from her chest wound. Drying blood was everywhere, but I managed to wipe the wound clean...sure enough, the skin had knit together. I assumed the internal damage had as well, though I had no way to tell. Her chest was a mass of scar tissue, such as you'd expect days after such a wound, not half an hour later. Her back wound had also closed up. But the sand beside her was caked with the blood she had lost.

Ariyl was pale and shivering with cold. She was going into shock. I had to keep her warm. I wrapped my shirt around her and laid her down. Then I dashed out and grabbed an armful of driftwood the tide hadn't reclaimed. Rushing back in, I raised Ariyl's legs a bit and piled sand over them. Then I squeezed in behind her, my back against the cave wall, a sort of sitting-spooning position, with her head on my chest, my shirt across her for a blanket, and my arm clamped around her. My glasses slid off my face during this, but I let them lie.

As I sat behind Ariyl, with my free hand, I built a teepee of sticks next to us. Then I fished a dollar bill from my wallet and shredded it. Legal tinder, it occurred to me. It might have been funny if I wasn't terrified I was losing her. I spent a frantic minute striking a rock against a bigger stone before I got enough of a spark. Finally I got the money to smolder, leaned over and blew on it as gently as if removing grit from cuneiform.

The bill flickered into flame, and eventually the thin sticks kindled into a little blaze. Ariyl was in and out of coherence all this time. I kept up a running patter. I couldn't let her slip into a coma.

"Ariyl, is that better? Feeling any warmer?"

"Mmm," she moaned, seeming to drift off again.

"Hey, don't you go to sleep on me!"

"David...am I dying?"

"Nah, you're too tough. Just promise me you'll stay awake. Keep talking."

She was short of breath, but she made the effort.

"'Kay. Feel so dumb...showing off. Didn't think I'd...catch a bullet."

"Lady, you took on nine cops with nine slugs apiece. You're lucky you didn't catch all eighty-one."

"That what it works out to...eighty-one?"

"You don't know what nine times nine is?"

"Don't need to...we just..."

"...ask N-Tec," I finished with her.

"Things sure come easy in your world, Ariyl."

"And hard in yours. You really spent...three years...just looking for the Minotaur?"

"Not specifically that. Just something that had the word Atlantis on it. But yeah, three years of my life."

"And then...you left it behind?" she marveled.

"Well, the roof was about to crush you."

"Yeah...guess you had no choice. I'm your ticket home."

Yeah. Just thinking about number one. You're welcome, you ungrateful ditz. But I kept that to myself. She was in no shape for it.

"Yeah," I said. "That must've been it." I could feel her head starting to roll to one side. Had to jumpstart the conversation. "Hey, now. Tell me about your favorite book. Or do you read?"

"I *can* read...I just don't."

"Okay, that's nice and depressing. So, tell me your favorite vidz."

"That's easy. *In Old L.A.*"

"Right, with the black-and-white taxis. What else?"

"Um..." she seemed to breathe a little easier when she focused on her vidz. "*Beijing Carjacker*, *Zero-Gravity Sex*, and of course, *Voyage to Atlantis*."

"That one may have been a bad influence."

"And oh, yeah, *The President's Brain is Missing*."

"Sounds like a comedy."

"It is. But it's based on a true story."

"I know. I lived through it."

As Ariyl explained it, vidz were movies beamed directly into your cerebral cortex, involving all five senses, in which you could either observe omnisciently, or move around as a participant, like the most vivid dream you can imagine. Most were open-ended with branching stories like video games, only orders of magnitude more complex. People could play the same one a hundred times and it was never the same.

To me it sounded like a recipe for societal breakdown and mass lunacy. But then, they once said that about TV. And compared to time travel, the vidz seemed downright benign. But there had to be more sophisticated fiction in the twenty-second century.

"Did you ever hear of *Romeo and Juliet*?"

"I hear you need a translator chip for it."

"How about *Lord of the Rings*?"

"Another flat-flick?" she asked, with all the enthusiasm of a toddler for a silent documentary.

"Okay, maybe you saw *The Godfather*?" She shook her head, mystified. "*Psycho*? *The Wizard of Oz*? Didn't they even remake them?" I kept getting that blank look. Well, I had to admit I probably wouldn't recognize most of the Broadway hits of 1913. But there must be some perennials. "How about *It's a Wonderful Life*?" Ariyl paused, unsure.

"Maybe. What's it about?"

"A man who was never born." I looked around the untouched cave, lit by our flickering fire. I had to ask.

"Why did you look up Sven in the phone book, Ariyl? Why not me?"

Ariyl took a beat.

"Or did you?" I pressed.

"Yeah, I did. You weren't there. Sorry."

We were five centuries away, but now I knew with dead certainty, if we jumped to 2013, this cave still wouldn't have a trace of my dig. It was a world without me.

"Well, now I know how George Bailey felt."

Ariyl gave me the blank stare.

Never had my life seemed more pointless. It wasn't just Sven who didn't know me. As things stood, none of my friends, not even my parents would. If *they* were ever born.

"On the other hand," I said, "At least I'm out from under my student loans."

Ariyl looked at me, full of pity.

"David, how do you stand it?"

"Oh, it's not so bad. Most don't rack up interest till you graduate."

"I mean your world. Knowing you have to...die someday."

"Oh, that. Well, everybody dies," I remarked, philosophical. Ariyl's terrified look told me the last thing she needed was a philosopher with a rotten bedside manner.

"Present company excepted," I hastened to add.

"But I *will* die. If I can't get N-Tec back."

I squeezed her hand. "We'll get it back."

She nodded, faintly reassured. "Know what? Without those glasses...you're kinda cute."

I nodded. "You should see me when I undo my hair." Her eyelids started to droop. "Wake up," I prodded. "I'm going to teach you something."

"Huh? What?"

"Repeat after me. Two times one is two."

She pouted a bit, but complied. "Two times one is...two."

"Two times two is four."

"Two times two is four."

"Two times three is six."

And so it went, until she knew everything up to twelve times twelve. It didn't take long. She had a remarkable memory, when she actually used it. And she seemed to grow stronger as she did.

Then Ariyl asked if I had a girlfriend.

"No," I said.

Well, technically, a fiancée isn't a girlfriend.

But why was I reluctant to tell her about Moira? Well, because maybe she might track down Moira, like she did me, and tell her...I don't know, something crazy.

"Did you *ever* have a girlfriend?"

"Well, sure." One, anyway.

"Why aren't you together?"

"Well, she's in Washington, D.C. now. She's assistant to Congressman O'Hare. I guess she kind of expected me to move there."

"Why didn't you?"

"Assistant professor jobs are hard to find. I couldn't just start over, dusting exhibits at the Smithsonian. I'd never have gotten to do the dig on Santorini."

"That was why? It wasn't another woman?"

"Of course not. I mean, she used to joke about being jealous of the head of my department, but there was nothing going on." At least, I thought Moira was joking.

"Was your department head pretty?"

"Dr. Dexter? She's actually pretty easy on the eyes. But I wouldn't let myself think of her that way. Even if I'd been unattached, getting involved with a colleague would be unprofessional. I would never let that interfere with my work."

"God, what a drudge. No wonder your girl dropped you."

"Who said she dropped me?" I was getting hot under the collar. "If you don't mind, I think we better change the subject."

"Okay. Here's a new topic. I'm starving."

"I'm on it." I was relieved to go outside. I found a fish stuck in a tide pool. It took me a while, but I caught it, then cooked it over the fire and fed her as much as she could get down. She was also dehydrated. I refused to bring her seawater, until she convinced me she was genetically adapted to drink it. Some gene-spliced microbe in her digestive system purified it for her. So I filled my shirt pockets, and she drank.

As she grew more lucid, I asked her everything I could about her era. Ariyl was long on social details, gossip and plots of vidz, but short and sketchy on how her world actually worked. Democracy still existed, but it was student government. Real control was vested in N-Tec. Well, who was I, from the era of unrecountable voting machines, to feel superior?

Any history before Ariyl had turned five was a blur. She knew little about it beyond stories of a devastating war between competing mega-computers in the mid-twenty-first century. N-Tec had emerged as the victor and their supposedly benign monarch. No one had made vidz about this period (hmm) so for Ariyl it barely existed.

Maybe this explained why she didn't have memory chips in her head to provide history or times-tables. It made sense, if part of N-Tec's programming was rigorous suppression of any separate computerized intelligence. As long as N-Tec was the only game in town—and remained devoted to humanity—such a system might just work.

Since the Change, work had vanished for almost everyone, along with crime, war and death. Life was a series of vacations, parties and trysts.

The only thing I could compare it to was Huxley's *Brave New World*, only with more sobriety: N-Tec closely controlled drug intake.

Maybe it was less Huxley, and more like the pleasantly useless existence of Bertie Wooster. Except P.G. Wodehouse's cushy pre-war

Neverland was, in 2109, combined with the kind of rampant, risk-free sex I'd missed by being born well after the Free Love era; and apparently, it was policed by an ideal of liberal political correctness that vanished from my world sometime before I reached voting age.

One welcome difference from our era: Despite the copious coitus, rape was nonexistent—which Ariyl couldn't explain. The entire concept of sexual assault against her will was alien to her. I presumed that meant, as with weapons, that N-Tec was somehow standing guard.

I kept reminding myself the world of N-Tec was a few years younger than Ariyl. It was still an evolving system. I was not sanguine about its future. The need to restrict drugs suggested a bored populace that craved stimulation. And the invention of time travel, and its use as a societal diversion, seemed insanely reckless, far worse than even our own nuclear era. Had a lunatic programmed this computer?

Even without Time Crystals, God only knows what effect unlimited wealth and the banishment of death would eventually have on parenting and basic morals. What kind of immortals would it produce?

In Ariyl's case, for all her carefree sex and gleeful violence, she came off as a sheltered rich girl. She seemed to have a decent streak, and despite her aggressive sexuality, a strong sense of propriety—or at least, some twenty-second century version of it. That probably didn't come from her indulgent parents. To put it in Wodehouse terms, I suspected it came from N-Tec being not only her digital Jeeves, but Aunt Agatha as well. Hadn't Ludlo even called it their digital nanny?

But now, Ariyl had been turned loose in the real world—worse, in her own past—with frightening power, zero guidance, and no idea of the consequences of her acts. I was starting to sympathize with Ludlo's mistrust of N-Tec.

But I still couldn't explain one thing: Why had N-Tec, supposedly the dominant entity in the year 2109, failed to stop Ludlo?

15

THE RETURN OF THE MINOTAUR

I awoke with a start. It was full daylight, and Ariyl was gone from my lap. One second I'd been talking to her, and the next...obviously, I'd nodded off. Great doctor, huh? I looked around for her, frantic.

"Ariyl? Ariyl!" I called.

"Here," came a voice, unexpectedly close. Ariyl's face rose into view. She was standing in a five-foot-deep hole, roughly where my excavation would someday be. Except not, because David Preston would never be born in this Ludlo-contorted timeline.

"What are you doing down there?"

"Digging," she said, bending over. She resumed her rapid scooping, propelling a remarkable stream of sand backward between her legs. She dug faster than a pack of Rottweilers attacking a luau pit. There was a huge pile of loose sand on the surface behind her.

"Should you be doing that?" I asked. Ariyl looked at me, puzzled for a moment.

"Oh, you mean the bullet hole!" she realized. "I'm all healed." Ariyl was wearing her SmartFab tank top, which had knitted itself up where the bullet had torn through. She lifted the top, again baring her bosom.

"Does it look okay?"

"Magnificent," I murmured.

"I mean the scar," she sighed, patiently.

"Right, right." What had been a gaping wound was now just a pink blemish between her breasts. "Good as nude. New!" Ariyl gave me a teasing pout.

"In your time, is it considered rude to stare?"

"Yes, it is. Why, are you planning to spank *me*?"

She smiled. "Not unless you ask me to."

I needed to look away fast, before I forgot I had a fiancée. I examined the cave wall for possible petroglyphs. Ariyl giggled.

I heard her leap out of the pit. "And your top mends itself, too?" I began.

"Yup! Take a look," said Ariyl, wiping sand off her hands on her dress. With one hand, she touched her shoulder, and said, "Clean up."

Instantly, all the wet sand sticking to her clothes dropped to the ground, like iron filings from a paper when you yank away a magnet from the back side. She was spotless again.

"Works on bloodstains, too," she added. Then she became serious. "David...um...thanks for, you know. Last night. You kinda saved my life."

"Kind of. You can thank me by promising never to take on an entire police force again."

"Oh, come on, you loved it." Then she saw I was serious. "Okay, I promise."

My eyes strayed to the pit, and they must have bugged out at what they saw, because Ariyl laughed at me again.

She had uncovered the corner of the temple's bottom step. And she had dug a very familiar hole beside it, whence had come a very familiar sand-clump, now resting on the edge of her excavation. Ariyl picked it up.

"What the hell?" I exclaimed. "That can't be..."

Before I could finish, Ariyl had crumbled the sand away to reveal the exquisite horns and head of the golden Minotaur.

"How can that be there?" I stammered. "We dug it up yesterday!"

"You mean five centuries from now. And *I* dug it up," she corrected. "But that was in the 2013 Ludlo erased, and replaced with a timeline where the Nazis won, and you were never born. Have you not been paying attention?"

"Here, let me," I said, taking the Minotaur. I still had a brush in my pocket. I sat on the sand and began cleaning the exquisite golden statue.

Ariyl sat beside me and watched. I kept looking for some difference between this Minotaur and the one I'd left to be incinerated in the eruption of Thera. "Are you sure this isn't just a mate to the other one?"

"No, it's the one from your dig. Except now that you were never born, I figured we might as well grab it..." she paused to calculate, "... uh, five-hundred-and-twenty-one years early.

"Hey, good subtraction."

"I had a good teacher."

"But if I'd managed to hold onto the other Minotaur, the one we dug up in *my* 2013..."

"I guess now you'd have a matched set. Weird, huh?" I just shook my head. She picked up a sharp driftwood stick.

"I think I figured how this changing-history thing works." With the stick, she drew a curving line in the sand. "We mark this 'D' for David's timeline." She put a big 'D' at the end of the line. Then she wrote down two dates at either end of the line.

"This is normal history, where the temple was buried in 1628 B.C., and you dug it up in 2013.

"When Ludlo left Atlantis, I think he went to 1939 and stole Einstein's letter to the president."

Ariyl marked '1939' at the line's midpoint, and from that point she drew a second curve branching off the other way, which she marked with a big swastika. "That created NaziWorld."

"In this timeline, they won the war, you weren't born, and the Minotaur was still down by the temple step, where Ludlo buried it. I figured I'd dig it up now, in 1492...because in this version of history, you won't be there in 2013 to dig it up."

Ariyl rubbed out the original line beyond the split. She made another hole way back before the '1939' above the date '1628 BC'. Then above it, she drew a smaller 'D' and 'A', meaning us.

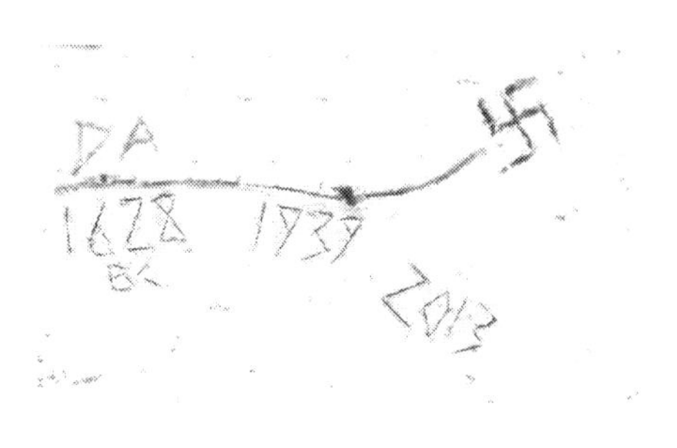

"And if you weren't back with me in 1628 B.C. while Ludlo was changing 1939, he would have erased you along with everything else that happened afterward." She rubbed out my original 'D', in case I missed the point.

I couldn't help a grudging smile. I knew what she was expecting.

"Okay, thank you for kidnapping me."

"My pleasure," she replied. "But actually, you grabbed my ass."

"Okay, then my pleasure. You know, for someone who didn't know her times-tables, you have a highly logical mind."

"Yeah, well, I'm ignorant, not dumb."

In a few minutes, I had cleaned off most of the Minotaur. I rushed the job, before something else blew up or someone burst in shooting. Ariyl peered at the remaining sand as I crumbled it away from the sculpture.

"That paper that Ludlo wrote down other places and times on...it was in that pouch, at least when we were at Dodger Stadium. Any chance it's still there?"

"After three thousand years? It would've rotted to molecules after the first decade. I expect he took it out before he buried the Minotaur."

Then, a chilling thought hit me.

"Listen, did Ludlo ever mention other objects he wanted to collect?"

"You mean like baseballs?"

"Yes, like that worthless one he traded to Andy Graise. That was kind of a stupid slip," I remarked. "Why did Ludlo give Ty Cobb a ballpoint pen to sign a 1908 ball?"

Ariyl put up her hand, embarrassed.

"My oops. I gave Ludlo this antique pen as a gift? He snuck it along on our trip, to see if we could smuggle stuff through time?"

"But why not use a fountain pen?"

"What do I know about the history of pens? Ludlo didn't catch it either. I thought the antique dealer said it was from 1894. But thinking back, I guess he said 1948." Ariyl giggled a bit. "Ludlo was so pissed when I told him. But then he figured your friend Andy wouldn't know the diff."

"Nice," I said sourly. "But that solves Sven's mystery about the two-hundred-and-sixty-year-old ink. If it was manufactured in 1948, it was well over a century old in 2109, and then Ludlo took it back to 1908, got it written on that ball, and then buried it till 2011, so it was, uh..."

"Two hundred-sixty-four years old."

"Now you're just showing off."

Ariyl grinned. "But what surprised me was, when Ludlo jumped into 1908 with that 1948 pen, N-Tec never caught it. And they didn't yank him back when he let Cobb sign the baseball. I mean, that didn't happen in history. But N-Tec let it slide. So Ludlo's all, 'Let's try for bigger stuff.'"

I regarded the golden statuette.

"Bigger than the Minotaur?"

"Oh, yeah. Swords and crowns and books and paintings. He's really big on artworks."

"That worries me. When he took the Minotaur, he knew it was going to be destroyed. But suppose he decides to take the original Mona Lisa, right after it was painted? That would rewrite history. Thousands of works influenced by Leonardo's painting might never be painted, or would be painted very differently. And God knows what else would be different in the world."

"But Ludlo wouldn't change history deliberately. That would definitely get us yanked home."

Suddenly those amazing purple eyes widened in alarm. "Oh, shit, the Time Crystal!"

She arose, dusting the sand off her legs.

"If I leave it off me too long, it automatically goes back to 2109."

I jumped up, alarmed. "How long? A week? An hour?"

"Uh, probably less than a day. Twenty hours? Something like that."

Ariyl was already dashing out of the cave to a big rock off which heat waves rippled in the blaze of the Mediterranean sun. I was right on her heels. There lay her Crystal, soaking up solar radiation. It was glowing again. The sand was hot enough to blister bare feet, and I cringed when I saw Ariyl grab the Crystal's chain and put it over her head. I figured her skin would sizzle. But she didn't even notice.

Curious, I ran my fingers along the chain, then the Crystal: Not even warm. "You could make a UFO out of this stuff," I muttered. Suddenly, I noticed my knuckles were resting on her breast. Ariyl had already noticed, with a funny smile.

"Oh, sorry." I removed my hand.

"I didn't say you had to take it away."

"Yeah, but I'd better."

"Why?"

I started to tell her about my fiancée, but something told me I shouldn't. For my fiancée's sake, I told myself. For Moira.

"So what else does he want to collect?" I said, getting back on topic. "Did he mention anything specific?"

"He went on and on about this...well, a baseball, I guess, in Philadelphia, one that a whole buncha guys signed."

"What team, the Phillies? Do you remember any of the players?"

"Um...Adams, Jefferson, Hancock?"

I waited a beat. She had to be joking this time. But no, she was not.

"Ariyl, was this 'baseball' by any chance called the Declaration of Independence?"

"Yeah, that was it! I figure it won a pretty important game."

"You could say that. It was a piece of paper signed by the people who invented America."

"Again with the pieces of paper? You and Ludlo would so get along."

"I can't wait to meet him," I muttered. "You remember what date Ludlo had for Philadelphia?"

"I do. 1976. July fourth."

"Of course," I realized. "The Bicentennial!" I got a blank stare. "You know what the Bicentennial is?"

"Duh. A two-hundred year anniversary. But of what?"

"Of the original Fourth of July! The day Congress adopted that piece of paper."

"*That's* what Fourth of July was? I thought it was the day they invented fireworks."

So depressing. But I let it go.

"Okay, the National Archives in D.C. are extremely well guarded, but in 1976 they might have lent the Declaration to Philadelphia for a display."

"What do you mean, 'might have'? I thought you knew everything about history."

"Only compared to you. I do know they lent it to Philadelphia in 1876 for the Centennial. In 1976...I'm just guessing. I'm not constantly hooked up to the Internet." I ran scenarios in my mind. "If it was there, I can see Ludlo's reasoning—a much bigger crowd at the Bicentennial, and it would be only a temporary exhibit. Security would be more haphazard. A little diversion, and Ludlo could easily overpower the guards—if he's anywhere near as dangerous as you."

"David, that hurts my feelings."

"Believe me, I wouldn't want to hurt you in any way."

"That's sweet. So where do we find it?"

"Like I said, I don't know...but the logical place to start is Independence Hall."

Satisfied, Ariyl touched her Crystal.

"Just a sec!" I blurted out, and sprinted into the cave for the Minotaur. I couldn't believe I almost lost it again. And there were my glasses, lying in the sand. Probably so scratched up as to be worthless, but I stuck them in my pocket anyway.

I ran back out and Ariyl took my hand.

"Okay. Independence Hall, Philadelphia, noon –"

"No, dawn. We don't want to miss Ludlo."

"Make that dawn, July 4th, 1976 A.D."

16

BICENTENNIAL MINUTE

We emerged at the rear of the hall. There was a reddish glow in the eastern sky. The air was cool and humid. I'd never actually been to Independence Hall, or for that matter, Philadelphia. The back of the building was unlit, and I wondered just how safe a neighborhood this was in the post-Vietnam, crime-and-drug-infested year of 1976. It was quiet, as I expected, nowhere near the peak tourist hours yet.

"Come on," I said.

Ariyl followed me, drinking in the sights. Suddenly she stopped.

"Oh, my God, I know why Ludlo wants the Declaration of Independence! This was in the vidz! There's like a treasure map on the back, right?"

"No, there isn't," I explained. "That's the plot of *National Treasure*." I paused. "You guys don't know what *The Godfather* is, but you remade *National Treasure*?"

"Well, if there isn't a map on it, why's it so important?"

I turned and pointed at the magnificent old brick edifice.

"Because in there, two centuries ago, our Founding Fathers

signed a declaration of war against the most powerful empire on earth. Our nation was born in this building."

"Uh-huh. Well, before the rest of your tour, can we do breakfast? I'm starved. All I had was that little fish and no offense, but it was nast'."

"Well, I'll have to reconnoiter. I've never been to Philadelphia. The closest I've been to Independence Hall is the fake one at Knott's Berry Farm. And since I burned most of my money, we should probably find a McDonald's." I scanned the city street. "That's odd."

"What is?"

"I don't see a McDonald's."

"That's a place to eat?"

"Or a Burger King. Or a Wienerschnitzel, or Jack in the Box. I don't see a single fast-food joint."

"Why'd I bring you along?" she exhaled, impatient.

"'Cause I know all about 1976."

"Like?"

"Like everything! Vietnam is over. Jimmy Carter is running against Gerald Ford. Tie-dye and bell bottoms are in."

"Really?" enthused Ariyl. She touched her shoulder and said, "1976, something hip." Her clothing morphed into headscarf, vest, tie-dye shirt and bell bottoms. "What else do I need to know?"

"Punk rock was just born. Next summer, Elvis will die."

"Who is Elv –"

"Please," I cut her off, "don't finish that question."

"Deal, if you find me food *now*."

The street was empty, with no traffic or pedestrians anywhere. My concern about the possible crime rate returned. I slid the Minotaur inside my sandy, bloodstained khaki shirt. My best hope was I'd look too crazy to harass.

"Nice quiet neighborhood," I observed. Ariyl shook her head.

"This Bicentennial blows. Where are the flags and fireworks and stuff?"

I turned around and took in the darkened landmark once more.

Though its wooden trim had been recently whitewashed, it looked empty.

"Yeah," I murmured, "Where *are* the flags? And the street lights? And the traffic signals and the parking meters?"

I stepped back, and felt flat stones beneath my feet. Historic paving right in front of the Hall, I might have expected. But it extended down the street for blocks, as far as I could see. Somewhere, machinery was chugging, but I heard no cars.

"And where's the asphalt? Ariyl, is something wrong with the Crystal? This looks more like 1776."

A brass bell clanged and a steam whistle blew. I looked down the boulevard and half a mile away, I saw a steam locomotive crossing a bridge. "Okay, 1876," I corrected myself.

Ariyl glanced down at a soggy newspaper on the road. She picked it up. *The Royal Philadelphia Gazette* headline screamed: "FRENCH INVADING PENNSYLVANIA COLONY!" She showed the masthead date to me: "July 3rd, 1976."

"Yesterday's paper," I agreed, my mouth dry as ash.

"So nothing's wrong with the Time Crystal," said Ariyl.

"But something's wrong with Time. While we were back in 1492, your pal Ludlo did something else."

"As big as Nazi America?

"Bigger. Now we have No America."

I skimmed the article, which summed up the ongoing war, and my heart sank. I heard more chugging, but this time it came from overhead. I looked up and above Independence Hall, emerging from behind the clock tower, I saw a quaint airship out of Jules Verne, with a filigreed gondola whose steam engine belched black smoke, and turned twin propellers, slung under a huge, decorated, gas-filled envelope.

"What's that, a 1976 airliner?" giggled Ariyl. "It's adorable!"

"Yes, very steampunk. We need to go. Now." I was tugging for all I was worth but Venus was still stuck in the sand.

"Not till I get some food!"

"Am I not explaining this right? This is *not* our 1976. Not mine, not yours. Something major went wrong with the timeline. None of this stuff belongs!"

"Can we at least just ask them?" She pointed to four fog-shrouded figures emerging from a shadowy alley, a hundred yards away.

"No!" I hissed, trying to clap a hand to her mouth.

"Hello-o?" she trilled. "Where's the nearest—David, please! —cafe?"

Three bare-chested warriors stepped into the orange beams of daybreak, in war paint and buckskin vests, with revolvers and steel hatchets. Behind them came a uniformed officer with a ridged helmet like the French wore in World War One, and carrying what looked like a Tommy gun.

"*Espions anglais! Tirez sur eux!*" he barked at his men.

"Don't shoot, we're not spies!" yelled Ariyl. In English, unfortunately.

We ducked behind a tree trunk as the Frenchman and the Indians opened fire. Chewed-up bark flew everywhere. Finally they stopped, out of bullets. I peeked around, and saw the warriors demanding more ammo. My French is only serviceable, but I knew their commander was telling them we were unarmed, and to just kill us. They came dashing up the road toward us, hatchets flashing in the rising sun.

"Get us out of here!" I exclaimed.

"If I do, we can't return for hours. We might miss Ludlo." She chewed her lip. "If he even wrote 1976."

"If? *IF?*"

"Well, he has truly sucky handwriting."

"Why did I bring *you* along?" I yelled.

And now discussion time was over. The warriors were upon us.

I didn't have a weapon handy, so I was forced to use the Minotaur. I blocked a warrior's hatchet with it, then I clubbed him hard. He fell to his knees, dazed. The second warrior came at me, but my parry didn't work so well with him. His hatchet caught the Minotaur, nicking it badly—I yelped as if he had sliced my flesh—as it flew from my grip.

The next instant Ariyl was there, grabbing my assailant under his arms and then turning into the path of the first warrior's hatchet, which he buried in his comrade's chest instead of mine. Ariyl dropped her human shield and laid out the first warrior with one punch.

I heard a war cry as the third warrior arrived. With dazzling speed, Ariyl sidestepped him and grabbed away his hatchet, breaking his wrist with an audible snap. Now he really let out a cry. Ariyl backhanded him, he hit the tree and was silent thereafter.

A sharp clack of metal came as the French officer slapped a new magazine in his machine gun. He started to fire at us, but in that same instant, Ariyl flung the fallen warrior's hatchet a hundred yards down the road, to imbed in the Frenchman's shoulder with stunning accuracy. He cried out, dropped his gun and sank to the pavement, moaning in pain. All was peaceful again.

"And that," said Ariyl, dusting off her hands, "is why you brought me."

"Thanks for the reminder."

Ariyl again touched her shoulder, commanded a cleanup and all the dirt, blood and war paint dropped off her clothes. "Now, who are these guys?"

"They seem to be a modern version of Algonquin Indians. I'm guessing the Delaware tribe."

She turned and stopped, seeing the first Delaware with his comrade's hatchet buried in his bloody chest. She let out a horrified gasp.

"Is he *dead?*"

"Of course he's dead. That's what I meant by dangerous!" I snapped. "Isn't this the kind of theme park entertainment you traveled back in time to watch?"

"Oh, my God!" she gulped. Then she bent over a bush. I

managed to grab her hair and hold it back just as she threw up. I cursed myself silently. Maybe Moira was right. I can be a dick sometimes.

After a moment, I laid a gentle hand on her shoulder. "Not like in the vidz, is it?"

She turned toward me, wiping tears from her eyes. "Oh, how would you know? Vidz are maximal gory."

"Well, okay, but, vidz don't feel this real. Right?"

"Yeah, they do," she said impatiently. "They feel exactly like real life. It's just...In my mind, I know they're only digital. But this guy is real. Or was real, before I killed him."

"His friend killed him."

"But if I hadn't grabbed him and pushed him into that hatchet..."

"*I'd* be dead. You saved my life. Does that make you feel any better?"

"No." I must have looked offended, so she conceded: "Well, okay. I guess. But why try to kill us? We weren't threatening them."

There was gunshot down the road. We whirled in time to see the French officer, who had somehow sat up to aim his weapon at us with his one good arm, slowly crumple to the street, dead.

Standing over him with a smoking revolver was another Indian warrior in war paint. Not a Delaware—from his hair I immediately knew he was a Mohawk. He picked up the dead officer's machine gun, slung the strap over his shoulder and approached us.

Like the Delawares, he was young, maybe 19. He had the air of quiet gravity you see in people who have to kill close up. There wasn't a flicker of humor to him. A smile on his face would have seemed a crime. Give him a buzz-cut and an olive drab camo uniform, he could have been a Vietnam vet...or in my era, in mountain gray-and-tan, just back from Afghanistan. But instead he had the original Mohawk Indian cut, and wore bandoliers and buckskin pants. He answered Ariyl's question in a near-Cockney accent.

"Why kill you? Because that's what the Delawares are paid to do," he said, still several yards away. "That's why the French use them...but you notice, they don't trust them with the machine guns, or a lot of ammo."

Even Ariyl sensed this was a situation. She whispered in my ear, "Do I kiss his ass, or kick it?"

I muttered back, "If what I think happened did happen, he's on our side, as long as he thinks we're English."

I called out to him in my best BBC British, "We are in your debt, sir. I am David Preston, this is Ariyl Moro."

"No point knowing your names," he replied as he came close, scanning us carefully. "You won't last long, the way you keep leaving your enemies alive."

He pointed his pistol to finish off the two surviving Delawares, but instantly Ariyl yanked it from his hand.

"Please don't," she said politely, as she passed the weapon to me. The Mohawk stared at her, then me. I gave him a hey-it-wasn't-me shrug, but held onto his pistol.

In a flash, the Mohawk unslung the machine gun, but even faster, Ariyl took the barrel in her fists. It took her three seconds to bend it to a right-angle. Now I saw a flicker of fear in the warrior's eyes, but he kept his cool.

"Why do you care about them?"

"I don't know," she replied. "I just do."

I looked at Ariyl with newfound respect. The Mohawk did too.

"My name is Joseph Erie," he said. "If you are not my enemy, will you give my pistol back?"

Ariyl frowned at the revolver. I could read her mind.

"You've mangled enough metal for today, my dear. Better let me hold this." I tucked his pistol into my belt-less pants.

"You're not English," said Joseph. So much for my being the male Meryl Streep. "But you're not French either. Where are you from?"

I dropped the accent.

"The United States of America?"

"The what?"

"Oh, come on," scoffed Ariyl. "Even I've heard of it."

I shook my head.

"This is what I was afraid of. There is no America in this timeline. Which means you definitely got Ludlo's date wrong."

"The entire country's gone?" she asked, skeptical.

We saw the flash and felt the radiant heat of the explosion an instant before the deafening sound came, with a hot blast wave that nearly knocked us off our feet. A bomb had gone off near the railroad bridge.

I looked up and saw the airship's envelope was painted with the French gold fleur-de-lis. A compact iron catapult on the airship lobbed a second bomb at the steam train below. This time it hit the rear car which exploded in flame.

The train was flying the Union Jack. Sharpshooters were trading shots with riflemen on the airship. The caboose was now ablaze. The airship dropped bags of ballast to quickly gain altitude. Somewhere behind the smoke, I heard a Cockney voice yelling, "Get the Froggie bastards!"

Ariyl, Joseph and I took cover behind that same protective tree, as a third bomb from the airship went astray and landed nearby. It made a crater in the street and showered us with gravel. My ears were ringing.

"Well, it's the wrong flags," I hollered at Ariyl, "but you got your fireworks!

"So, you're saying nothing in this 1976 is the same as the real 1976?"

"Nothing except for Joseph's haircut!"

Ariyl turned to look, and at that moment the young Mohawk seized the opportunity to bolt towards where his British comrades were making their stand.

"America never won its freedom," I shouted over the din. "So in this world they had another French and Indian War. Or wars. England and France are still using local tribes to fight over their colonies. Apparently, no French Revolution either, so no tricolor flag for them."

"But why don't they have jets and cars and all that stuff I saw in the vidz?"

"Maybe because so many modern inventions came out of nineteenth century America—steamboats, telegraph, telephone, light bulbs, gramophone! After independence, we had a thriving economy, a fair patent system, strong public education, and best of all, a mostly peaceful democracy that encouraged investment in people like Fulton, Whitney, Morse, Edison, Tesla, Bell, the Wright brothers. I'd bet that this colony—maybe this whole damn world—has had none of that. Just two centuries of slaughter and stalemate, draining manpower and capital. So those inventions came along later, scattered in different places. No wonder their tech is so far behind."

I looked up again at the hovering ship, nervous. "I sure hope they know how to extract helium."

"So all this weird stuff is because Ludlo stole the Declaration of Independence?"

"Right. But on July 4th, 1776. Thanks to you, we're two hundred years late."

The Brits on the troop train had yanked the canvas off a rotating cannon mounted on a flatcar, and aimed it upwards. Their first shot arced below the rising airship.

"I just don't see how one piece of paper could make such a difference," said Ariyl.

The stray cannonball exploded the Hall's tower. We ducked as flaming debris landed around us, and a big bronze bell inscribed "Pass and Stow," with an inscription from Leviticus, fell, hit the pavement with a sickening *clong*, and split in two. The cannon kept on firing at the airship.

I was explaining at the top of my lungs now: "Fifty-six men signed the Declaration! If they lost the Revolution, it would have been their death warrant! What if the very day they approved it, Ludlo stole it right from under their noses?"

"They didn't make copies?"

"The Founding Fathers didn't have a FedEx Office!"

"What's that?"

"All they had was Jefferson's handwritten draft! It went to the printer the afternoon of July fourth!"

"Think that's when Ludlo took it?"

"Yes! Imagine the effect on their morale. Even in our history, the Revolution almost failed. Washington only won two battles before Yorktown!"

"Who's Washington?"

"He batted cleanup for the Yankees," I snapped. "Let's go! If we want to undo this mess, we have to stop Ludlo before he grabs the Declaration!"

BOOM! The cannon scored a direct hit on the airship's envelope, a hundred feet up. It exploded in a huge fireball, just like the *Hindenburg*.

"Oh, man! Definitely not helium!" I bellowed. The whole flaming mass descended towards Independence Hall—and us. Ariyl grabbed her Time Crystal, and I grabbed for the Minotaur...which, inevitably, was not there. It was on the ground eight yards away, where the Delaware warrior had knocked it.

"The Minotaur!" I cried. I started to dash for it, but Ariyl had my hand and pulled me up short. She was right, I'd never make it. Ariyl called out, "Destination: Same location, ten A.M., July 4th, nineteen—"

"Seventeen!" I screamed.

"1776 A.D.!"

I could see, just as everything went dark and distorted, the Minotaur becoming a golden puddle amid the furnace of blazing wreckage.

Not again, I thought.

17

THE STATE HOUSE, 1776 A.D.

IN THE DARK GRAY FLICKERING, THE FLAMES VANISHED. The Hall stayed the same, but around it I saw the steampunk Philadelphia deconstructed from industrial city to agricultural-era town, as a series of trees retracted limbs, and shrank into the ground, abruptly replaced by huge versions that likewise dwindled into saplings, then vanished into the earth. After four or five of these cycles, we returned to the full-color world.

It was sunny and bright, not terribly hot yet. It felt around 75 degrees Fahrenheit...a pleasant late morning for the Atlantic seaboard in July. The trees were generally smaller than they had been in 1976. Most of the big brick buildings of the alternate 1976 had vanished, along with the railroad bridge, the tracks, and the paved streets. Independence Hall, known in the Colonial era as the Pennsylvania State House, was intact. In fact, it was in fairly good shape, being only thirty years old.

The town was not quite silent: Cocks crowed, cattle lowed, insects buzzed, a dog barked here and there, but compared to my automobile-humming West L.A. neighborhood, it was as quiet as a tomb.

A farmer was leading his cow down the road. He glanced back at us, and nearly got trampled by the animal. He hurried on, with many an anxious backward glance.

"At least this looks like 1776," I observed. "But we're not exactly dressed for it."

"I won't be a minute," winked Ariyl. Then she touched her shoulder and murmured, "Philadelphia, 1776 A.D., something casual."

In a second, Ariyl's jacket morphed into a shawl, her hairband into a bonnet, her top and bellbottoms into longer, homespun Colonial clothes. She still looked fairly spectacular, but no longer anachronous.

I looked down at my own modern (and bloodstained) shirt, pants and shoes. "Great. Now it's just me who looks like a freak."

"Yeah," said Ariyl, plainly not impressed with the attire of her escort. "Wait a sec." Before I could object, she sprinted around the back of the State House. Oh, no, I thought to myself. I rushed to the window on the left side—the room where the Continental Congress met—with fingers crossed that there were no witnesses around. Luckily, the room was deserted. Somewhere within, I could hear Ariyl breaking down a door.

I was quite a nut on American history when I was a kid, and on my bedroom wall I'd hung a copy of the famous John Trumbull painting of the presentation of the Declaration. I was disappointed to see now that Trumbull, who began painting the scene a decade after it happened, had gotten the room wrong. Instead of Trumbull's restrained white walls and mounted flags, the 1776 room was tarted up with paneling and faux Roman columns.

Ariyl came back to my side, holding a brown frock coat and a tricorn hat. She started helping me into the coat.

"Ariyl, where'd you get these?"

"Jeez, quit bitching. It nearly fits. And the color really sets off your eyes."

"Don't you get it?" I protested. "Stealing even this coat could change history!"

"I told you about the inertia thing. What, you think the owner will die of pneumonia? It's July!" She slapped the tricorn hat on my head. "Now let's *eat!*"

The tavern's front window had a view of the street leading to the State House. If Ludlo showed up, we could spot him. Or rather, I could. Ariyl was hungrily shoveling in her fourth helping of stew. She was starting to attract stares from other patrons. I leaned in and spoke to her *sotto voce.*

"I know you worked up an appetite, but for God's sake slow down. These people have never seen a locust swarm."

Ariyl looked up at the others, mouth half-full. "It's just so good!" she said. Everyone immediately avoided her gaze. To me, she added quietly, "The faster I eat, the less I taste."

The porcine tavern keeper eyed me and Ariyl. His gaze was, respectively, suspicious and lascivious.

"We need to figure out how to pay for this," I murmured.

Ariyl looked the tavern keeper up and down, and shuddered. "You have any of that money stuff?"

I automatically reached for the wallet in my pants, then realized all I had in it was maxed-out plastic, and a couple of bills imprinted with Washington's face and the name of a country that would not exist for another two hours.

"No, sorry," I admitted. As I withdrew my hand, something in the pocket of the frock coat jingled. I felt inside, and pulled out a worn silver sixpence, and a shiny new gold guinea bearing George III's supercilious profile. I grinned at Ariyl.

"I will not hear of it!" announced an outraged Southern voice. I looked around. The voice was coming from the corner table, but I could not see its owner, since my view was blocked by a pair of men exiting. One of the departing patrons was a tall, sad-eyed man in his fifties, with hair pulled severely back, and the other a dandy with long graying hair, prominent nose and smug mouth.

As I said, I was a history nut. I could identify many of the Declaration's signers in the Trumbull painting. I had no doubt that walking past me were Roger Sherman of Connecticut, and Robert R. Livingston of New York. Not just any two signers, mind you, but members of the Committee of Five appointed to draft the Declaration.

Before I could think of anything to say to them, they were gone. Instead, I found myself staring at the three men still sitting at the far table. One was a short, pudgy, bewigged man of forty poured into a tight black velvet suit. The second was a rather tall man in his early thirties, in waistcoat and shirtsleeves, with reddish hair peeping out from under a brown day-wig. The last was a portly, balding septuagenarian in a rumpled brown suit, with gray hair falling to his shoulders, and bifocal glasses. Trumbull, painting the trio in later decades, may not have gotten their clothing exactly right, but the faces were quite accurate. These were definitely the other members of the committee.

"What is it?" whispered Ariyl. "You look like you're gonna cry."

"It's them!" I breathed. "John Adams. Thomas Jefferson. Benjamin Franklin."

"The ballplayers?" I shot her a look. "Oh, oh, right, the Founding Dads," she said. Then she peered at me closer. "You *are* gonna cry, aren't you?"

"Shut up," I suggested. Ariyl went back to vacuuming up her stew, as I strained to eavesdrop without being noticed.

I couldn't believe my luck. The future second and third presidents of the United States, and the greatest scientific and governmental genius of his age, all sat close enough for me to chuck a bread roll at. They were arguing about the final wording of the Declaration itself. This afternoon, the fourth of July, the Continental Congress would vote to approve it. Jefferson's handwritten Original Rough

Draft, the seminal document of our republic, lay on the table before him!

"'Life, liberty and *property*'?" drawled Jefferson, spitting out the last word in contempt. "You will not move me on this. We must make it clear to the world this is no mere economic dispute."

"Still, I know you to be an admirer of John Locke," persisted Adams, seemingly bent on further irritating Jefferson. "And that, in fact, was Locke's original phrase, which you saw fit to alter."

Jefferson slowly nodded, looking Adams in the eye, "As *you* are insisting we alter 'inalienable rights' to 'unalienable rights'." He tapped at the disputed passage.

"That is the more correct form," insisted the flinty Bostonian. Adams spoke in a clipped accent, clear ancestor of the "Baastin" speech of my father. Though unlike Dad, I couldn't imagine Adams using "wicked" as an adverb.

"Hang your corrections, sir!" snapped Jefferson, taking another sip of rum.

"John, for heaven's sake," sighed Franklin. Of the three, Franklin's diction sounded the most British. As one might expect of the poor boy whose rise in Philadelphia society required a proper image in the minds of his fellows. And who, only months before, had been in London, trying in vain to convince Parliament to seat representatives from the Colonies.

"'Kay, let's go," said Ariyl, setting down her spoon.

"Have some more. It's all-you-can-eat," I murmured.

"Believe me, this is all I can eat," she grimaced.

"Just wait," I said.

"Aren't we here to catch Ludlo?"

"In a minute!" I hissed. She looked hurt. How could I explain it quickly? "Ariyl...I could spend a month questioning any one of those men."

"Boy, I bet they'd love that."

"Ludlo obviously hasn't gotten the Declaration yet. So we just stick close and make sure he doesn't."

Ariyl rolled her eyes, sat back and folded her arms.

I discreetly glanced over at the corner table. I knew over the last three days the wording had already been edited and amended and was about to be presented for the final vote. Was it possible Adams was still agitating for one last change...or was he simply agitating Jefferson?

"In any event, Thomas, so long as slavery exists, you must admit certain rights are indeed alienable."

Franklin smiled grimly but said nothing.

"Hang both of you," glowered Jefferson. "It was *you* who removed my denunciation of the slave trade."

"I feared it would ring rather hollow coming from a slaveholder," remarked Adams. "Or have you freed the Negroes who work your plantation since last we discussed this matter?"

Jefferson smacked down his tankard, nearly spilling rum on the document. I gasped. "Being a lawyer by profession, perhaps you do not comprehend the indebtedness which is the farmer's lot."

"My father was a farmer. I still farm that land," flared Adams. "And I pay free Negroes to work it."

"Then I trust you do grasp that I cannot emancipate slaves who do not fully belong to me. Even if I could, it would not alter the institution one whit. But someday..." Jefferson began, then stopped himself. "However, I do not believe I invited your opinion of my financial affairs."

"You are being unfair, John," Franklin put in. "Jefferson did not create the world into which he was born. He proposes to change it. I predict the eloquent words he has written here will have positive effect far outweighing his private life." Then he fixed Jefferson with a look. "And we have already made our compromise. We cannot succeed without the southern colonies."

Jefferson accepted Franklin's reproof. He respected the old man. And though Adams' words stung, undoubtedly he felt their truth as well.

I knew Jefferson was destined to spend the rest of his life sinking into debt. Unlike the successful Washington, he would never free more than a handful of his own slaves—not even his lover Sally Hemings. Strange how we owed so much freedom to a man who could not grant it to those whose lives he affected the most.

Of all the Founders, Jefferson always wrote the angriest words... watering trees with blood of tyrants and patriots, strangling moneyed corporations in their infancy. Maybe he was angry with himself, even today, the original Fourth of July. Exactly half a century from this historic day, he and Adams would both die, their friendship finally healed from their many quarrels.

Brooding, Jefferson stared into his rum. "Sooner or later, this nation shall end slavery. Delay will cost it dearly."

Franklin nodded. "But first, sir, we must *have* that nation."

The innkeeper arrived and set down bowls of stew for the men. Now was my opening. Ariyl caught the look in my eye.

"Where are you going?"

"I've got to ask them something." She took hold of my wrist.

"David, no! What if you start an argument, and change history like Ludlo?"

"Relax. History is my business. I'll be discreet. Here, leave a good tip."

I tossed her the sixpence from the coat pocket. She let go of my hand to catch it, and I headed over to their table. Alas, I overestimated the lull in their conversation. Just as I reached the table, Franklin cocked his head toward Jefferson, concerned.

"I recognize that our friend John is ever spoiling for an argument. But may I inquire, Thomas, what has you in so contentious a humor?"

"What, indeed!" exclaimed Jefferson. "If any man had cause to insist upon the *in*alienable right of property today, it is I."

Adams now noticed me, and didn't seem to welcome my proximity. If I were to ask anything, it had to be now. Half a dozen historical riddles that I might solve fought for my attention: Did they intend to guarantee unfettered ownership of firearms, or only in the context of a state's militia? (No, stupid. With the Bill of Rights more than a decade off, Jefferson might not even be considering the question yet.) Did any of them envision women's suffrage in the republic's future? Adams, married to bright, assertive Abigail, seemed the most likely. What about the alleged right of secession? Corporations treated as persons under the law?

I seized on the shortest, most direct query for these titans of the Revolution. "Gentlemen..."

Jefferson seemed not to hear me. He continued, heatedly to Franklin, "Yes, sir, I say property. Not an hour ago, I was working at the State House and when I went to the anteroom, I found my coat purloined, and my hat as well."

My question lodged somewhere between my vocal cords and my tonsils.

"That brown one," inquired Adams, "With the candle wax on the sleeve?"

I looked down at the sleeve of the coat Ariyl had pilfered for me. Wax drops. I instantly clasped my hands behind my back.

Jefferson nodded at Adams, "And a gold guinea and sixpence in the pocket."

Well, only a guinea now, I realized. I couldn't swallow. I started to back away, hoping to melt into the crowd, but Franklin addressed me.

"I pray you forgive my companions' distraction, sir. What was your inquiry?"

My tongue stuck to my palate. The question had fled my mind and left no forwarding address. To this day, I cannot remember what I was going to ask.

Franklin was staring at me, puzzled.

Adams was giving me his most dyspeptic look. Especially at my trouser cuffs, which I suddenly realized were far lower than was fashionable for the time. Thank God they covered my shoe tops. I needed to get their eyes off my clothing.

"Ah...I was wondering...um..."

I had nothing. Finally a question occurred to me.

"How is the stew?"

And now, finally, Jefferson turned. He looked me up and down, and frowned.

"Sir, might I presume to ask where you acquired that coat?" As polite as the phrasing was, there was cold steel in his tone.

"Uh...well, you see..."

Suddenly Ariyl was at my side. "Come, husband. We must not tarry."

Even in Colonial homespun, Ariyl was stunning. Her effect on Franklin in particular was, well, electric. He straightened in his chair, brushed back his hair, and lifted an approving eyebrow. Jefferson's clenched jaw went slack. Adams choked on his hard cider and blushed. Belatedly recalling their manners, they rose.

"Madame, I have no wish to delay you," began Jefferson. "But I do seem to have some business with your husband."

"Good sirs, I beseech you, forgive my poor David any offense he has given." The Crystal's language chip was supplying her with quite a vocabulary, if not a perfect accent. "His mind has been feeble since our horse kicked him in the head."

What the hell?! I shot her a how-could-you look. But the tragic fact was at that moment, I couldn't think of a better story, nor any story at all.

Jefferson's expression softened. He gave me a sympathetic look.

"Ah. I see. At first, Madame, I imagined that his coat had a familiar look. But upon closer inspection, I see I was mistaken. Godspeed to you both."

Jefferson, Adams and Franklin all bowed to her.

Ariyl continued, pressing our luck. "Mr. Jefferson, Mr. Adams, Mister—"

"Doctor," I whispered.

"D*octor* Franklin...though David be of unsound mind, he has an unfailing instinct for greatness in men. I am quite certain that centuries from this day, your names shall be inscribed upon great monuments, and your labors shall be celebrated."

The three beamed, flattered. Ariyl stepped back, preparing to withdraw. I had to say *something*.

"Uh, yeah. That goes double for me." Ah, eloquence.

Franklin laid a gentle hand on my shoulder.

"Our stew, lad, is most palatable," he said, as if indulging an eight-year-old.

I gave him a sickly grin, then turned and followed Ariyl to the door. As we departed, I glanced back and saw Jefferson watching Ariyl. He raised his tankard.

"Gentlemen. To the pursuit of happiness."

"The pursuit of happiness," chimed in Franklin. And even Adams, albeit without enthusiasm. I heard the clank of their tankards as we stepped out into the fresh air.

Before the door closed, I heard Jefferson say, "Then I believe our task here is complete."

In a miserable daze, I scuffed my way up the dusty street, away from the State House.

"The chance of a lifetime. I could ask them any question. And what do I ask? 'How's the stew?'"

"I'm sorry, David," said Ariyl, taking my arm.

"It's not your fault. *You* were great. And I don't just mean the vocabulary. You thought fast."

"Thanks. I did, didn't I? No, I just meant, I'm sorry I stole Jefferson's coat."

"Oh, yeah." Now reminded, I was ready to get mad at her all over again.

"But still, it was cool!" she put in quickly. "I mean, you got to talk to your heroes."

"Who think I'm a thief. And a jacko."

"Would you rather be digging up old broken pots?"

Sadly, I had to think that over. Call me Jack Benny.

"Lighten up!" she continued, poking me playfully. "Admit it, David, we're having fun!"

"I guess," I conceded. "At least, when we're not in mortal danger. Which unfortunately, we've been pretty much the whole time I've known you."

"Anyway, wasn't Thomas nice about it? I had no idea he was so hot!"

Now, I'm no prude—well, actually, I kind of am. Still...that definitely crossed a line.

"Thomas," I stated, "is old enough to be your great-great-great-great..." I lost generational count as I realized we were passing a wooden sign that read, "John Dunlap — Printer." It hung outside a modest brick building that exuded the sweet scent of ink. I stopped.

"This is it. This shop printed the Dunlap Broadsides. The first official copies of the Declaration." I looked down the road, and saw Jefferson, Adams and Franklin leaving the inn, headed away from us, toward the State House. I estimated that within an hour the vote would be taken, and then John Hancock and Charles Thomson, President and Secretary of the Congress, would sign the approved draft.

"Then they'll bring the signed document up the street to this shop," I informed Ariyl. "Now, you stay here and keep an eye out for Ludlo, and I'll go watch the Continental Congress."

"Uh, maybe you watching Congress...not so much," Ariyl advised.

"Why?"

"Thomas might think you came back for his shoes."

I stared at her for a long moment, but I knew she was right.

"Damn it!" I was screwed. This was now officially the most frustrating day of my life.

"Okay, you..." (this was killing me) "...you watch the signing of the Declaration. And I'll, I'll observe this historic print shop."

Ariyl patted my shoulder.

"Tell you if I hear anything cool!"

I nodded, without optimism. She headed off to the State House.

The breeze was pleasant, but standing in the sun in that coat was not an option. I sought out a shady spot where I could loiter unobtrusively. I tried to look at the bright side: If I could somehow have been convinced two days ago that I would see Dunlap's historic, long-vanished print shop in action, let alone get a pat on the shoulder from Ben Franklin, I'd have turned cartwheels.

The State House clock tolled twelve o'clock. Then, an eternity later, it tolled one.

By the time two o'clock rolled around, I couldn't stand it anymore. Something must have gone wrong. I marched back toward the State House.

Ariyl was nowhere in sight. The windows were now open. It must have gotten warm in there. As I approached the building, Benjamin Franklin emerged, swatting at a swarm of flies. He was carrying that same leather folio. I ducked behind a large tree to one side of the steps.

Then light flashed on the side of the building. I peeked around the other side of the tree. Ten yards from me, I saw the side of the building ripple. Then the man I met at Chavez Ravine seventeen months ago materialized.

Jon Ludlo was already costumed for the era, in frock coat and tricorn hat. He stood with his back to me, swaying, momentarily dizzy. Could Franklin have seen this? No, Ludlo was around the corner of the building, and not beside the window. But Franklin turned in the direction of the flash of light, which he had definitely seen. He started towards the back of the building. I couldn't let him blunder right into Ludlo's hands!

But what could I do? And where the hell was Ariyl?

Jefferson and Adams stepped out the front door.

"Where are you going?" inquired Jefferson.

"It's quite odd," Franklin told them. "There's not a cloud in the sky. Yet I could have sworn I saw lightning back there."

The old man was almost to the corner of the building when

Adams gently took his arm. "Come along, Franklin. We've no time to find you a kite."

Jefferson chuckled quite a bit at this, as they passed the tree. The last I saw of them, they were joined by Sherman and Livingston... headed for Dunlap's print shop, and immortality.

Now I turned to spy on Ludlo. He was staring intently at the Founders. I couldn't see why he didn't pursue them. Of course, he still had time. He might be planning to steal the Declaration from the printer. Could I prevent that? My hand went to Joseph Erie's long-barreled revolver, still stuck in my pants. I couldn't very well draw a futuristic gun on Ludlo in the presence of three prolific writers, who certainly would record such a weird event for posterity, and thus alter history profoundly. But if Ludlo waited until after they left, it would be just him, and John Dunlap...and me.

Then Ariyl walked into view from the far side of the State House. She and I both could see the Founders heading up the road. But I could see Ludlo, and she couldn't.

Ariyl followed the men at a discreet distance. Then a funny thing happened. As Ariyl moved into his field of vision, her back was to Ludlo, but I could tell he recognized her instantly.

He looked stunned.

Then he put his hand to his Time Crystal, and vanished.

"So what?" Ariyl asked, when I caught up to her a minute later.

"You don't think that's suspicious?"

"No."

"He somehow changes your world so it isn't there anymore..."

"By accident," she interjected.

"Then he takes a letter that changes the war so Hitler wins."

"He didn't know that would happen, David. He just wanted the letter."

"And just now, if he hadn't spotted you, he would have taken the Declaration of Independence, and erased America."

"Well, good. Me showing up changed all that. Problem solved. What are you complaining about?"

"I don't think *any* of these were accidents. He's no dope. You said he's a genius. I think he's deliberately changing history."

"That's ridiculous!"

"Then why try to steal the Declaration on the very day it's signed? And why not talk to you when he saw you?"

"Well...he wasn't expecting me. He told me to wait in Atlantis for him. Maybe he's picking up another present for me, and doesn't want to ruin the surprise."

I ran my fingers through my hair, trying my best not to rip it out by the fistful. I took a deep breath. "Ariyl, you saw Ludlo's list. Can you remember any other dates on it?"

"I can see the whole thing in my mind."

"I thought you always forgot dates!"

"Only dates that I hear. If I see it, I remember it."

"You have eidetic memory?"

"I guess. That's what Ludlo calls it. He's sorta jealous...they added it to the genome after he was born."

"So you know Ludlo's entire list!"

"I couldn't see the *whole* list. The first one was 1908, the Alpine Tavern..."

"Getting Ty Cobb to sign the ball."

"Then 2011, Dodger Stadium...to meet your friend Andy. And then Atlantis, 1628 B.C., for the Minotaur. After that was August 2nd, 1939. And then here, July 4th, 19—I mean, 1776. He kinda had those two dates off to the side, with a question mark. The dates below those, at least what I could see, were pretty much in order."

"From most recent to most ancient, right?" Ariyl nodded. Ludlo's scheme was starting to make sense to me: "You know what? I think 1776 was an experiment. I think he stole the Declaration just to test what would happen. Coming from the past, from 1492 to 1976, we just stumbled across the results of his test. And maybe that explains 1939 too. If we did nothing to fix them, and he'd seen how radically he'd changed history, then I think he would have had to put them back himself."

"Why?"

"Because if he really wants to steal historic objects, he can't change the history that produced them. He has to start in the most recent era, and move backwards. You have to take everything you want from American history, before you erase America."

"David, I'm telling you, he wouldn't do that!"

"He already did."

"Well, now that he saw me here, he won't come back. So he can't erase America anymore."

"But he could undo a hundred other events! Ariyl, we got lucky here. In 1776 he bent a branch of history that we weren't on. We climbed up behind him and straightened it out again—that's what you just did, by scaring him off. But sooner or later, he's going to get behind *us* and saw off the branch we're sitting on. We'll cease to exist. We have to find him before that! Now, what was the most recent date you saw on his list?"

"Uh, October 4th, 1945."

"You're sure this time? No more sloppy penmanship?"

"I'm positive," she snapped.

"Okay. First, we have to make sure we win World War Two. Take us to August 2nd, 1939."

"Right, the place was Pec-Pecon...?"

"Peconic, New York," I finished. She looked impressed. "Einstein's vacation home, where he wrote his letter to FDR. No way could Ludlo think stealing *that* letter wouldn't change history."

"Well, not everybody lives and breathes this stuff like you do. Sure we don't want to go to 1945 first?"

"No, whatever he was after there would be different if America lost World War Two. We have to fix 1939. And pray that he hasn't changed anything else."

She looked at me funny.

"You pray?"

"Not since I was a kid. But in the last twenty-four hours, yes, quite a bit. We need all the help we can get."

Before we departed 1776, I slipped in the rear door of the State House and left Jefferson's coat and hat where Ariyl had found them. I felt fairly sure the distortion to history would be within N-Tec's limits.

It would be quite some time before I realized there was something else of Jefferson's that I'd neglected to return.

18

PECONIC, LONG ISLAND, 1939 A.D.

OUR TRIP FROM 1776 PHILADELPHIA TO 1939 LONG Island seemed to take less time than any of our previous hops. Either the Crystal moved us at a more or less steady rate of seconds per years, or else I was just getting used to the vertigo.

On the warm, sunny morning of August 2nd, 1939, we arrived in the town of Peconic. Ariyl was still hungry. We had no spendable money, so I was forced to pawn my antique Panerai diver's watch. At least it belonged in this era. The old pawnbroker gave me a disgusted glance—the words 'Kampfschwimmer' on the case no doubt convinced him I was a Nazi frogman. But America was still neutral, so he paid me twenty-five dollars in crisp new bills, which would be worth twenty times that much in my time.

We ate at a local diner. I had the breakfast special. Ariyl had three.

Then we walked up to a vacation cabin on Old Grove Road out on Nassau Point, a narrow, sand-rimmed triangle jutting out into Peconic Bay. The cabin actually belonged to a Dr. Moore, but I knew Einstein was living here the second I laid eyes on it: A shady, unkempt yard, a screened-in porch, and a bicycle leaning against the house.

Ariyl rang the doorbell.

I had to watch from the cover of shrubs down the road—my bloodstained khaki outfit would not have made a good impression. But I had no doubt Ariyl would, as her SmartFab clothes had morphed into a 1939 female postal uniform which managed to contain, just barely, her curvy charms.

It was Einstein himself who opened the door. He had the sorrowful expression I'd seen in a hundred photos, though his wild hair was not yet the all-white mop I was expecting. He wore an old undershirt and rolled-up trousers. Rather sloppy attire for the world's most famous scientist, in an era where style counted. If Mrs. Einstein had still been alive, she'd have pitched a fit. But at age sixty, it was clear the old widower would be taking no further advice on his personal grooming. I was dying to talk to this colossus of modern science...but I told myself I must not interact with him. Especially not while my attire suggested that I worked in a slaughterhouse, without an apron.

So I spied from down the road, watching as Einstein's eyes tracked up Ariyl in amazement.

"Good morning, Professor," trilled Ariyl.

"You look like a Rockette," he beamed. "I had no idea postmen were so pretty on Long Island."

"Thank you! Any letters to go out today?"

"Such service!" he chuckled. "*Ja*, my dear. A most important one. But too important, I fear, to entrust to anyone but my friend, Professor Szilárd. He will be along shortly to pick it up."

The old scientist indicated the lid of the small black mailbox beside his door, under which was wedged his historic letter, inside a big manila envelope, all ready to go.

"Well, you know best, sir," said Ariyl.

Einstein's face crumpled back into sadness.

"Do I, indeed? I almost wish it would not reach its destination.

But the alternative is too terrible to contemplate. Now, if you will excuse me..." The great man stepped outside, closed his door, and walked down the steps to his bicycle.

"I believe I will feel better after a nice long ride."

Ariyl saluted him. Evidently, she thought her postal uniform made her part of the military. She walked away from the house, as if heading to her next stop. The old man pedaled gracefully down the road, and was soon lost from view. Then Ariyl ducked behind the shrubbery with me, concealed, waiting for Ludlo.

"He seemed so bummed. What exactly did he say in this letter?" Ariyl asked.

"Sh!" I said, finger to lips. Call me paranoid. I had the distinct feeling we were being watched, and I didn't want any more disruption of history. I went on, in a whisper: "He informed President Franklin Roosevelt that a single bomb could be built that would level a city. That it would be made from uranium, and that was why the Germans had already stopped all sales of uranium from their mines in Czechoslovakia. It took two more years to get the ball rolling, and without this letter, I don't believe Roosevelt would ever have supported the Manhattan Project, which built the bomb and won the war."

"But if Ludlo had got here today before us, and stole it, couldn't Einstein just have written another one?"

"Maybe. Maybe not. Szilárd would have found Einstein gone, and no letter. It took weeks for them to agree on the wording of this one. They might start wrangling all over again, with more weeks going by before Einstein finally signed off on it. It might be months until Szilárd could hand the letter to FDR's advisor...and by then, what other events might delay or prevent its being read, and acted on? And meanwhile, if Ludlo got the original letter to the Germans... no, it has to be this letter, and it has to go out today, if we're going to put history right."

"Well, I sure hope Ludlo shows up soon. I still can't believe he'd do something that dumb."

"You still think you know him. I don't think you know this guy at all. He sounds like a psychopath to me."

"He is not!"

"Grow up, Ariyl."

Just then, a whirlwind scudded down the street. Like a miniature tornado, it picked up leaves and candy wrappers, and headed right for Einstein's porch. The wind caught the FDR letter, whipped it loose, and deposited it somewhere inside the thick hedge growing alongside the house. If we hadn't seen where it went in, we might never have found it. Nor would Ludlo have, unless he had been right there to see it.

Ariyl gave me a superior look. I fumed.

"Go ahead and say it."

"Told you. Ludlo would never have done something like that."

My ears burned, something they hadn't done since seventh grade. That's why I went into archaeology, where I could take years before publishing a theory, to be absolutely sure I'd considered all the other explanations before committing myself to a position. Sven always said I waited too long for things. Well, I hate being proved wrong. Like now.

"All right, all right. Maybe this is a fluke, a closed time-loop Ludlo had nothing to do with. Maybe, like the butterfly wing starting a hurricane, all this time travel into past eras snowballed into the breeze that lost the letter."

"Easy fix," said Ariyl.

She dashed to the hedge with her usual frightening speed, located the letter and brought it to me. Einstein had not bothered to seal the envelope. Szilárd no doubt would want to proof the letter before passing it on.

I slid out three typed pages. One page was a short version; the other, a two-page letter. Both were signed at the bottom in Einstein's tiny scrawl. It was a thrill to hold in my hands a letter that had literally changed the world. I saw it wasn't stained or damaged in any way. I paused another moment, thinking this really belonged in a museum. Idiot. Someday it would be. I slid it back into its envelope.

Ariyl hurried up the road and wedged it back under the mailbox lid. She came back to me.

"Can we go, now?"

"Not yet. I want to be absolutely sure it gets into Szilárd's hands."

The sun rose higher, the air got warmer. The sound of the waves lapping nearby made waiting in this heat even more unbearable. Ariyl fidgeted, restless.

"So, after this, 1945?"

"Yes. September 3rd, the day after the official Japanese surrender. If the war is still on, or if Hitler's still alive...we've got a problem."

"But if everything's okay there?"

"We check 2013. If nothing's different in my world, you can try going home."

"Oh." She paused. "You mean, my world will be back, too?"

"If you and I somehow caused a breeze that derailed World War Two...then that would have derailed your future. Once we restore my world, yours should be back too."

"And you'll owe Ludlo an apology."

"He still erased America!"

"Temporarily. And by accident."

"Maybe. Just make sure they never let him near a Time Crystal again."

"No, duh." She paused, and chewed that pouty lip of hers. "David, what if things are still wrong with history?"

"Then, like Sven said, we have to find Ludlo, and stop him."

"How would we do that?"

"Find him, or stop him?"

"Either one."

"How should I know? I'm making this up as I go along."

Ariyl laughed. "Did you just make *that* up?"

"No. It came from a movie."

"Really?" She sounded impressed. "Look, while we're here, you want to do something?"

"Like what?"

"I dunno. Catch one of those flat-flix you keep talking about?"

"You want to see flat-flix?" She nodded. "Even if they're not in color?"

She cringed. "Really? What about sound, they have that, don't they?"

"Yeah, for about a decade they have. Look, Ariyl, under ordinary circumstances, I'd love to take you to a movie, but..."

"C'mon, you've been telling me how great they are. Pick your favorite."

I shook my head. "You're really hitting below the belt. I mean, this is 1939. We'd have an embarrassment of riches. Besides *The Wizard of Oz*, there's *Mr. Smith Goes To Washington, Only Angels Have Wings, Ninotchka, Wuthering Heights, The Hunchback of Notre Dame, The Women* and *Goodbye, Mr. Chips.* John Ford with three of his best, *Young Mr. Lincoln, Drums Along the Mohawk*—in color, you'd like that—and *Stagecoach.* Bette Davis in *Dark Victory.* Or Basil Rathbone, the all-time best Sherlock Holmes in *The Hound of the Baskervilles.*

"I suppose we could even see *Gone With the Wind.* Terrific cast, incredible production, and it's in color."

"Cool! It's about people in a hurricane?"

"Uh, no. People in slavery days."

"So they fight slavery?"

"Actually, no. They own the slaves."

"You're kidding!"

"I wish. Yeah, let's forget that one."

"To be honest, they all sound kinda depressing."

Perhaps a little too deep-dish for Ariyl, I thought.

Maybe just a classic action picture—*Gunga Din, The Four Feathers,* Cecil B. DeMille's *Union Pacific.* Errol Flynn playing a cowboy in *Dodge City,* or Tyrone Power as *Jesse James.*

Or better yet, how about a zany comedy? Laurel & Hardy in *The Flying Deuces*, W.C. Fields in *You Can't Cheat an Honest Man*, or the Marx Brothers in *At The Circus*.

Or some Universal horror: Lugosi as broken-necked Ygor in *Son of Frankenstein*, deftly stealing the picture from bolt-necked Karloff (revenge for Boris stealing Bela's place as Hollywood's monster man.) Meanwhile, Lon Chaney Jr., who would soon be raiding both their careers, was warming up as Lennie in Steinbeck's heartbreaking *Of Mice and Men*.

"I'd have a hard time picking just one," I said. "And as great as 1939 was, we jump ahead another year or two and we have classics from Disney, Hitchcock, Preston Sturges, Billy Wilder, John Huston...and Orson Welles."

"Orson," she giggled. The very name amused her.

"Welles. One of the all-time geniuses of film."

"I know the name. Ludlo talked about him."

"Poor Orson only got to make one truly great picture, *Citizen Kane*, before they yanked it all away from him. By the end of his life, he was doing talk shows and ads for cheap wine so he could make home movies that he never finished."

"What do you mean, yanked it all away?"

"Welles' second film, *The Magnificent Ambersons*, was taken out of his hands by the studio and cut to ribbons. A third of the story gone. They slapped on a happy ending that plays like the last reel of another movie. Then, to add injury to insult, the studio destroyed the leftover negative, so he could never restore it. One of the biggest crimes against art ever committed."

I don't want to pretend I'm an expert in Hollywood history. I'm not. When it comes to old movies, I'm a dedicated fan rather than a scholar. But I did know some famous stories, and I rambled on about great movies I'd seen. Amazingly, she seemed to be interested, if only to recognize where plot elements of her favorite vidz had originated.

We'd been talking for nearly an hour when Leó Szilárd arrived, a passenger in a black sedan. A bulky man, wearing a suit despite the summer heat, he puffed up the steps and rapped on the door, then rang the doorbell. There was no answer. He saw the letter clamped under the mailbox lid. He pulled it out, opened the envelope and read it through. He nodded in satisfaction. He looked down at the spot on the drive where Einstein's bike had been leaning. The physicist chuckled to himself. He knew where his friend had gone.

Szilárd got back in the car, which was driven by a balding man I could not see well. It wheeled around and rumbled off in the direction of New York City.

I exhaled. I'd been holding my breath, without realizing it. Maybe, just maybe, this nightmare was over.

"So, what are we going to see?" pressed Ariyl.

"First, we check on 1945. No, wait...December 26th, 1946."

"Why?"

"It's the day my father was born."

"Aw, you want to see your father as a baby? That's so sweet!"

"No! God, no! What if I give him pneumonia or something? Talk about asking for a paradox. No, I'm staying miles away from Boston. But the day before— Christmas morning—a bus crashed and burned outside New York. On board was a returning war hero, one of the guys who liberated Dachau. He broke a window and led eighteen survivors to safety—not a single death. It was a miracle. Especially since he came within seconds of missing that bus. Grandma said it was in all the papers the day Dad was born. That's why she named him Richard...after the hero."

"So you figure, his story was so unlikely, that any change to history would have altered where the hero was that day?"

"You're getting good at this."

"Thanks. Okay, just name the time and place."

I brushed myself off, and we walked up a driveway to a shuttered house, where our departure wouldn't be observed.

I hated to admit it, but Ludlo had never showed up. At least as far as we knew.

19

THE RAINBOW ROOM, 1946 A.D.

"YOU SAID YOU'D TAKE ME TO THE BEST CLUB IN Manhattan. You didn't tell me your idea of a date is reading a bunch of newspapers," moped Ariyl.

"It's not a date, and I can't relax until I know we're out of the woods." But the newspapers all agreed—the miracle of the bus crash had happened yesterday, exactly as Grandma Sara had told me. Other articles mentioned Hitler's suicide, discovered by the invading Red Army in May 1945, and the Japanese surrender on the *USS Missouri* on September 2nd of the same year, just like I put on my seventh grade history exam. (Got a hundred, thank you very much.)

I wanted one more assurance, however. I asked our waiter for a telephone. He plugged one in to our table, and I placed a long-distance call to Massachusetts General Hospital in Boston. It took five minutes for the operator to call back with my party.

"Hello, this is Sara Preston," said a woman's weary voice. It was also the voice, half a century younger, of my Grandma Sara.

"I'm sorry to disturb you. I'm a friend of your husband Sam," I said. "I understand congratulations are in order?"

"Yes," my twenty-five-year-old grandmother yawned, "Born at two-twenty this afternoon. His name's Richard."

Everything just as I remembered it about Dad's birth. It looked like I would be born, after all. In another four decades.

"I won't keep you. Good night, Gra—uh, Sara. And God bless." I hung up.

History was back on track.

So why didn't I feel more joyful?

History was just as I remembered it, but millions were dead. Naturally I was glad the Nazis were defeated and the Japanese military machine dismantled. The horrific practice of waging modern war on civilians, which began with Guernica and Nanking, had been turned back on the nations responsible. But in the process, my country and its allies had obliterated whole cities like Hamburg and Dresden and Tokyo and Nagasaki. I tried to tell myself they started it. But no one was innocent anymore.

Not even Ariyl and me—now that we had played a part in it.

Damn it.

I had to remind myself that millions were also alive. Like my whole family. And the rest of Boston. Restoring this particular timeline meant I could go home.

And honestly, that was a relief. For the first time in more hours than I could count, I felt the tension ebb from my weary muscles. I'd forgotten what it felt like to relax.

"Hey." Ariyl passed her palm across my eyes to bring me out of my trance. "Are we gonna celebrate?"

"Sorry. Lost in thought."

"You want to dance?"

"Here?"

"No, down on the ice rink, so we can both fall on our ass. Come on, handsome." Without waiting for my assent, she took my arm and drew me to the slowly rotating dance floor. It was crowded with other couples, but they all moved back a bit to make room for Ariyl. And to give her the once-over while they were at it.

Ariyl's outfit was now a clingy burgundy velvet number, which in this era would have had shoulder pads, except that she didn't need them. My worry that my "assistant" would be spending all her time conditioning was groundless: Ariyl's SmartFab chapeau actually sent out an electrostatic charge that parted her luminous hair Veronica Lake-ishly over one eye. Those lovely tresses caught the Technicolor spectrum of the overhead lights magnificently.

I was wearing a tuxedo that Ariyl had recently liberated from a closed Saks Fifth Avenue. "We'll put it back after dinner," she'd promised, while bending apart the iron bars on a back window with depressing ease. "I just want you to look nice."

So, dressed to the nines, we danced. I mentally thanked Mom, who'd insisted I learn to ballroom dance, back in the late Nineties when it ranked just above Egyptian mummification as a lost art.

The music was peppy, a big band swing number I couldn't identify. Ariyl was a bit clumsy at first, crunching my toes twice in the first few steps. But once she saw how the others did it, her inbred coordination kicked in, and in moments she was gliding like Ginger Rogers, if Ginger had been six-three. Thank God she wasn't wearing heels.

I finally understood why people back then danced. In my arms, Ariyl felt amazing. If I'd been struck deaf that instant, I still would have followed every note of the music through her firm waist and hips as she moved.

Then the girl singer stepped up to the mike for a slow ballad. She launched into a beloved Gershwin standard. Everyone moved in and got chummy with their partner. Ariyl looked around, noted the change, and came in close.

Though she had nearly four inches on me, slow-dancing with Ariyl wasn't unpleasant. Not in the least. By the second refrain, she knew the words and sang along. Despite her breathy, high speaking voice, Ariyl sang in a lower register like Grandma's fave, Lizabeth Scott. In my ear, she purred the lyric about how she needed...well, you might chuckle at the idea of this amazon needing anyone to watch over her. A day ago, I would have too. Tonight, I just felt special.

Maybe too special. I gradually became aware of the eyes of others, staring at us. We did stand out from the crowd, me with my unoiled hair, and Ariyl with her, well, her everything.

It made me nervous. These people were noticing something they didn't see in 1946 Prime—an incredibly striking woman in the Rainbow Room the night after Christmas, whom they might remember the rest of their lives.

Was our dance merely a butterfly flutter that would dissipate against the inertia of history? Or might we be generating another self-magnifying cyclone that would alter the future?

"I think we should sit down," I murmured to Ariyl. She drew back, looking a bit hurt. "Nothing personal, but we're now in a public place where we didn't exist, in the first draft of history. We might change something for someone. Like that guy over there."

I nodded at the burly guy at ringside, with slicked-back hair, all but drooling over Ariyl, while his wife (to judge from her ring) glared at him icily. Ariyl cocked her head, skeptical. I persisted.

"Maybe they get in a fight tonight about you, and get divorced, and never give birth to a great genius."

"Or maybe he's so turned on they go home and *make* a genius," countered Ariyl. But she got my point. "Okay, fine, killjoy." We made our way off the floor.

I paid the check. Man, filet of sole, prime rib with all the trimmings and cherries jubilee, plus a magnum of champagne, and a long-distance call...and a decent tip...in one of Manhattan's swankiest clubs, and we got away for under twenty bucks. There's no time like the past.

We rode the gleaming brass elevator to the street and strolled outside, the frigid air biting our ears. Right across 50th Street stood a glittering fairyland edifice of neon signage, topped by a towering, lit Christmas tree—Radio City Music Hall. I read the marquee.

"Oh, God, this is perfect."

"What?"

"Something we can enjoy without drawing a crowd. Come on."

I slapped down silver money at the ticket kiosk.

"The show already started, sir," said the lady inside.

"That's what I get for pawning my watch," I sighed. "How much have we missed?"

"The stage show, the newsreel and the Donald Duck cartoon. If you hurry, you'll be in time for the feature."

I thanked her and pulled Ariyl (to the extent that was possible) through the palatial lobby toward the auditorium.

"What's the hurry?" wondered Ariyl, as a pimple-faced usher, uniformed like a Ruritanian palace guard, opened the auditorium door for us.

"Sh!" I whispered. "The movie's started. You're not supposed to talk."

"Really?" she asked at normal volume.

"Shh!" reminded the usher.

We took our seats near the back. The house was only half full... no doubt due to the blizzard outside. The faint acrid smell of someone's cigarette tinged the aroma of fresh buttered popcorn. We'd just missed the opening credits.

There on the screen, in glossy black and gleaming white and thousand silver shades of gray, but now fifty feet high, was the movie I'd seen and loved every year since I was twelve. "Adeste Fideles" ringing softly on a celesta. Snow fluttering down on a small town. Voices murmuring prayers, all for the same man. Then a soft chorus sang Gounod's "Ave Maria" as the camera pulled up, up and back into a starry night sky, until the Earth itself was lost. Then came voices from the interiors of glowing nebulae.

"Who's that, aliens?" asked Ariyl.

"*Shhh!*" hissed a woman in front of us.

"Angels," I whispered.

"*Angels?*" Ariyl repeated, rolling her eyes.

"Give it a chance."

The celestial scene proceeded. Ariyl shifted in her seat, which creaked in protest. But when the film moved to an icy pond back on Earth, as ten-year-old George rescued his brother from drowning, she stopped creaking. She smiled, delighted by two small girls, Mary and Violet, already vying for the boy that Mary would love "till the day I die."

By the time George had saved the druggist from accidentally killing a child, gotten his ear slapped bloody for his trouble, and vowed never to tell, as the grateful Mr. Gower dissolved in tears... Ariyl was a wreck. So was I. Again.

Then the scene shifted to a young man in a luggage store, stammering as he explained just how big a suitcase he wanted.

The adult George Bailey held out his arms, and was captured in a freeze-frame.

Ice water shot through my veins.

"We have to go," I told Ariyl. "Right now."

"I love this flick!" she whispered, brushing away tears. "I want to see how it comes out!"

"SHHH!" hissed the lady in front.

"We're leaving now," I said, and strode up the aisle. I took one more look back at the screen, to see if maybe the champagne was scrambling my vision.

But no. On screen in sharp focus, playing the lead in *It's a Wonderful Life*, was the still-boyishly handsome Henry Fonda.

20

RADIO CITY MUSIC HALL, 1946-1961 A.D.

We went to the theater lobby and I struck up a conversation with the girl at the candy counter. She was a dedicated movie fan, and read all the mags. In between popcorn sales, and with very little prompting, she informed us that James Stewart didn't star in *It's a Wonderful Life* or any other pictures since his return from World War Two. Jimmy had made it through twenty-some bombing missions without a scratch...only to be tragically slain at RKO Studios last year, on the night of October 4th, 1945. It was a time of violent labor strife in Hollywood, and police said Jimmy might have just been in the wrong place at the wrong time. He'd showed up for a meeting with a famous director and had gotten caught in the crossfire. His killer had not been found. I gave Ariyl a significant look: Stewart had been shot dead on the very next date on Ludlo's list.

The candy girl opined that Stewart would have made a much better George Bailey than Fonda, who she loved but said was "kinda stiff in this one."

I knew the clock was ticking—the fact that we were in a changed future meant Ludlo must have already altered 1945 and was no doubt planning to meddle elsewhere, earlier in time. But I felt compelled to see just what this change would mean for the future. I mean, besides a dozen upcoming film classics sucking without Stewart in them.

Standing outside Radio City Music Hall, I had Ariyl jump us ahead to the first Thursday after the next few presidential elections. Just a minute's stay, always at five in the morning, to avoid being seen. I fed the newsrack a nickel at each stop.

November 1948: Truman still eked out his victory over Dewey, though so closely that the iconic headline gaffe, "Dewey Defeats Truman" was committed not just by the *Chicago Daily Tribune*, but also the *New York Times*.

November 1952: Eisenhower and Nixon had been elected. Not much difference I could detect except that the speech about his dog that had saved Nixon's political ass mentioned not a cocker named Checkers but a pit bull named Gordon. And Gordon had viciously attacked a *Washington Post* reporter late in the campaign, making the Republican win over Adlai Stevenson more of a squeaker than a landslide.

November 1956: Nixon had resigned the Vice Presidency in July for "health reasons"...and running with Eisenhower was Ronald Reagan, who had left the Screen Actors Guild presidency in 1953 to win a seat in Congress. If it was possible, this Reagan was an even more militant anti-Communist than he had been in his original version...though his twinkly movie star smile smoothed the edges off the angry accusations that were to make homely, charmless Joe McCarthy so despised in my timeline.

November 1960: Reagan would succeed Eisenhower as president, elected on, among other things, a promise to "do what needs doing in Cuba," which had fallen to Castro right on schedule. Reagan, on the other hand, was president twenty years ahead of time. The *Times* profile said Reagan's staunch stand against the Reds was inspired by the murder of his close friend James Stewart by "commie labor goons."

Ariyl and I started hopping a month, then a week at a time, as the Cuban crisis deepened. Unlike John F. Kennedy, Reagan fully supported the CIA's Bay of Pigs invasion in April 1961. However, even with full U.S. air support, the war bogged down in urban guerrilla fighting, with Castro abandoning Havana to command the resistance in the hills. Castro had correctly judged Reagan's antipathy was a mortal threat to his regime, and was already deep in the Soviets' embrace.

Reagan's version of the Cuban Crisis, therefore, took place only weeks after he took office, instead of twenty-one months. Unfortunately, to judge from the paper, no missiles had been spotted by U-2 flights, as Kennedy had learned in our version of October 1962. So neither Reagan nor anyone else in his government knew there were already Soviet nukes in Cuba, let alone where they were. They were Castro's secret trump card.

On May 20th, 1961, amid heated debate in Congress and throughout the nation over his tough stance, the *Times* reported that right before an address Reagan had joked over a live microphone, "I just signed legislation which outlaws Russia forever. The bombing begins in five minutes." In my timeline, Reagan had waited until 1984 to make that wisecrack; by then, the crumbling Soviet Union was dispirited, and desperate enough that it was about to install reformer Mikhail Gorbachev. But in 1961, the effect was rather different.

We couldn't buy a paper on May 21st, because the newsrack had been incinerated, along with Radio City and most of Manhattan.

Once again proving that the essence of comedy...is timing.

It didn't matter who gave the order, Khrushchev, or the Soviet commander in Cuba, or (most likely) Castro himself. Nor was it any comfort that undoubtedly every inch of Cuba and every major city in the U.S.S.R had also been consigned to the ash heap of history. Nor that in this timeline, Reagan had single-handedly brought down the Berlin Wall, along with every other wall in Europe.

This wasn't a future I wanted any part of.

21

HOLLYWOOD, 1945 A.D.

In the Los Angeles of my era there is a big masonry sphere with all my favorite continents, atop the southwest corner of the Paramount Studios soundstage at Melrose and Gower. I feel like I must have passed it every week, and I never even connected it with where else I'd seen that famous globe. But on the windy morning of October 4th, 1945, I now realized that corner was originally the site of Paramount's modest next-door neighbor, whose symbol it bore.

What clued me was the prop radio tower that was now atop the sculpted world: A neon-and-steel replica of the Radio Keith Orpheum logo that beeped R-K-O in Morse Code as animated radio waves emanated, signaling the start of *King Kong, Gunga Din, Bringing Up Baby, Cat People,* Wheeler & Woolsey comedies, and the classic Astaire and Rogers musicals. Also Orson Welles' *Citizen Kane*...and, to the studio's eventual regret, his production of *The Magnificent Ambersons.*

Ariyl and I walked past dozens of fans congregated a couple of blocks east, at the Italianate, filigreed Bronson Street gate of Paramount. There were also angry picketers at that entrance.

As we walked west to the RKO gate, I eyed the radio mast. In the next decade, Howard Hughes would buy this fabled studio, run it into the ground, and sell it to Desilu; TV's Lucy was probably the one who had the tower taken down.

At RKO, we saw no picketers, and few gawkers waited to see if their favorite star would enter the gates of this compact dream factory. The ones who were there gaped at me, still in my tux at ten in the morning, and at Ariyl, still spectacular, though more appropriately dressed.

I slid a nickel into a *Variety* newsrack. From what I could glean, a bitter strike had been going on for six months, some impenetrable dispute between two unions about who should represent set decorators. But neither the picketers nor the fans knew what Ariyl and I did—that Oscar winner, war hero and all around good-guy James Maitland Stewart would bleed to death on the pavement outside RKO's gate tonight.

And I knew somehow Ludlo was responsible.

No fans turned a head at the dark, energetic, balding little man in a loud shirt, who waved breezily at the guard as he drove up to the RKO gate. I nudged Ariyl.

"That's the director he's meeting?" she asked.

I nodded. We walked a block to use the payphone at Nickodell's Restaurant. I dropped in a coin and dialed.

Ariyl was smirking. She found the idea of needing metal discs to get reading material or communicate or obtain gumballs amusing.

My party answered.

"Th-this is Jim, Jimmy Stewart, haire," I drawled. Ariyl looked at me in bafflement. I did an excellent Stewart, if I did say so. "May I speak to Frank Capra?"

I was connected immediately. The director spoke in a rapid, helium-pitched voice.

"What's up, Jimmy?" he answered. "We still on for our meeting?"

"Wal, that's why I'm *cawling*, Frank. I-I, uh, I don't thank I can *make* it till next wake."

Ariyl was doubling over in silent laughter. I made a cut-it motion across my throat with my finger. She cupped her hand over her face, but kept snorting into it.

"Did you read the script yet?"

"Uh, no, no, nawt exac'ly, but I, I'm shurr it's gud."

"So what's the problem? Did Wasserman say anything about it?"

"N-no, Frank, lissen, I, I just need a little more *taw'ime.*"

"You sound kinda funny, Jim. Anything wrong?"

"N-nawt a *thang*. Why?"

Capra chuckled nervously. "Well, you sound like someone doing an *impression* of Jimmy Stewart."

Ariyl had to walk away, in convulsions.

"I'm fine! Just a li'l rusty, is all. Been in the Army, remember?"

"I know the feeling, Jim. You know, I was just about to call Wasserman, and ask you to come out to the house instead. Lu and the kids are dying to see you. How about Wednesday?"

"Th-that'd be great, I'd like to see them too. I'll have Wasserman set it up. S'long, Frank."

I hung up. Ariyl was wiping her eyes.

"He doesn't really sound like that, does he?"

"It happens to be an excellent impression," I asserted. "You just do your part right."

I dialed MCA, and handed the phone to Ariyl, who posed as Capra's secretary calling for Stewart's agent. Wasserman's aide promised to call back to firm up the details for Wednesday the tenth.

"Well, that was easy," said Ariyl, hanging up. "When's our next stop?"

"We're not leaving yet. All we've done is save Stewart's life tonight. I hope. We still don't know why Ludlo killed him."

"Ludlo would never kill him!" bristled Ariyl. "I'm sure this was all an accident."

"All right, whatever. Now, you said you'd heard of Orson Welles before?"

"Ludlo's mentioned him."

I thumbed through *Variety*, and luckily, there was a picture of Welles, with some casting announcement about his current film, *The Stranger*.

"Does this guy look familiar?" I asked.

"Yeah! Except he had a mustache, and kinda gray hair. He was in this old, old photo on Ludlo's wall. It was like the pride of his collection. The stamp said it was from some place called The Players, October 4th, 1945."

"Well, this is Orson Welles. Ludlo's photo must be why he picked this date. It showed him where he could find the man out in public. He wants something from Welles. And if he's running true to form, I think I know what it is."

The Players was a white, three-story nightclub with its name in cursive above fanlight windows on the first floor. It resembled a Southern plantation house, and was set into a steep hill on the north side of Sunset Boulevard, across a narrow side street from Chateau Marmont. As I said, I'm not a true scholar of old L.A., so I'd never heard of the place, but as it turned out, I had eaten there before. In my time, it's a Pink Taco.

But in 1945, despite competition from famed clubs on the Strip like The Garden of Allah and Ciro's, this joint was jumping. Living up to its name, it had actors everywhere: Spencer Tracy dining with Kate Hepburn; James Cagney; I think Errol Flynn (I couldn't be sure, he was facing a rather young lady he never took his eyes off); Judy Garland and Vincente Minnelli, Groucho, Harpo and Chico Marx with brother Gummo (their agent, I gathered) celebrating someone's birthday, and only straight man Zeppo missing. I was pretty sure a blonde with her back to me was Marlene Dietrich. Bogart and Bacall dining with director John Huston. Barbara Stanwyck and Robert Taylor. Ingrid Bergman and (I guess) her husband, with Alfred Hitchcock and his wife Alma Reville. W.C. Fields, face studded with gin blossoms, looking like he was at death's door, but determined not to pass through sober.

Betty Hutton was onstage, singing "Murder, He Says." Her presence doubtless explained such a big late dinner crowd. She was amazing—hilarious and hammy and adorable, with more energy than anyone I'd ever seen, outside of Ariyl in a fistfight.

A man with a pencil-thin mustache, a prodigious mop of tousled hair, and a bemused expression sat in the booth at the southeast corner, with the air of a benign prince holding court. This had to be the owner. He had a view of the distant, moonlit Pacific, and the glittering, patchy grid stretching out to it that was mid-century Los Angeles. Beside him sat a pretty brunette I didn't recognize, and around the booth, half a dozen bit players with the funniest collection of mugs I'd seen outside of a Preston Sturges comedy. And then I realized that's exactly where I'd seen them. William Demarest was the only name I could come up with.

An owlish young man with spectacles table-hopped and deadpanned with a German accent to the owner, "Preston, ve miss you at de studio. Now dere's only one genius at Paramount. Me."

"You were saying that before I left, Billy," said Sturges to his rival Wilder.

I would have given anything to spend just twenty minutes eavesdropping in this room, soaking up the wit.

Or even just gazing at the glamour on display. Every woman was dressed to kill; every man wore a crisply pressed suit and a tie, cufflinks and tie clip. They all looked like they'd been dressed by a costumer, to be *in* a movie. Where and when I come from, it's a big deal if someone wears a jacket to a club. Alas, I was a bit overdressed for The Players, still in my stolen Saks tux.

Regardless, we had a mission to accomplish.

Bob Hope and Bing Crosby passed us on their way out. Crosby winked at me: "Sorry I missed the wedding." Hope growled comically at Ariyl. She smiled wanly. She had no idea who they were.

A flash went off in the corner of the room. Ariyl nudged me and pointed to where Orson Welles sat with sinuous, copper-haired Rita Hayworth. Welles quickly filled out an address card for the girl who had snapped their photo. He gave her a five and a wink. Bingo. We had just seen the pride of Ludlo's collection being created. We wound our way over to the table.

As soon as the photo girl left, the high-wattage smiles were turned off. Rita looked neglected, Orson looked bored. At least until he got a gander at Ariyl.

"Good evening, Ms...uh, Miss Hayworth, Mr. Welles," I began. Orson pushed on the table, a modern affair cantilevered to swivel out for easy access. This was handy, given Orson's already husky physique. Courtly, he stood up to greet Ariyl. Rita looked daggers at him.

"You have the advantage of me," he purred in his radio baritone. Despite his baby-face, he looked older than his thirty years, thanks to the mustache...and because he had not bothered to wash out the gray hair at his temples from today's shooting.

"I'm David Preston, this is Ariyl Moro." Orson shook our hands, then indicated Rita. "My lovely wife, Rita Hayworth."

"Hi!" said Ariyl brightly.

"Charmed," said Rita, charmlessly. She remained seated, watching Orson like a hawk.

"I'm a huge fan of you both," I said. Rita smiled patiently. Orson was delighted.

"Will you have some wine? It's a 1937 Clos des Lambrays. It's quite good, though I'm going to lay a few bottles away. I think they sold it before its time." Ariyl reached for a glass but I intercepted her hand. She would need a clear head tonight.

"No, thank you. We need to talk to you about *The Magnificent Ambersons*. The complete version."

Welles paled. Without taking his eyes off me, he cleared his throat. "Darling, I need to discuss business with these people. Would you mind heading home without me?"

"Why should tonight be different?" Rita snapped, shoving the table out of her way. As she marched for the door, she uttered a Spanish curse word that was new to me.

Welles watched her go, and exhaled, embarrassed.

"She's been suspicious of me from the day we were wed, even though I gave her no reason."

"So do you give her reason now?" asked Ariyl.

I burned her with a look. After a beat, Orson guffawed.

"Excuse me, I think I'll find a bathroom," said Ariyl, taking my hint. Welles raised an eyebrow.

"You mean, you want to powder your nose," I prompted.

"Isn't that illegal in 1945?" she wondered. I gave her another look, and she got it. "Oh, like makeup! *That's* what you say instead of peeing. Yeah, gonna do that." That language chip could use some updates.

Orson got to his feet again and bowed slightly.

"Please hurry back," he said as she departed. We sat down again. "Quite the valkyrie, isn't she?" admired Orson. "Are you two...?"

"In a big rush? Yes. Now, please sir, about *Ambersons*."

"Ah, God. What a marvelous picture that would have been." He was misty-eyed. "What I gave them was twice as good as *Kane*."

"Do you have the original print?" I asked bluntly.

Welles looked around cautiously, like the war criminal he was playing in his movie, then murmured under his breath.

"Not at the moment. It's on its way from Brazil. I take it Ludlo sent you."

"Mr. Welles..."

"Orson."

"Orson. Ludlo is not who he says he is."

"Isn't he?" Orson looked troubled. His manner became frosty. I figured I was back to 'Mr. Welles' with him. "Well, I can assure you of one thing. When he wires money, it arrives. Who exactly are *you?*"

"We're film collectors. For the New York Museum of Modern Art. How much did Ludlo promise you for your cut of the movie?"

Welles sat back and appraised me. One thing I knew about his career was that after the failure of *Ambersons*, he could never again afford to turn down a paying gig. I myself first heard those amazing Wellesian tones when I was four, and he was voicing Unicron in my favorite cartoon, *Transformers: The Movie.*

"He promised me ten thousand, cash on delivery. He's already wired five thousand to my associate. Could it be that you are as serious a collector as he is?"

"Deadly serious. We'll double his offer," I lied, wondering where Ludlo had stolen the money he'd wired, and how *that* theft might screw with future events. Ariyl's pal was clearly trying to add Welles' lost masterpiece to his collection. My only advantage was that I probably knew 1945—and Welles—better than he did. I tried a different tack.

"But is money your only criterion, Orson? Would you rescue your greatest work...just to let a private collector hoard it for himself?"

"I plan to prevail on his better nature, to let me strike off an internegative."

"He doesn't have a better nature. He wants it for himself. Whereas we'll preserve your work in a museum, where everyone can see it." I said this with sincerity; I did hope somehow we could. Anyway, at the moment I needed Welles to believe it.

"*Ambersons* in a museum?" marveled Orson. "God, that *is* a wondrous notion. Are you sure you don't operate out of a lunatic asylum? Because I've been advocating that for years, and people think I'm joking."

"You're just ahead of your time. But please, you have to tell me everything Ludlo said."

Welles stared into his wine glass, pondering.

"He first phoned me on Monday. Which is odd, because when I finally met him here tonight..."

"Ludlo's here?" I exclaimed.

"He left twenty minutes ago."

Damn. Too bad the bloody Crystal wouldn't let us jump back half an hour, to grab the fool.

"Anyway, when we met tonight I must admit, his behavior was mysterious. He offered money—which he'd already wired—and asked for my phone number—which he obviously already had—and basically, spoke as if we hadn't already arranged everything. I assume he was worried we might be overheard."

My interpretation: Ludlo first arrived tonight, October 4th, met Welles, got his number, then jumped back in time three days to phone Welles at home, and arrange for getting the film sent from Brazil. Now he would jump back to this night, to meet Orson some hours from now...and somehow, this scheme would get Jimmy Stewart killed.

"On the phone, Ludlo said he'd already been at RKO, to search their film vaults. Do not ask me how he possibly could have gotten leave to do that." I didn't have to ask. With a Time Crystal, Ludlo wouldn't need permission to get into any location.

"Of course, he could not locate my 132-minute cut of *Ambersons*. I explained that all they had left was that 88-minute happily-ever-after abortion they released. On the bottom of a double-bill with *Mexican Spitfire Sees a Ghost*!" Welles shuddered at the memory, and polished off the burgundy. Then he poured himself some more.

"Needless to say, despite the charms of the late Miss Lupe Velez to draw the crowds, *The Magnificent Ambersons* was a monumental flop. RKO washed their hands of it, and burned my unused work for its silver content."

Again tears welled up in his eyes. He looked away for a moment, and only turned back when he'd composed himself.

"However..."

Welles paused, with a conspiratorial wink. Then, like a magician, he did his reveal.

"I *also* told Mr. Ludlo that I knew where I could lay my hands on my original cut. It's the composite workprint my editor Bob Wise sent to me in Rio de Janeiro, where I was doing my patriotic duty, working for the government. While those Judases at RKO butchered the best picture I ever made."

Welles carefully slanted his story to put him in the role of victim, but it really boiled down to how he abandoned *Ambersons* in post-production to fly down to Rio to film the Carnival. He was doing his bit for the Good Neighbor Policy with South America, shooting his ill-starred, unfinished *It's All True*...and partying in Wellesian style. After a Brazilian drowned in the sea performing for Welles' camera, the wunderkind had been summoned home...to find *Ambersons* ruined.

"I was careful not to tell Mr. Ludlo where the print was—five years in this piratical business have taught me the value of judiciousness, to say nothing of misdirection."

"But he wired the five thousand for you anyway?"

"We had to pay a premium to grease the wheels and get that print on a plane to Los Angeles. RKO's man in Rio, Gonzaga, had the workprint. He's a bit of a cineaste himself. Had I but known what treachery would ensue here, I would never have left Rio without it. Only a few months ago, Gonzaga took it upon himself to disobey the studio's direct order to destroy the print. Can you imagine?"

"So where is it now?"

Welles massaged his whitened temples.

"Irony of ironies, at midnight it will be delivered to RKO."

"What?!"

"This morning Gonzaga cabled me that he had put it on a plane. He must have gotten confused. He had ignored my specific instructions to send it to my house in Brentwood. No doubt out of habit, he addressed it to me at RKO. Where I have not had an office for three years, since those bastards gave me the boot!"

I was beginning to see why RKO had tired of their feckless boy genius.

"Could it be you didn't *tell* Gonzaga that RKO fired you? Because then he would have asked for even more money for slipping you their property?"

"*Their* property?" roared Welles. "That was a year of my blood, sweat and tears. And they told him to burn it! You dare call it theirs?"

He was right. I should have been more respectful.

"Look, I'm on your side, Orson. I want to preserve your work as much as you do. But if I do, you cannot tell a soul about this. We will be receiving stolen property, and if this gets out, you *will* wind up in Alcatraz. We both will."

Welles swallowed hard, and nodded. Orson surely knew he wouldn't last a balmy afternoon behind bars.

"All right," I said, "I'll help you."

Orson clapped a hand to my shoulder. "Come, let's away to prison; We two alone will sing like birds i' th' cage."

Orson's gallows humor worried me.

"Yeah, King Lear. Not a guy whose ending we want to emulate."

"Indeed not," nodded Orson. "I shall be the soul of discretion."

"Okay. Ariyl..." I looked around, and realized that she had not returned. "She should have been back by now."

Orson scanned the room. "I certainly hope Rita didn't lure her outside. I think my dear wife is capable of anything at this point."

Ariyl's musical laughter erupted from across the room. Orson and I walked over, to find her at a table with a trio of actors. They were several drinks ahead of me, as was Ariyl.

One, whose back was to me, was shaking his head: "Lew says it's about an angel. I dunno, that's just too 'too' for me. After what the world's been through, does anyone still believe in angels?"

The second thespian raised his glass to Ariyl and drawled, "Wull, *I* do."

"Aw!" cooed Ariyl.

I cleared my throat. She looked up at me.

"Oh, hi! We've been having so much fun! David, meet Duke, and Dutch, and Jimmy."

The three handsome movie stars rose to shake hands with Orson and me. They each politely told me their full names even though everyone in America knew them. I felt a pang of nostalgia for the Minoan and Revolutionary eras, when I'd been looked up to as a giant. Everyone at this table was an inch or more taller than I was, though only Duke was taller than Ariyl.

"Gentlemen. Ariyl, we need to go."

"Naw, come on, li'l lady," coaxed Duke. "You don't wanna go, do you?"

"Wellll," hedged Ariyl. I gave her a look.

"The night is yet young," grinned Dutch.

"N-now, don't listen to *him*, he's a family man," drawled Jimmy. Ariyl giggled at his voice. I really did have him down.

"Would someone tell me what I'm sayin' that's so darned funny?" Stewart demanded of the others.

"Dutch, don't you have to get back to Lake Arrowhead?" needled Duke. "Does your wifey even know you're down here?"

"Well..." said Dutch, his eyes downcast as if reading a radio script before him, though there was nothing, not even food. "Jane knows I'm here on Guild business." That's right, I realized, Jane Wyman. They divorced right before she won an Oscar. A decade later, Nancy Davis would become his second wife.

"And what are you so high-and-mighty about?" Dutch added with growing irritation. "Is your divorce final yet?"

"No," growled Duke, his merry mood suddenly gone, his narrow eyes narrowing even more at Dutch.

It was starting to feel a little tense at the table.

"I do have to go," said Ariyl, getting up.

Duke kept glowering at Dutch through those slits of his. Dutch didn't look worried. Duke had a good thirty pounds on him, but then again, Dutch had a bulge under his coat that I suspected would even the odds, if it came to that.

"Now, now, wait a second, Duke, we're havin' a friendly dinner," soothed Jimmy, signaling the waiter with his glass for refills. He gave Ariyl a grin that was equal parts shy and sly. "These married men get kinda surly when they're out with a single fella."

"Huh! Tell 'er where *you* were all afternoon, Don Juan," laughed Duke, his mood as fluid as his dinner had been so far. He didn't wait for Jimmy's reply, but leaned toward Ariyl, with a mocking smirk. "Flyin' kites at the beach with Hank Fonda."

"Really?" chuckled Orson. Jimmy caught a whiff of something in that.

"There something wrong with kites, Orson?"

"Not in the manly hands of decorated veterans like yourself and Fonda," replied Orson with expertly feigned humility.

Orson glanced over at another table, and a wicked twinkle came to his eye. He knew Stewart wasn't gay, and he had just spotted a woman who apparently could testify to that.

"Oh, look, there's Marlene!"

Dietrich was reputedly insatiable, having exhausted just about every straight actor in Hollywood, married or single. Jimmy and Duke, who I got the idea had each been around the block with her, turned and shrank down in their seats.

"We should get going," muttered Duke.

Jimmy nodded, "I haven't had my vitamins today."

"Not till I get my darned steak," insisted Dutch.

"Shall we?" Orson said to Ariyl and me, indicating the door.

As he escorted us out, Orson paused to whisper something to Jimmy, who nodded.

At the door, Ariyl almost collided with Cary Grant.

"Hel-*lo*," Cary beamed. She beamed back. I did my best to scowl like she was my gal and pull her along.

It was twenty minutes to midnight.

22

RENDEZVOUS AT RKO

ORSON WELLES WAS THE GREATEST RACONTEUR AND the worst driver I have ever known in my life. As he ferried us from the Sunset Strip to RKO Studios, he mentioned he had just gotten his license a month ago. He then told three hilarious stories, of which I can recall not a single detail. Each of my laughs was punctuated by a gasp of terror as I pointed to stop lights, pedestrians or oncoming vehicles he should be aware of. He was amazingly inattentive, but not timid; he sped at a clip you or I would only attempt in a video game. Ariyl, typically, enjoyed it as if she were on a roller coaster. She could afford to, considering how hard she was to injure.

"You ought to be flattered. I had already asked Jimmy Stewart to accompany me on this adventure, but I withdrew the invitation when you two made your offer. After all, this coupe only seats three. Professor Preston does look stronger than Jimmy. And of course, you, Miss Moro..."

"If you only knew," I said.

"By the way, I should mention that Ludlo will not be alone," Orson added as we careened down narrow, pitch-black Gower Street at sixty-five miles per hour. "Because of the strike, all the studios have extra security. I noticed the boys camped out by Warner Brothers looked particularly formidable, and I recommended that Ludlo might offer after-hours employment to some of them as a security force of his own. He was quite taken with the idea."

"You told him to hire thugs?" I asked, flabbergasted. I now realized it wasn't Frank Capra that Stewart had been destined to meet at RKO. It was Orson Welles who, in Ludlo's twisted version of history, had gotten Jimmy killed. And now instead, Ariyl and I were in the hot seat.

"They're hardly thugs. I expect they're out-of-work carpenters and set decorators. Although I understand one of the unions did bolster their ranks with a few mob types, and the other has several Communist Party functionaries who are quite prepared to employ violence to usher in the dictatorship of the proletariat."

"Orson, are you insane?"

"Oh-ho, the times I've been asked that," he chuckled. "But worry not. We're all sophisticated people. Let me handle the negotiations." My heart sank.

Reaching Melrose Avenue, Orson yanked his car into a skidding U-turn and parked outside the RKO gate.

Sure enough, there was a quartet of desperate characters waiting by a black sedan outside RKO, all chain-smoking cigarettes. Except for one trembly character, who finished one Hershey bar and began another.

"Unless I miss my guess, that man is a heroin addict," rumbled Welles knowingly.

Ludlo, however, was not there. That no-return safeguard might delay him for hours, I realized.

I got out of the car.

"Scram, asshole," advised one of the thugs, clearly their leader. The trembly guy headed for their sedan.

"Benny, where you going?" demanded the leader.

"I'm jonesin' bad, Aldo," whispered Benny.

"Leave that shit till we're done! If you wasn't my flesh and blood..." Then he turned back as Orson slid out from behind the wheel. "I told you, scram!"

"Not until I conclude my business with your employer, Mr. Ludlo," Orson explained.

"Hey, ain't I heard you on the radio?" queried a third thug. "You're The Shadow! You're...whatshisname."

"*Don't* tell him your name," I hissed. Orson bowed with ostentatious modesty.

"Your obedient servant, Orson Welles."

"Hey, Aldo! This is Orson Welles!"

"Who gives a shit?"

"I do," said the Shadow fan.

Then Ariyl got out of the car. Benny dropped his candy bar, while Aldo and the Shadow fan stared at her.

"Can we talk?" she asked me, with some urgency. I nodded.

We strolled a few yards down the street as Orson chatted with his adoring public.

"David, this *Ambersons* flick...it's really great, right?"

"The Holy Grail of lost films. I'd kill to see it intact."

"Then...why should we stop Ludlo from saving it?"

"We have to stop him from doing anything. Even if he donated the print to a museum. Especially if he does. Because that's not how our history turned out. Look, you're the time traveler. I'm just along for the ride. But I do know this: In my history, Welles spent the rest of his life mourning the loss of that movie. It affected every other film he made. If we rescue it, Orson's life changes. History changes, and not just film history. My 2013 would be noticeably different. And magnified over a century, your 2109 could be *radically* different. No. Much as I feel for Orson, and the world of art...we have to put history back the way it was, or as close as we can get it, without these people suspecting a thing."

Suddenly, I realized there was a large shadow behind us that had not been there before. We turned and there, silhouetted in the glare from the streetlight, just like the reporter in the projection room in

Citizen Kane, was Orson Welles, speechless for once, hanging on our every word.

"Uh, hi. How much of that did you just hear?"

"Enough," said Welles, eyeing us in awe. A swell job of fixing history we were doing.

Just then a delivery truck pulled to a halt at the gate.

On the back of the truck were four octagonal steel cases in which I presumed were packed twelve very full reels, some eleven minutes apiece, of 35mm film. As expected, they were addressed to "Orson Welles, RKO Studio."

The guard at the gate, sporting a sidearm, stepped out to converse with the driver.

Orson walked rapidly away from us and up to the driver. "Good evening, my name is Welles," he said brusquely. "As you can see, those film cases are addressed to me." I walked over to join them. Welles glanced at me as if I were a hallucination only he could see—then turned back. The elderly guard shook his head.

"They're addressed to the studio, Mr. Welles. If you're working here, they'll be waiting in your office first thing tomorrow."

"But I'm going to need them tonight."

Click. Aldo cocked his gun and aimed it at the guard.

"Stand still and keep your trap shut."

Instead, the old fool went for his gun—and he wasn't exactly fast on the draw.

"No!" I yelled, knocking Aldo's gun aside and grabbing the guard's arm. I knocked his hand against the doorframe and he dropped the pistol. Aldo shoved me aside and stuck his gun in the old man's mouth.

"Siddown!" he roared. The guard obeyed, then glared balefully...at me.

You're welcome for me saving your life, I thought.

"Tie him and gag him," Aldo ordered the fourth thug. Then to the Shadow fan: "Carmine, get the cases."

The truck driver, by this time, was on foot, running for his life.

"Put that away," said Welles, offended. "There's no need for gunplay."

"Jesus, Aldo, these things weigh a ton!" groaned Carmine, straining as he yanked two of the film cases off the truck, and carried them to their car.

"Not so fast," declared Orson. "Where's Ludlo?"

"He ain't coming. We bring these to him."

"You most assuredly will not. Our deal was that he would pay me on delivery. Since he has breached his promise, I shall take possession of my property."

Aldo put his gun to Orson's nose. "Shaddap, Slim."

"Slim?" repeated Welles, his face clouding over in outrage.

"That was rude," commented Ariyl, who was suddenly at Orson's side, grabbing the pistol out of Aldo's hand. She tossed it away into the dark. Aldo threw a vicious left hook that Ariyl caught an inch before her face. Then he tried a right cross but she just caught that one too. She held his fists as easily as she might a child's. He thrashed, helpless in her grip. She simpered at him.

"Got any other bright ideas?"

He did. He head-butted her. Ariyl wasn't expecting that, and winced in discomfort. But the bridge of her nose was a lot harder than Aldo expected.

"Ow, Jesus!" he cried, as his forehead began bleeding.

"That hurt," frowned Ariyl. She then tightened her grip, crushing Aldo's right fist. I heard soft snaps of carpal bones, then him howling in pain.

"Carmine! Louie!"

Carmine, who was struggling with the last two cases, left them and ran to Aldo's aid, as did Louie, the fourth thug, both drawing their pistols. Moving in a fast blur, Ariyl slapped their guns aside—one discharged, the slug ricocheting off a film case. Jesus, the only print of *Ambersons*!

Ariyl grabbed both men by the shirtfront, hoisted them in the air and slammed them together, hard. Both expelled an involuntary "Ooof!" and she let them drop senseless to the pavement.

Now I ran to check the damage to the film. A bullet hole was drilled through the rim of the case, but it seemed to have entirely missed the nitrate ribbon inside.

I looked back to tell Ariyl, just in time to see skinny, sweaty Benny emerge from the sedan behind her. He gaped at his whimpering brother and the pair of groaning men at Ariyl's feet. Then he struck her neck savagely with a tire iron.

Ariyl gasped in discomfort, whirled, and snatched away the tire iron. She went into her usual steel-bending act. Benny looked suitably impressed—possibly crapping his pants. Then as Ariyl turned away from him, he did something I never imagined a junkie would do.

He jabbed Ariyl in the neck with his fix.

"Ow!" she yelped, her eyes widening in surprise as he pressed the plunger, emptying the syringe into her. She yanked it out, seized Benny's collar and threw him over her shoulder into the street. He landed hard, with a cry of pain.

"Ariyl!" I yelled.

"Hm?" she turned to me, smiling blissfully. She took a step, then keeled over on the sidewalk.

I ran over and kneeled beside her, but suddenly a foot buried itself in my diaphragm. Carmine may have had the wind knocked out of him, but now he was back on his feet and feeling vengeful.

I wanted to breathe, but his next couple of kicks made that impossible. I got a mouthful of pavement, tasted my own blood, and wondered when I would be able to inhale again. Benny helped his brother Aldo to his feet. Then Benny pulled a gun and pointed it at Ariyl.

"Want I should finish her?"

"Not yet," seethed Aldo, trying to move his broken fingers. "Take her along! I want this to be slow, and I want the bitch awake for it!"

I kept telling my lungs to inhale, but they were on strike.

If Carmine thought those film cases were heavy, they were nothing compared to the unconscious Ariyl, who required three straining men to load her in the trunk. They retrieved their guns. Carmine started back for me, but stopped as he heard a police siren wailing.

Carmine dashed to the black sedan, grabbing the last film case. They took off up Gower with a screech of tires.

Finally, I was able to gulp in some air. I staggered to my feet. Orson's coupe was gone, no doubt driven at top speed by Orson. I could hear the siren approaching on Melrose from the east. The delivery truck driver must have dropped a nickel on these goons. But the cop car sounded a mile or more away, and I didn't want to lose the sedan. I stumbled over to the guard and pulled his gag down.

"I'm going after them," I panted, "Tell the cops to follow me!"

"I'll tell them to shoot you down like a dog, you stinking punk!" He turned and bellowed, "Help, police! He's one of 'em!" Exasperated, I put his gag back in. Explaining all this to the cops would take more time than I had. I got in the delivery truck. I had to hunt for the starter button, before I could tear off after Ariyl's kidnappers.

I saw the tail lights of the black sedan nearing the north end of Gower. I floored it and closed the distance. The mopes made a skidding left at Hollywood Boulevard, then wheeled right onto Cahuenga. I kept with them, far enough back that they wouldn't see me, while I kept checking my own rear-view mirror for signs of police pursuit.

We followed the winding road through Cahuenga Pass. I was disoriented by the lavish Spanish-style homes occupying this gap in the hills where I was used to seeing the Hollywood Freeway. But once we climbed the hill up Barham Boulevard, I knew where I was. To my left was sprawling Universal City, to my right the reservoir, and at the bottom of the hill, the L.A. River, a golf course, and Toluca Lake.

And just east of the main road, another small city of soundstages,

Old West storefronts, New York brownstones and mid-American houses: The new Burbank lot of Warner Brothers Studios.

The sedan swung left onto a side street. I cut my lights and parked on the road, outside Warner's fortified studio wall that was bedecked with billboards for upcoming releases like *Rhapsody in Blue, Mildred Pierce,* and *Christmas in Connecticut.* I watched the sedan roll into the driveway of a derelict bungalow with untrimmed ivy strangling it on every side. I left the truck and slunk closer on foot, as fast as I could.

When I heard the sedan doors open, I ducked behind some trash cans. I watched Aldo, holding his mangled hand like a useless T-Rex paw, as he directed Louie, Carmine and Benny. They half-carried, half-dragged Ariyl's limp form into the darkened house.

I stole into the side yard and peered through a couple of windows before I found the back bedroom into which they had dragged her. With considerable effort, they beached her on an iron frame covered with just a bare bedspring.

"Watch the doors," ordered Aldo. Louie and Carmine nodded, pulling out their pistols.

"We gotta get someone to fix your hand," said Benny. "Lemme call Doc."

"Okay. But tell him, he brings any more goddamn skag for you, I'll kill him."

"Aldo, please, I need somethin'." He fingered the bruise he'd gotten flying headfirst onto the street. "Jesus, I never saw anyone as strong as this bitch!"

"Tie her up, and lemme know the minute she comes out of it!" said Aldo. Using his left hand, he awkwardly checked the chambers of his pistol, probably suspecting he'd need a full load to kill her. Then he turned and kicked Ariyl in the thigh, viciously. She didn't stir, but he gasped and swore in pain. He limped from the room, leaving only Benny.

Benny went to work with the rope, expertly lashing Ariyl's wrists and ankles to the bedposts, so she was spread-eagled. Benny hiked up her dress, revealing a considerable portion of those track-star thighs. Which, of course, he paused to run his hands over.

I could cheerfully have shot him at that point—I still had Joseph Erie's pistol—but even if I took Benny out, I couldn't outgun all three of his pals. She was breathing, but judging from her deep repose, Ariyl would be out for at least another hour. I remembered that N-Tec didn't allow drugs...she had no tolerance at all.

I needed help. But the cops weren't going to believe me, not after what the watchman at RKO was telling them. And they might not act on an anonymous tip. And none of my friends in this city were even born yet. Except Sven, and even at age nineteen, he wouldn't be much use in a brawl.

What I needed was the cavalry.

23

THE BATTLE OF WARNER BROTHERS

I MADE IT BACK TO THE SUNSET STRIP IN RECORD TIME, driving most of the way on Fountain Avenue. Police sirens, likely looking for this stolen delivery truck, were wailing down Sunset.

I parked the truck just below the boulevard on Harper, a side street across from the Players, but as I approached the door, I was swept backwards by the exodus of Hollywood's finest.

"What's happening?" I asked no one in particular.

Short, overripe Mae West, accompanied by a much younger muscleman type, shook her head. "Say, that guy Sturges is nuts. He wants to get smashed with his pals so he kicks everyone out."

"Well, at least we didn't have to pay," grinned her buff companion.

"When did *you* ever pay?" sighed West. She gave me an appraising glance before sashaying to her car.

Desperate, I searched the exiting faces. Finally, I saw Duke, Dutch and Jimmy. They were weaving as they left the door, and they were not happy.

"I never got my damn steak," groused Dutch.

Duke spotted me, and laughed, "Hey, look, here's the headwaiter."

I ignored the crack. "I need your help. Somebody kidnapped Ariyl."

"Huh. Some joke," scoffed Jimmy, unamused.

"No joke. We went with Welles to pick up his damn film at RKO. It all went bad, a guard and I got roughed up. Some of those strikers doped Ariyl, and took her."

"Then why don't you call the police?" asked Jimmy.

"That's no good. They think I was in on it."

"Aw, sounds like bullshit to me," said Duke.

Dutch shook his head. "I don't know, Duke. Those strikers are pretty desperate characters. Jack Warner told me they're a bunch of Commies."

"That why you're carrying the hogleg?" observed Jimmy, his finger lifting Dutch's lapel to reveal the shoulder holster. Dutch yanked his coat closed again.

"One of these days, you fellas are going to wake up to what's going on in this town."

"I've been saying it for years," said Duke.

My ethical dilemma: I could take the time to explain that these mopes were more likely to take orders from Sicily than Moscow...or I could sound the charge.

"Reagan's right," I said. "These Reds are armed and they're going to kill her. Are you guys going to sit on your hands, or are you going to help me?"

The three exchanged a wary look.

"Oh, excuse me," I snapped, "I guess it's harder to be a hero when the bullets are real." I turned to go.

Jimmy seized my lapels and pulled me in an inch from his nose. He was furious, breathing hard, eyes wet and haunted. "The *krauts* had real bullets. I saw what they did to my men, close up."

I met Jimmy's stare without blinking.

"I know you flew a bomber. That's why I came to you." His fury ebbing, Jimmy nodded, and let me go.

"Well, I *would've* flown, if it wasn't for my damned eyesight," said Dutch.

"Near-sighted," snorted Duke. "From reading the scripts for all those training films?"

"At least I was in uniform!"

"I hadda keep working. I got four goddamn kids!" protested civilian Wayne, ready to punch someone.

"You mad? Good! Save it for those Commie goons!" I barked, and turned toward the truck. Would anyone follow?

"If we don't come back in an hour, call the cops," said Jimmy, falling in with me.

"Aw, what the hell," said Duke.

"Wait up," said Dutch.

When I looked back, I saw three heroes following me.

As we were about to cross Sunset, I saw a police car shining its spotlight at the stolen delivery truck I'd parked down the hill. What a time for the LAPD to get efficient!

"We have to take one of your cars," I said.

"Mine's right here," volunteered Duke, pulling out his keys. He fumbled them and they fell on the concrete roadway.

"I'll drive," I said, scooping them up.

As we climbed into Duke's car, Orson's coupe lurched to a halt, and he got out, wild-eyed. "Jimmy, stop!" he commanded. "Don't go with him, any of you."

"Why not?" demanded Jimmy.

"I overheard him talking to that giant blonde. He never intended for me to get back *The Magnificent Ambersons*. He wants to bury it again."

"Orson, it flopped." said Dutch, "Why wouldn't you want it buried?"

"Because it's Art!" thundered Welles. "And there is more..." he added, ominous. "Much more. They are not from this century.

They're time travelers, from the future, trying to alter how history comes out."

The three looked at me. I did my best innocent shrug.

"Aw, hell, I thought you were gonna say, they're from Mars," drawled Duke. Jimmy and Dutch burst out laughing.

"Yeah," agreed Jimmy. "Fool us once, Orson..."

They piled in Duke's car and we took off.

"I still say, we should call the cops," whispered Jimmy.

"Yeah," I nodded, sarcastic, "Because the word of three drunk movie stars is going to make them forget all about why they're after *me*."

It was after two A.M. I couldn't tell you how long we'd been scouting the house, waiting for an opening. As long as Ariyl was out, she was in no immediate danger. I figured the longer we waited, the soberer my squad would be.

We'd first stopped by Wayne's house, awakening his estranged wife, to get guns for him and Jimmy. She'd nearly shot us with one, but we escaped with just a tongue-lashing.

I didn't like the guns, but I wasn't taking a chance on letting Aldo kill Ariyl. I'd sweat the risks to history later. Besides, I had a plan that I hoped would make the guns unnecessary.

Now we were at the northeast corner of the lot, toward the rear of the house, able to see into the windows of both the back bedrooms, and the living room. I signaled to Jimmy to wait there, then beckoned for Duke and Dutch to move toward the front with me, keeping low. As we reached the front, I signaled for them to halt.

"Are we going in, or not?" groused Duke.

"On my signal. Now shut your eyes and lean back." I went behind Duke, took the sack of flour we'd liberated from Casa Wayne along with the guns, and combed it into Duke's hair.

"Of all the goddamn stupid ideas," he fumed. "I never played an old man in my life."

"You'll do fine. If those mooks—these *commies*—see a young movie star knock on their door, they're going to smell trouble. So remember, you're an old man, looking for an address." To complete the disguise, we put Dutch's horn-rimmed eyeglasses on Duke. On a dark porch, he'd pass.

"No, hunch over, Duke, like you got arthritis," coached Dutch.

"Everybody's a director," snapped Duke. Then a thought hit him. "Jesus, Jack Ford better not hear about this. He'll never let me live it down."

"Remember, don't shoot unless you have to," I whispered. "Think of the publicity." Not to mention the disruption to history if a dozen of these mobbed-up bastards' descendants instantly ceased to exist.

"I'll try," declared Dutch. "But if there's gonna be a bloodbath, then let's get it over with." I shook my head, but said nothing.

I crept back into the side yard, where Jimmy waited. We could see Louie in a chair facing the front door, reading a *Racing Form*. Aldo was smoking nearby. His hand had been attended to while we were gone—it was now bandaged and splinted. He also had a bandage on his bruised forehead. Jimmy had reconnoitered the rear bedroom on the far side: Carmine was dozing there.

Now Jimmy pointed at the window—Ariyl was waking up! Benny hurried out to report. Seconds later, Aldo strode in, by himself. His right hand was useless, but he had a gun in his left, and murder in his eyes.

I urgently signaled Duke at the front. I couldn't see Dutch now, but assuming he was following the plan, he had already flattened himself against the wall on one side of the front door, waiting to follow Duke in.

Duke, white-haired and bespectacled, coughing and sniffing, holding a crumpled piece of notepaper, shuffled up the front porch steps. After that, he was out of my line of sight.

In the back bedroom, Ariyl's eyes fluttered. Aldo laid his gun alongside her inner thigh, and waited to savor her reaction.

Brrring! went the front doorbell. Aldo looked up.

In the front room, Louie put down his paper and went to the door.

Jimmy and I padded to the back door as we counted to five, long enough for Duke to say in a gruff voice, "Excuse me, young fella, but I seem to be lost."

Jimmy reared back to kick the back door, then on impulse, I tried it. The idiots hadn't locked it. That was 1945 for you...even mobsters left their doors unlocked. I opened it soundlessly and we went in.

At the end of the hall, which ran the length of the bungalow, I saw Louie's back as he peered out the little gated peep-hole in the front door.

"You got the wrong address, Pops. Beat it."

"You said it," said Duke. BAM! He kicked the door off its hinges, knocking Louie on his ass. Before Louie could recover, Duke leaped on him and started punching. Dutch dashed in after, gun ready.

Meanwhile, Jimmy burst in the right bedroom, while I took the left. I threw open the door, only to find Aldo sitting on the bed, leaning over Ariyl, who was just realizing what deep shit she was in.

Aldo swung his gun barrel to me. I pulled the trigger on Joseph Erie's gun—nothing! The damn thing had a safety, and it was on. It was life-before-my-eyes time, except that with two simultaneous snaps, Ariyl popped her legs free of the ropes and clamped her thighs around Aldo's chest in a scissor hold. She rolled to one side, throwing his aim way off. His shot missed me by two feet.

Then she flexed. Her thighs swelled, there was a sickening crunch, and Aldo dropped his gun. After a beat, she opened her legs and Aldo sank to the floor panting for air, as he had every reason to do with a chest full of broken ribs.

Shouts from the other bedroom, as Jimmy duked it out with Carmine. Ariyl snapped free of the ropes on her wrists. We rushed in just as Jimmy knocked Carmine to his knees and slammed a wooden chair down on his back, finishing him off. Jimmy stared in wonder at the chair, which was intact.

"In the movies, this woulda *broke!*" he said, his voice cracking.

Shots from the front room.

"Christ, Dutch, don't shoot *me*!"

We ran to the front room, to see smoking bullet holes near the doorway, just beside Duke's head. Duke shoved his borrowed specs back on Dutch's face.

"Here's your damn glasses!"

Meanwhile, Benny was high-tailing it down the street holding his injured ass. He went a few more steps, then collapsed whimpering on the pavement.

Louie was laid out on the floor, seeing stars.

And being stars, their first call was not to the Burbank police. Dutch put in a call to Jack Warner. His boss shook off slumber and barked instructions that I could hear even though I wasn't on the phone:

"Say nothing to no one until I get there. I mean, *no one*."

Ariyl and I busied ourselves tying up the battered hoods—all except Aldo, who wasn't going anywhere without an ambulance—and then I delivered what first aid I could.

The actors waited. Dawn was approaching. Duke was growing suspicious that Warner would slant the publicity for this heroic raid toward Dutch, a Warner contract player. He suggested Louis B. Mayer would do the same for Jimmy.

"Well, now why would he do that?" wondered Jimmy.

"Aw, hell, do I hafta spell it out? He wants you back under contract. You're the big war hero."

Stewart's eyes flashed and he leaned into Duke's face.

"Now, listen, goddammit. I told Wasserman I won't allow any publicity about that. Not a word. I just did my damn job, same as a million other guys. Same as you would've. Why do you...I mean, you talk about it like, like going to war was a stroke of luck. I didn't see my men get shot to pieces so Louella Parsons could gush about it! I don't want to hear another goddamn word about publicity!" By now, he was shaking with anger.

"Okay, Jim," said Dutch, quietly.

It shut up Duke for a while.

We'd saved Ariyl, but I was in despair. I'd failed our larger mission. I saw no way a story this big could fail to change history. Another half hour passed.

"Five minutes, then I'm calling Herb Yates at Republic," Duke muttered to Dutch. "He's been giving me a big buildup. He knows how to get ink for a story like this."

I was in the back bedroom with Ariyl when an extremely upset movie mogul named Jack Warner charged into the bungalow. I stepped into the hall to see what he did. Behind Warner came what looked to be ambulance orderlies, and studio carpenters. The former began attending to the injured while the carpenters started cleaning up all evidence of the battle: repairing the door, patching the bullet holes in the wall.

"Where are the cops?" wondered Jimmy.

"And the photographers?" added Duke.

"Fellas, I need to speak to your pal Dutch in private," said Warner. Duke fumed, but there was no dissent. I ducked back into the bedroom where Ariyl sat, and heard Warner and Reagan walk into the bedroom across the hall from us and shut the door. Warner tried to keep his voice low, but his sharp pitch and staccato delivery made it easy to overhear what he was saying.

"Ronnie, you've put me and the studio in a very bad position. And yourself."

"How's that, J.L.?"

"Do you have any idea who those guys you beat up were?"

"Sure. Commie labor goons."

"No, they weren't! That's the *last* thing they were. How do you think they wound up in a house across from the studio?"

"You tell me."

"A man named Willie B, who I can always count on when I need labor peace, arranged for these men to come out here. They're strike-breakers, Ronnie."

"Wait a minute, you're saying these are *your* goons?"

"This damn strike has gone on for six months, and over what? Forty-three set painters! It's costing the studios millions—and union members are out a million in wages. It's crazy, and it's gotta end."

"I agree. But these S-O-B's nearly killed that girl."

"That wasn't part of their job. And from what you say, she nearly killed one of them. I'd say we're all even."

"You're not having them arrested?"

"You don't think they've been punished enough? Do I need to count up their broken bones? And the guy you shot in the ass? Look, you're a smart guy, Ronnie. And cooperative. The kind of guy I'd love to see keep working, and move up in the Guild, too. Keep this thing quiet, help me settle this strike so everybody wins...and you show me you're the kind of guy I can do business with. You follow me?"

"Well...sure, J.L. But you're going to have to help me sell this to Duke and Jimmy."

"Leave them to me. First, I wanna meet Wonder Woman."

A moment later, Reagan knocked on our door. Without waiting for a response, Jack Warner strode in. Dutch, joined by Duke and Jimmy, stood in the doorway, watching with a mixture of admiration and foreboding.

Warner was a dapper, feisty little guy, with a tiny mustache so sharp you could open letters with it. He shook Ariyl's hand.

"Miss Moro, is it? Jack L. Warner, head of production at Warner Brothers. I am delighted to make your acquaintance."

"Thank you. This is my friend David."

He looked at me for a quarter of a second.

"Hiya. Now, Miss Moro, can I call you Ariyl?"

"Sure."

"Ariyl, hm. Might want think about April, or Amber. Anyway, I have an eye for talent, and I can see you are full to bursting with it. You're Jane Russell plus Alexis Smith. Hell, *times* Alexis Smith. Have you ever considered a career as an actress?"

"Uh, not really."

"Well, sweetheart, you have got *It*. I'd like to take you under my wing." (I'd like to have seen that.) "Sign you to a seven-year contract. You learn to act, sing, dance, ride...all while drawing a salary. We'd start you in small parts, but with a little work, I could easily see you starring opposite Reagan or Wayne, or Stewart here. Probably not Alan Ladd, unless we dig you a real deep hole to stand in." He cackled at his own witticism.

Ariyl stood up, towering over Warner. "Jack, you're sweet, but I really don't want to be an actor. Pretending seems like a silly way to spend your time."

Then she turned to Jimmy and squeezed his arm with absolute sincerity.

"Except for that angel flick. You totally have to do that one."

Jimmy looked pleased. Warner looked pole-axed.

"But baby, you could make millions out here!"

Ariyl looked at me.

"Again with this money thing? What is it with you people? It's so sad." She turned back to Warner. "You know, in a hundred years, there isn't going to *be* any money. No war, no poverty, no one will have to work for anybody else, and everyone will be given everything they need. Now, if you don't mind, we need to go." And she left. I hurried after her.

Warner turned to the three actors, aghast.

"Oh, my God. She's a fucking red. You schmucks rescued a goddamn Commie!" The three schmucks looked properly stunned.

The last thing I heard as we left the house was Warner screaming at them: "You like your careers? You want to keep the FBI out of Hollywood? Then repeat after me—*nothing* happened here last night. You follow me?"

As day broke, Ariyl and I walked down the street toward the

studio, watching the picketers and the scabs and the rest of the strike-breakers and the Burbank police all take up their positions at the gate. Hollywood labor history was not my field, but I did know there had been a violent confrontation outside Warner studio in October 1945, complete with fisticuffs, tire chains, reinforcements from the LAPD, and tear gas fired by Warner's security guards. Apparently, that was all going down today.

Between J.L.'s strong-arm tactics at his gates and with the three actors in the bungalow, I was pretty confident the events here would be successfully buried.

We turned back to the house. Down the porch steps came two of the three caballeros, looking chastened.

"I finally get in on some fighting, and I can't tell anyone about it," groused Dutch.

"I wouldn't call that a fight. When you're in a real fight, you won't want to talk about it," mused Jimmy, softly. "Say, what's keeping Duke?"

Now Wayne came down the steps, shaking his head. Little puffs of flour dust were still coming off his hair. He fired up a cigarette.

"Well?" demanded Dutch.

"Aw, J.L. just was tellin' me I looked good with the white hair. Said he'll talk to Howard Hawks about me for some picture he's casting, needs an older guy for it."

Jimmy looked at Dutch and remarked dryly, "Hawks, huh? Wal, guess that tells you who the big star is *now*. We're just a coupla has-beens, Ronnie."

Wayne looked at Stewart, a bit ashamed. "Aw, hell, Jim, you're the real actor here. You're the guy with the Oscar."

"You'll get one," I told Duke.

Duke snorted. "Oh, sure. I tell ya, though, I'd give my right eye for one."

"Make it the left, and you got a deal," I prophesized. (Oh, like he was going to figure that one out.)

"What about me," grinned Dutch, "Think I'll get one?"

"Nope."

Reagan lost a little of his smile. Jimmy noticed.

"Wal, *you'll* probably be our president pretty soon," Stewart allowed.

"Of the United States?" exclaimed Duke.

"Even worse, the Screen Actors Guild," deadpanned Jimmy. "I tell ya, Duke...Dutch here has *ambition*."

"You had me scared," said Duke.

Dutch bristled. "If *you* could get an Oscar, I guess I could be President of the United States."

"An actor? Haw! Over my dead body," scoffed Wayne. He ground out his cigarette, then he winked at Ariyl. "Well, so long, shrimp."

"Thanks, you guys," she smiled.

We watched from a distance as they got into the waiting studio limo, and departed. On their heels came Warner and his crew, carrying off the battered hoods and all traces of the battle.

Ariyl looked both ways, then said, "I have to show you something."

24

TWELVE REELS

ARIYL LED ME INTO THE GARAGE. STACKED JUST INSIDE the door were the four steel cases containing Welles' once-lost, now found cut of *The Magnificent Ambersons.*

"When I was coming out of the drug, I heard Benny telling Aldo he left them here."

"I wish you hadn't showed me this, Ariyl."

"Why?"

"We can't leave the film here."

"I know we can't give it back to Orson. But what if we bury it? Then maybe in a hundred years..."

"It's nitrate film. Highly unstable. If it doesn't burn, in fifty years it'll decompose into goo. And if someone digs it up before then, history changes, and we don't get home."

"We could take it back to my time."

"The post-apocalyptic wasteland, which we're hoping to erase? I mean, if we're lucky?"

"If we can't take it to the future, and we can't leave it, and we can't bury it, what do we do with it?"

I couldn't believe the sacrilege I was about to utter.

"Burn it."

"You're kidding."

"Either we burn this print, or we burn our future. We don't have a third choice."

I undid the snaps on the case with the bullet hole. Inside were three reels, undamaged, giving off a heady chemical smell. I found a box of wooden matches on the workbench.

"David, please don't," said Ariyl. She could've easily stopped me. But she didn't.

I took one reel outside and set it in the backyard incinerator. I took out a match, pressed it against the rough striking surface on the box...and held it there tensed, for what seemed like an eternity.

If I was doing what had to be done, why wasn't I doing it? With maybe billions of unborn souls depending on me, was I going to wuss out over a damned movie?

Maybe...maybe we had time to race back a century with them, stash them in a past that wouldn't be rewritten by...

"Mr. Ludlo!" I knew those orotund tones, echoing from the street. Hurriedly, I took the reel back in the garage, returned it to the case and closed it up.

"Hide these," I told Ariyl. The four cases probably weighed thirty pounds each. She gathered them up like so many empty hatboxes, and stacked them inside a 55-gallon drum. On the workbench I found dusty squares of corrugated iron and pieces of galvanized rain gutter, which I placed atop the cases. It looked like a trash can full of scrap metal.

A moment later, Orson Welles entered the garage. He was hung over, and his eyes had not adjusted to the darkness inside. He was wearing an overcoat over his shoulders like a cape against the early morning chill, and a dark slouch hat. He stuck an enormous, unlit Cuban cigar in his mouth and started to pat himself down for a light—but stopped when he saw us. He waited a long beat, as if composing a speech in his head.

"Forgive me if I speak softly, but I have a monstrous headache. I overindulged in the Clos des Lambrays last night. I assume what I overheard you two discussing at RKO was some fantasy movie scenario. And from my confused reaction, you may have thought me even worse of a lunatic than is my general reputation. Let's just say I can barely recall whatever passed between us. I simply want to conclude my deal with Mr. Ludlo."

"He's not here," I said.

"That is puzzling," said Welles. "He left a message with my secretary. He was quite specific about the time, and about the garage at this address."

"Look around all you want," I bluffed. "Ludlo's not here. And if you recall *anything* from last night, it should be that you have nothing to sell him. Not after you ran off and left those gorillas—that *you* told him to hire—with the film cases." That was true enough, as far as it went.

"With all due respect," said Welles, "I believe my film is in this garage. I'll take you up on your offer to search the premises." He brushed past me and began inspecting its various filthy nooks and crannies. He peered at the dusty scrap metal in the drum, but did not dig into it.

At that moment, I happened to turn and saw a fading shimmer of light through the small window at the rear of the garage. I glanced at Ariyl for her reaction—she was already out the door.

"Excuse me," I muttered, heading outside.

I hot-footed it to the rear of the property, toward a narrow setback between the garage and the back fence.

Ludlo must have materialized seconds before. He wore a suit and a snap-brim fedora. The small whirlwind of leaves he'd set off was just dying down. Ariyl stood behind him. I was behind both of them, peering through a ropy curtain of the untrimmed ivy that was gradually swallowing the garage whole.

"Jon?" whispered Ariyl.

Ludlo whirled, surprised.

"Ariyl!"

She ran and hugged him. He again looked stunned, as if he'd seen a ghost. He held the hug longer than she held it. He seemed genuinely happy to see her.

No, that's wrong. Not happy. *Relieved.* I wish I'd understood then just what that difference meant. Why I even cared, I couldn't have said. After all, I was engaged. I had no interest in this madwoman. And she was practically off my hands. I was just eavesdropping to make sure she didn't need any help.

Ludlo held her face in his hands. "You have no idea how I've missed you, Ariyl."

"Where have you been?" she asked. "Or should I say *when?*"

"You'll laugh," he said.

"Try me."

"I was on Cleopatra's barge. Honest to God."

"Why?"

"To get a look at her, see what all the fuss was about." Ariyl lifted an eyebrow, waiting for the answer. He snorted, contemptuous. "She was a scrawny, big-nosed bore." Ludlo shook his head. "How history gets inflated in the retelling."

Ariyl didn't laugh.

"Anyone else you visited?"

"Helen of Troy. She was even worse. The face that launched a thousand scows."

"So while I was going through hell, you were checking out chicks?"

"Believe me, Ariyl. These so-called legendary beauties –anyone born before gene-splicing for that matter—compared to you they all look like apes in drag."

"Oh, bag the sweet-talk, Ludlo. Why didn't you meet me in Atlantis?"

"What are you talking about? I'm on my way there now. I just have to rescue this film here. It's a classic."

"I know all about *The Magnificent Ambersons.*"

"You do?" he asked, puzzled. "Well, great. I was going to make you a present of it. I arranged for someone to come over and authenticate it." He smiled to himself. "Quite an authority, actually." He started for the garage.

"No!" Ariyl grabbed his arms. "No authenticating! And no presents! No more Minotaur paperweights, no Declaration placemats. Omigod, Ludlo, you hafta stop jacking stuff! You don't know the unholy mess you made!"

"What do you mean?" he asked, the soul of innocence.

"You utterly zeroed out our whole world! N-Tec is history. Or more like, *not* history!"

Ludlo took a deep breath.

"Ariyl, I know. I just didn't realize you did. You're right, there is something wrong with N-Tec. I knew that when I saw you in 1776."

"Why didn't you say something if you saw me?"

"I was afraid of crossing your timeline. Until you mentioned the Declaration just now, I didn't know if you'd been there yet, or were going there next. Look, I know I made a mistake somewhere in time, but we can repair it. We just have to figure it out."

He was saying all the right things, with an earnest tone in his voice...but I didn't like the way his gaze kept flicking over to the garage. Couldn't she see it?

Ariyl exhaled in relief.

"No sweat, I met a friend who can help us figure that out." No, she couldn't see it. She trusted this creep. Well, I didn't.

"What friend?" inquired Ludlo.

"That'd be me," I said, stepping out from behind the garage and cocking Joseph Erie's revolver. This time, the safety was off. I aimed at Ludlo's heart. In movies, people always aim between the eyes, but as a target, the head leaves little room for error, and I wasn't any kind of marksman. I figured if Ludlo jerked right or left, there were other vital organs in his torso I would still hit.

"First, we'll take your Time Crystal," I said. "Ariyl will hold onto it until we've finished undoing whatever you've done."

Ludlo peered at me, possibly trying to read how fast I was on the trigger. I halted twelve feet from him. I felt pretty sure I could squeeze off a shot before he could jump me from there.

Rather than test my assumption, Ludlo put up his hands. He gave Ariyl a charming grin, with just the right tone of nervousness.

"You did say 'friend', right?"

Ariyl turned to me with a wide-eyed "stop that" look, then addressed Ludlo with determined cheer: "Jon Ludlo, Professor David Preston. David was the one who discovered the Temple of the Dolphins."

"Congratulations?" said Ludlo, lowering his right hand for me to shake.

I stayed put. "I've seen Ariyl in action. I assume you're as strong and fast as she is. So I'll just say thanks from here."

"Put that down," said Ariyl, her patient manner thinning. "You're making an ass of yourself."

"Take his Time Crystal. Then we can all discuss what an ass I am."

"How dare you point that at him?" she demanded.

"How about, because he erased America?"

"I did not!" exclaimed Ludlo. Even I thought he sounded sincere. And, damn him, *technically* he was correct.

"Actually, you sorta did, Jon," Ariyl put in. "Only then, we jumped behind you in time and stopped what you were about to do."

"Ariyl, I would never do anything that reckless. I mean, that'd be jacko. There must be some other explanation."

"What about the Einstein letter to FDR?" I demanded.

"I've never even been on Long Island."

"Then how did you know that's where he wrote it?"

"From history."

"I knew we were being watched! You were there, spying on us. If we hadn't showed up, you would have stolen Einstein's letter, like you did before."

"That's an insane lie!"

This is where the logic got so goddamned frustrating. By figuring out how Ludlo changed history, we'd jumped behind him in time, got there first so he *couldn't* change it—but *our* changes also erased his crimes.

"Is it just me, or is this guy completely paranoid?" Ludlo asked Ariyl, offended. "What are you *doing* with him?"

Ariyl looked away, a bit sheepish.

"Ariyl, you cannot let him time travel anymore," I insisted. "Don't you see how destructive this guy is?"

"Says the guy who wants to burn *The Magnificent Ambersons*," pouted Ariyl.

"He what?" exclaimed Ludlo.

"You know we have to, and you know why," I said.

"Ariyl, you can't let him *do* that," protested Ludlo.

"You hypocritical son of a bitch!" I said. "You're wiping out history right and left, but I'm the bad guy?"

If I were a bad guy, at that point I should have blown his head off.

Suddenly, Ariyl stepped between me and Ludlo. I jumped aside, again aiming for his heart, but in an eye blink she was blocking my shot again. We kept this up for several seconds:

"Get out of the way, Ariyl!"

"I trust him!"

"Then why doesn't he trust you? Give her the Crystal, Ludlo!"

Ludlo slowly took hold of his Crystal.

At that moment, there was a loud FOOMPH! from inside the garage.

"Fire!" I heard Orson bellow. I heard his rapid footsteps on the gravel drive, then a second later the entire garage exploded in flame.

Ludlo shouted, "Previous destination!" and dove. I fired, but my shot only went through where he had been, before he vanished in a rush of wind and color. His fedora, with a bullet hole, landed on the ground, as the dust-devil whipped up by his departure subsided.

"Damn it, Ariyl!"

A blur of flesh and the next instant, my revolver was in Ariyl's hand.

The garage was now an inferno.

Ariyl scooped up Ludlo's fedora and we ran for the open side yard. Smoke and flames shot out of the garage windows.

On the far side of the flames, I caught my last, rippling glimpse of Orson Welles, standing safe on the driveway, smoking a Cuban cigar, but not savoring it. He looked as forlorn as Christmas lights in February. Flammable nitrate film, that bullet hole in the case, a falling tobacco ember: From his expression, it was clear Orson understood the hideous irony that, for the second time, he had doomed his own masterpiece.

Hot, choking smoke abruptly shifted toward us. Ariyl smashed her way through the wooden fence behind us, and as we made our way into the clean air, we found ourselves in an alley. I grabbed for the pistol. She held the gun out of my reach.

"Give me the gun!"

"You boys just love these toys, don't you?" she fumed. I hadn't really had time to appreciate Joseph's alternate-1976 pistol, but it *was* an elegant firearm, combining a design like the Navy Colt with a long, tapering seven-sided barrel and Art Nouveau-like designs etched into the steel. I'd never seen anything like it. And I never would again.

"Ariyl, don't!"

But she was in a temper.

The forged steel slowly gave in her hands. Arms trembling and face red with effort, she forced the gun barrel into a loop. She'd made her point, but she wasn't done. She then pushed the gun sight into the loop. Technically, she had just tied the barrel into an overhand knot. A pretty impressive feat: Vaudeville strongmen built careers on a stunt like that, but I was too furious to applaud. Then she clucked her tongue with mock dismay, "Aww! Toy's all bwoken."

She set the contorted pistol into my palm. I immediately dropped it because it was burning hot—distending metal, I realized a second too late, heats it up. I blew on my hand.

"Freud would have a field day with you," I seethed.

"Who's Freud?"

"You better get past your compulsion to turn phallic symbols into pretzels, because next time we see Ludlo we're going to need a weapon!"

"*If* we ever see him again, now that you scared him off," she snapped.

"I don't scare him, Ariyl. You do."

"Excuse me?"

"That's why he tried to get rid of you."

That shut her up, for about four seconds.

"You have issues," she said finally. She glared at Ludlo's fedora in her hand, with the bullet hole I'd put in the crown. Now the hat morphed back to its undamaged SmartFab form, a white headband like Ariyl's.

"You said Ludlo worships art, right? And you're pretty ho-hum about it. So why'd he give *you* the Minotaur?"

"What are you trying to say?"

"He didn't count on you having trouble with me, and dragging me back to Atlantis. He thought you were going straight to 2109 to drop off his 'gift' like he told you, so you would be in 2109 when he erased it."

"Why would he do that?"

"To be the only time traveler left."

"You're crazy! He loves me!" She stalked off. I pursued her.

"You dumped him. He wouldn't be the first guy to take that hard."

"He's no killer. He's intelligent. He's deep. He collects antiques!"

"And erases billions of lives to get them."

"That was an accident! He'll fix it!"

"What if he won't?" I insisted. "What if he flipped out? What if he's decided he *likes* screwing with history? What if the only way to stop Ludlo is to kill him?"

Ariyl halted in her tracks, then turned on me with icy fury.

"I must've been out of my mind to think we have anything in

common. A primitive like you couldn't possibly comprehend someone like Jon!"

She clutched her Crystal. "I'm going to show you how wrong you are!"

"How? Do you have the slightest idea where he's going next?"

"No. But I know where he's *been*. We can meet him on his first stop on this trip. In 1908, when he met Ty Cobb. And before he had any bad memories of you."

"I have a few bad memories myself," I shot back.

At this point, all I cared about was the useless revolver. I scooped it out of the puddle where it fell. Now that it looked like the timeline would be pretty much the way I learned it in school, I didn't dare leave a deformed version of alternate history lying around.

Ariyl held out her hand. In case I had any doubt that she was angry, she didn't wait for me, but immediately began speaking into her Time Crystal. "Destination: Alpine Tavern, Altadena, California, noon, March 1st, 1908 A.D."

I took her hand at the last second.

25

YE ALPINE TAVERN, 1908 A.D.

The Time Crystal was a bit off. We arrived not at any tavern, but at a Mission-style power house on whose Spanish tile roof was the sign "Echo Mountain." It sat atop a hot, dry, scrubby hill in the San Gabriel Mountains. It seemed the Crystal had split the difference between Altadena and the Tavern—which was located way up the steep mountainside in federal forest land. Altadena was just the nearest post office, not even a true city, but a pleasant, unincorporated hillside town, home to a small population of businessmen and orange growers. A century later, it would boast 45,000 residents, many of them avid hikers to this spot...and would still not be a city.

We emerged from the rear of the power house and walked out onto a broad stone foundation, that had been recently charred. I'd hiked up to this spot in my own era, and knew that from 1900 to 1905, several brushfires had swept over this ridge, consuming a dance hall, a zoo, a chalet, an earlier power house and a domed hotel known variously as the White City or the Echo Mountain House. Less than a decade after their construction, all were in ashes. But despite the blistering summers (and autumns and springs) of the San Gabriels, and the native chaparral that actually germinated in fires, the local optimists kept rebuilding, as this latest structure proved.

The Mount Lowe Railway had been built by Civil War balloonist Thaddeus Lowe—an engineering marvel by a remarkable visionary, but his little narrow-gauge line was a money-loser and he had been forced to sell out.

Now, in 1908, it was part of the Pacific Electric rail empire. The fact that Lowe's "railway to the clouds" still existed, and its power house flew a flag with forty-six stars, was evidence that history as I knew it was still pretty much on track, at least up to Teddy Roosevelt's second term.

Below us were Lowe's steep funicular tracks descending 1,300 feet to a car barn down in Altadena proper. From there passengers could ride the roomy Pacific Electric Red Cars downtown and all the way west to the Santa Monica Pier for a nickel. Now *that* was mass transit. Another half century and it, too, would be gone, torn up to make room for cars and freeways.

Ariyl and I were bound for the other end of the line, a few miles east along the mountainside.

"*Ye* Alpine Tavern?" frowned Ariyl at the sign on the depot. I shook my head.

"'The.' Old typesetters used 'Y' in place of 'th.'" I fleetingly wondered that if I met Ludlo here and now, whether that would explain why Ludlo thought he had recognized me at Dodger Stadium. But how could he remember my changing history before I did it? Had I always been destined to meet him? The paradoxes were maddening.

We boarded the little electric trolley.

Ariyl, batting her eyelashes, convinced the driver that she'd dropped our tickets on the ride up the incline. He let us slide. It helped that even swathed from neck to ankle in a SmartFab Edwardian sundress (and fetching straw hat), she needed neither bustle nor corset to achieve a Lillian Russell hourglass figure. In Ariyl's case, more like an hour-and-a-half.

I studied the rickety wooden tracks and power poles that wound along the mountain ridge climbing up to Mount Lowe. The route was more than a decade old and had weathered many a storm. No doubt it was state-of-the-art for 1908, but I was sure it would not pass an amusement park inspection of my era.

"All aboard for Ye Alpine Tavern," called out the driver. Ariyl gave me a superior look.

"It's 'the'," I muttered.

The driver clanged his bell and with a lurch the trolley rolled off. In sullen silence, we sat at the rear, on seats that faced sideways and outward. The trolley was much wider than the tracks, so we essentially dangled our feet out over the San Gabriel Valley, a quarter-mile below us. Spread out at our feet were poppy fields, orchards and farms; there were some roads, but what I really noticed were the many rail lines. Further south was fast-growing Pasadena, and then the Monterey Hills; beyond lay the rest of the basin, all the way to the cliffs of Palos Verdes and the Pacific. On the horizon stood a pair of hazy blue humps—Santa Catalina Island.

Even in 1908, there was haze, but it was ozone from plant decay, and wood smoke trapped by the mountains and the inversion layer. It was nothing like the toxic mix Angelenos would be breathing by 1950. Today, all I smelled were orange blossoms and sagebrush.

We headed for a wide looping turn that hung way out over a vertical drop, the San Gabriels' answer to the Grand Canyon. I felt a need to talk instead of sightsee. The driver certainly wouldn't hear us over the rattle of the trolley. And I was still trying to divine Ludlo's motives.

"How did Ludlo find out Ty Cobb would visit here? Cobb lived in Georgia. He played ball for Detroit. There was no pro ball out here."

"I told you Ludlo collected all this ancient stuff from when he was a kid," she answered. "He had this crusty old postcard, that someone sent from Altadena saying they'd just met this ballplayer Cobb at the Tavern. It was dated March 1, 1908."

"Just like how he found Welles through the nightclub photo."

"And Ludlo figured the safest way to get an autographed ball was at a place almost no one knew Cobb had been."

"Makes sense. Less disturbance to known history." I held my tongue for a moment. "I guess that was when he was still being careful about it."

Ariyl worked her jaw and said nothing.

A wiser man would have let it rest there, but something still gnawed at me.

"Am I missing something? You told me your Crystal won't take you back to a moment you already visited."

"I didn't go to 1908 with Ludlo, remember?"

"Oh, right."

"He made me wait at Dodger Stadium."

"Right. Almost like he didn't trust you."

Ariyl's gaze turned glacial. But I had to ask the next question.

"Ariyl, how is it Ludlo could change the American Revolution? Forget baseballs, forget the Minotaur. We both saw that he erased America in 1976. Why did we have to stop him? The Time Crystal won't let you meet yourself back in time. So how could it not have yanked him back the instant he took the Declaration?"

"Hell if I know. Ask Ludlo. He's the one whose grandpa invented N-Tec."

Good thing I was sitting down or I might have been knocked right off the hillside by that one.

"What?!"

"Yeah, Marcus Ludlo. Maybe not *invented* N-Tec, but you know, designed a lot of the softstuff."

"Software!"

"Whatever."

"Jesus!" I exhaled.

"What?"

"Marcus must have put in a backdoor!"

"Yeah, it led right to their pool."

"Not in his house, in N-Tec! Ariyl, every software designer leaves himself a way to get into his program and fix it. Or create mischief, if he's not such a nice guy."

"Except, Marcus Ludlo's dead."

"I thought you people were all immortal."

"We have a choice. Most people don't want to die. But I just remember Marcus as this weird old dude who didn't want clone parts or anti-aging meds. He kinda hated what the world had become, I guess. Ludlo's dad argued with him a lot, but the old guy wouldn't budge."

"When Marcus died, how old was his grandson?"

"Jon? He was ten, I think."

"Ariyl, I think Marcus gave a password to his grandson. That's how Ludlo got past all N-Tec's safeguards."

"You don't know that."

"It's the only explanation that makes sense!"

"Maybe to you. It doesn't to me. I've known Jon my whole life. He's not twisted like his grandpa. He's just kind of a...bad-boy," she simpered.

"You make it sound like he has piercings and plays thrash metal. This maniac derailed the space-time continuum. Twice!"

"Now listen to me, David. I do not want you butting in this time. You don't say a word, you don't even show your face. You just wait at the trolley. I'll handle Ludlo. Got it?"

"Ariyl, this is the fate of the universe, and you're being swayed by sentiment, or woman's intuition, or hormones, or God knows what. No matter what bullshit story he gives you, you *cannot* let him get away again. I won't let you."

She plucked the ruined revolver from my waistband and held it up to me.

"*You* don't have a choice. You saw what I did to those cops. You don't think I can handle you?" With an infuriating little smirk, she set the useless weapon in my hand. "I will talk to Ludlo, alone. Then he and I will drop you back at your dig and erase everything ourselves."

"Fine!"

Angrily, I flung the gun off the cliff. Who gave a damn about history anyway?

For a minute, we just watched the scenery roll by. At last, Ariyl said, "Incredible view up here."

This girl was unbelievable. She was acting like she hadn't just threatened me. Again. I ground my teeth, silent.

"You ever ride this trolley? I mean, in your time?" Now, I guessed, she was feeling guilty. She put her hand near mine. I moved mine away.

"This is all gone, long before I'm born."

"What happened?"

"What didn't? Windstorm. Flood. Fires. The Great Depression."

Ariyl wrinkled her brow.

"What was so great about people being sad?"

"Mind if I just enjoy this quietly while I can?"

We rumbled through a gap between two big boulders. After a long pause, she tried again.

"David...when I stop Ludlo from doing everything he did after he met Ty Cobb, and history all goes back the way it was before we met...then you're never gonna meet me, right?"

"Not unless you find another excuse to turn my life upside down."

"It's just, you know, the logic bugs me. So, I'll still remember you...but you'll totally forget me?"

"Don't worry," I assured her. "That'll never happen."

She warmed, visibly.

"Really? Why?"

"Because you're going to let Ludlo get away again."

She gave me a look that would have frozen oxygen.

The trolley reached the end of the line. Nestled among the trunks of tall, shady oaks like some fanciful tree-hotel was "Ye" Alpine Tavern, a long, three-story structure with a river rock foundation, overlooking the broad valley. With its wooden balconies and balustrades, crisscross log patterns and rustic warped-wood railings, the Tavern was part Swiss chalet, part Craftsman mansion, and a bit of pre-Disneyland.

"End of the line, folks," announced the driver. Glowering at me, Ariyl stepped off the trolley.

"Just wait here," she commanded.

She marched past the bent trunk of a huge pine, around which the stairway had been constructed. She ascended to the lobby level—just as Ludlo walked out the door, looking natty in his 1908 suit.

I couldn't hear them, but I could mentally dub in the conversation: He looked amazed, since he thought she was waiting for him at Dodger Stadium. He would be unaware that that had been days ago for her.

I watched from the trolley, sitting in the shadows so he would not notice me, though of course, to the pre-Chavez Ravine Ludlo, I would be just some stranger dressed for a formal dinner, at noon.

Ariyl said something to Ludlo that stunned him. My guess? She'd told him if he truly loved her, he had to come home right now, no questions asked. She was pretty good at that kind of manipulation.

He peered all around, then mumbled something to her—possibly reminding her they mustn't talk about such matters in public, that any violation of history would end their trip. Then Ariyl took his arm and they went inside the hotel.

Maybe she could talk sense into him. Maybe they'd come out all smiles and she'd introduce us. Maybe here, at his first destination in time, Ludlo was still rational. Maybe he only flipped out later, as he became obsessed with his power. At any rate, I hoped so. I had to trust Ariyl. It was out of my hands.

I got off the far side of the trolley, and walked to a railing along the cliff. I gazed stonily at the view for I don't know how long, as it slowly turned golden in the light of the lowering sun.

A black janitor in his forties came along from the west, sweeping leaves off the promenade. From the eastern end of the path came a man my age or a bit younger, to judge from his tight skin and athletic stride. But his unpleasant face was a decade older than the rest of him: Sour. Haunted. And oddly familiar. Where had I seen him? And what was he clutching in his right hand?

The janitor swept a little too vigorously just as the man walked by, and dust landed on his shoes. As if it were the most natural thing in the world, the younger man swatted the back of the janitor's head, knocking his hat off.

"What the hell you doing, boy?" he snapped.

The janitor took a second or two to compose himself as he picked up his hat. Then he turned to the younger man, even-tempered.

"I'm sorry about the dirt, mister. But it was an accident. You got no call to lay hands on me."

The younger man's eyes widened in outrage. Judging from his drawl, he was new to California and expected a lot more deference from its Negroes.

"Why, you uppity mugwump!" With one powerful hand, he grabbed the janitor by his collar and shoved him against the rail.

I'm not a violent man, but I'd had enough attitude for one day. I took hold of the Southerner's other arm and twisted it behind his back until he yelped. He dropped whatever he'd had clenched in his fist, and it bounced off my toe. I held fast.

"Let him go!" I growled. I wrenched his arm harder, making it clear I was prepared to break it. He released the janitor. "Who the *hell* do you think you are, anyway?" I barked at the back of his ugly head.

"Ty Cobb?" came the answer. But not from the man I held. From someone behind me.

Oh, Christ. *That's* where I'd seen that nasty, buzz-cut mug before. On a yellowed baseball card in George Rath's shop.

And when I turned around, I saw the voice behind me belonged to Ludlo.

The wind was knocked out of me.

Not from seeing Ludlo. From turning my back on Ty Cobb. I'd loosened my grip on his arm, and the Georgia Peach immediately sucker-punched me in the kidney. His next blow, a fast left to my jaw as I turned back, laid me out on the promenade.

Somewhere, a bell clanged. Was the first round over? I heard the trolley driver call, "All aboard for Echo Mountain."

Cobb whirled on Ludlo, fists ready.

"That's right, I'm Cobb. Is everybody in this pesthouse looking for trouble?"

"Not me," said Ludlo, politely raising his straw boater in greeting. "I just want your autograph."

Ludlo had a piece of hotel stationery in his hand. But then his eyes lit on the horsehide baseball that Cobb had dropped on the path. It was a century newer, but it was the same A. J. Reach ball Ludlo would trade to Andy.

"In fact, on that ball, if you would be willing to part with it."

Ludlo produced an old-fashioned (though not old enough) ball-point pen—Ariyl's gift. And a five-dollar gold piece—no doubt part of their Travel Agency mad-money.

"I'd buy it from you, of course."

Cobb snorted, amused, and took the pen and the bribe. "Hell, why not?" Ludlo scooped up the baseball and handed it to Cobb, who squinted at the ballpoint. "Newfangled, huh?" Cobb gave the front end a little shake, as if it were a fountain pen that needed priming, then began to sign.

"And would you please date it?" added Ludlo.

Meanwhile, the janitor helped me to my feet.

"Thanks, mister," he murmured. "Do you want me to call the house detective?" I shook my head. "Then you take care, now," he advised, moving off.

Cobb finished dating his signature. He handed Ludlo the ball and the pen and gave me a parting, lethal glare before he headed into the hotel. The trolley bell clanged a final time, and it rumbled off.

I expected to see Ariyl somewhere near Ludlo, but he stood there alone, blowing the ink on the ball dry.

Then he looked over at me with bland detachment.

All I could think of to say was, "Have we met?"

He scanned me with utter lack of interest.

"I've never seen you before in my life." He dropped the ball in the new leather bag.

"True," I admitted. His smugness annoyed me, so I added, "Newfangled is putting it mildly." Now he frowned at his pen, perturbed. I told myself he'd have figured it out anyway. But I realized as soon as I said it, that it was a dangerous jibe.

So I turned and walked toward the trolley tracks, wondering where the hell Ariyl had gotten to. Then, looking down the line, it struck me that the girl at the back of the departing trolley, two hundred yards away, looked an awful lot like...hell, there *weren't* any other six-foot-three women in that exact dress. It was Ariyl, and even worse, she was chatting animatedly with Ludlo.

I looked back at *this other Ludlo*, a few feet from me on the promenade. That same damn Ludlo who was on the trolley was also here beside me, in the same damn SmartFab suit, only this Ludlo was wearing a straw boater.

And the other Ludlo, disappearing around the bend of the mountain, was hatless. And then I realized.

The son of a bitch had doubled back on us.

I began running down the tracks, as fast as I could.

26

THE GREAT INCLINE

THE TROLLEY WASN'T THAT FAST. IF I REALLY PUT A burn on, I could catch it within a mile. But what would I do then?

Normally when faced with a crisis, I sit back, analyze all aspects of the situation and decide on a prudent course of action. If I'd done that, I would have hunted up a pistol, or a posse. I could have accused Ludlo of kidnapping Ariyl and chased him down the line with a dozen armed men.

Instead, I acted instinctively. Just like when I tackled Ariyl. Something about this woman brought out the idiot in me. So here I was dashing after a trolley, without a gun or any other weapon. By the time I caught the trolley, I would be completely winded. And I still had no idea whether Ariyl was even in danger. Maybe she had figured it out on her own, and was even now, outwitting Ludlo.

But probably she wasn't. I kept running.

I rounded the bend in the tracks, and stepped to the rocky cliff edge to look over. I saw the trolley emerge from a switchback, three dozen feet below where I stood.

Now, the weathered Jurassic rocks of the San Gabriels are among the oldest in California. Some you can crumble in your hands. Or just by standing on them.

And thus it was that a second later, I was sliding down the rough cliff, shredding my formal pants on Mesozoic stone. If I didn't do something fast, I would land on the tracks in front of the trolley. So I spread myself out flat, and tried to dig my heels in as I slid. That slowed me, just enough so that when I fell, it was onto the trolley roof. Several of the rocks sliding with me banged off the roof and landed beside the tracks.

"Whoops!" chuckled the trolley driver below. "Don't worry folks," he called back to Ariyl and Ludlo. "These old mountains are always dropping rocks on us. That's why we got that steel roof. You're plenty safe."

I clung to the trolley roof. The driver didn't stop to check for damage. That gave me some time before we arrived at Echo Mountain and Ludlo discovered me. I still didn't have a weapon, but at least I'd be fully rested when he tore me apart.

Though if I talked fast, at least I could warn Ariyl.

I was right above her and Ludlo, and by pressing my ear next to a vent, I had no problem eavesdropping.

She'd had time to tell most of her story. My heart sank at what I was hearing now.

He was doing his best Hugh Grant impression.

"Ariyl, I-I swear I have no idea why we weren't yanked back. I mean, I know you wouldn't lie. I just can't believe I took—well, that my future self is *going—was* going to take—those things. I-I must've lost my head. And obviously, there's a glitch in the N-Tec monitoring program. When our trip's over, we'll warn N-Tec to fix it."

"What do you mean, when our trip's over? It's over right now, Jon. We have to go home before anything else happens to history!"

"Ariyl, be reasonable. If we went back now, they'd erase our trip from ever happening. And they'd never let us go back in time again. We'd lose all these irreplaceable memories."

"Jon, we don't have a choice."

"Sure we do. We take our same trip as planned, but now that you've warned me, I swear I won't touch a thing. Trust me, I'll be ultra careful."

That goddamned liar.

Ariyl wavered. "But...what about David?"

"Who gives a shit about him?"

"Not me. He's a total zed. But...he did save my life. I can't just leave him stranded out of time. Either we go home now and erase our trip totally...or, if we cover things up like you say, we have to make sure David gets home."

"But he'd go home with foreknowledge. He could change his own future—which may I remind you, is our history."

"Trust me, he won't. He's not like that."

"You mean, he's not like me?" There was a chill to his tone. Ariyl didn't reply to that.

"No. No, we have to prevent his ever meeting you," decided Ludlo. "It's simple. We go back to Thera, the week *before* we were there, and we take the Minotaur then. So the Minotaur isn't there on May tenth for earlier-me to bury for earlier-you. You never go to Preston's dig. He never sees the Minotaur. He never meets you. Essentially, we erase you from his mind."

"Yeah, well, he doesn't like me much. I'm sure he wouldn't care."

That's what I'd been thinking all afternoon. But maybe I would.

"And what about you, Ariyl?"

"What do you mean?"

"I can make it so *you* won't remember *him*."

"What?"

"You stay here. I go back to Thera alone. I take the Minotaur. Then I'll take you—the earlier 'you' from Chavez Ravine—with me on the rest of our trip. You would never meet *him*. The 'you' I'm talking to right now, would no longer exist."

"You want to erase *me*?"

"No! Not you. Just the last couple days of your life will never have happened. You forget them like a bad dream. After all, it's what you just suggested both of us do, by going home and erasing this trip. Only *my* way, the two of us can start over."

Jesus, Ariyl, don't trust this psychopath!

There was a pause.

"No, thank you," Ariyl replied, and from her tone, I sensed that Ludlo's suggestion gave her the willies.

"You just said he meant nothing to you."

"I'll decide what memories I keep, thank you."

"Ariyl, I just don't want to see you hurt."

"And just so you know, Ludlo...there is no 'us'."

I wanted to cheer. But I had a sense of foreboding. Ludlo's scheme did not rely on Ariyl's cooperation. In his mind, if he jumped back in time and removed me from the equation, he still had a shot with her. But the current, wised-up, disapproving version of Ariyl... how long would it be before he decided there was no point keeping *her* alive?

We pulled into the station.

"Echo Mountain, end of the line," announced the driver. He climbed off and headed for an outhouse.

Twenty yards away, the funicular rail car was clanking its way up what looked like a forty-five-degree incline to the power house carrying its white-haired operator, and a gaggle of female tourists in giant sun hats and suffocating Edwardian garb.

Ariyl got off the trolley, but Ludlo caught her arm.

"You're telling me we're through?"

"You and I were never *not* through."

"Then have the honesty to tell me one thing. Where did I go wrong with you?"

Now this slimeball wanted pointers to use on her earlier self! But Ariyl was chewing something over that he'd said before.

"Waaaait a minute," she said slowly. "You *can't* go back to me at Chavez Ravine. The Time Crystal won't let you return to the same time moment you were already in."

"Let me worry about that. There's a way."

I dropped to the ground.

"You bet there's a way, Ariyl. That backdoor I told you about. The truth is, he's already doubled back in time."

Ludlo looked stunned. But it wouldn't last for long. I had to talk fast.

"I just left the original Ludlo at the Alpine Tavern. That one still has his hat. This is Ludlo *after* he dropped that hat outside the garage in 1945."

Speechless, Ariyl reached into her jacket pocket. She pulled out Ludlo's SmartFab headband, and stared at Ludlo's bare head.

"Oh, my God. You've been lying to me this whole time!" She turned to me. "I'm sorry, David. You were right."

I would have liked a full second to savor that. But before I knew what hit me, Ludlo grabbed my arm and leg, and threw me over the cliff. If the cable car had been a second slower arriving, I would have overshot it and fallen to my death. As it was, my shoe tip caught on the top of the open car and I crashed to its deck, headfirst.

I heard Ariyl scream my name.

Despite the pain shooting through my head, I could see, blurrily, what was happening. I just couldn't get up. Ludlo slapped her savagely, knocking her to the ground. My brain ordered my body to move but someone somewhere down the spinal column wasn't relaying the message.

"You whore!" raged Ludlo. "You dump me, but you let that Neanderthal paw you?" He clutched the chain of her Time Crystal and dragged her to her feet.

"Let me go!" screamed Ariyl, thrashing.

"When I'm done with you!" snarled Ludlo. By this time, the ladies on the car were all screaming. I heard the car operator release the cable clamp and engage the brake lever. The ladies on the cable car scuttled into the power house. So did the elderly operator, who knew he was no match for this madman.

Ariyl punched and kicked at Ludlo. She dug her nails into his face. His wounds healed almost as soon as they bled. He got his arm around her throat, and now had her in a chokehold. With his free hand, he yanked her Time Crystal off her neck and hurled it over the cliff.

"Now you're coming with *me!*"

He dragged her over to the cable car where I lay, still groggy, blinking blood out of my eyes. Even deprived of oxygen, Ariyl was putting up a terrific fight, and it was all Ludlo could do with his free hand to grab the brake lever and rip its entire mechanism out of the cable car. The next moment, I was racing down the incline.

As I fell, I heard Ludlo yell a lot of words, but I only understood "May first." I barely glimpsed the flash of light that told me Ludlo was gone, taking Ariyl somewhere I couldn't follow, years or decades or centuries from now.

27

ALTADENA-BOUND

I WAS MAKING A 1,300 FOOT DESCENT AT TERMINAL velocity but as the joke goes, it was only that last foot that would be the problem. A burst of adrenaline let me drag myself to the edge of the funicular car. I was zooming on a collision course with a big steel Pacific Electric train on the rails at the base of the incline. Not what you'd call a soft landing. Screaming passengers abandoned the Red Car as the funicular hurtled toward it. Rocks, boulders, and sheer cliffs raced by. I had about five seconds to find something less bone-breaking to cushion my fall.

A last patch of chaparral looked unpromising, full of sharp branches and twigs, but I was in no position to be picky. I jumped.

If anything, hitting the brush at sixty miles per hour was even more painful than I expected, but I was only conscious of it for a second. I heard the collision of the cable car and the train, and then abruptly, crickets.

It was pitch black. Either I'd gone blind, or it was night. As pain dragged me back to consciousness, I realized it was the latter.

I was lying in the middle of tall brush. As my eyes focused, I beheld a riotous profusion of stars above me, thanks to the clear night air and the absence of streetlights. In my time, you'd have to drive for hours into the desert to witness it.

Apparently no one had seen me fall from the cable car. At least, no one had come looking for me. Every part of my body was either aching or painfully lacerated—except, for some odd reason, my left thumb.

I crawled out onto the hillside. A blazing searchlight raked the night sky atop the power house, nearly a half mile up the hill. Below me, I saw nothing but dark landscape for miles. The night was warm and windy. Somewhere down in the fields of Altadena, coyotes yipped madly, excited at making a kill. That made up my mind.

I began clambering up the funicular tracks. The climb was grueling but rather dull, except when I slipped, grabbed a rail tie, and got a painful splinter in my left thumb.

I reached the top a half-hour later, and found the power house locked up. The trolley didn't run that late. I set off along the trolley tracks. I managed to limp the three-and-a-half mile route in about an hour.

Ye Alpine Tavern looked even more magical by night, strung with hundreds of colorful paper Japanese lanterns around bare light bulbs, to light its walkways and trails. It was an inspiring tribute to the indomitable, can-do Yankee spirit, that in the driest, windiest forest in the U.S.A., the Tavern's owners didn't worry one whit about fire. It's amazing the place lasted the few years that it did.

I limped into the nearly empty dining room, with its broad granite fireplace. I put on my scratched glasses to read the welcoming quote from Emerson inscribed on the beam above: "The Ornament of a House is the Guests Who Frequent It."

Then I caught my reflection in a dark window: Tie and collar gone, tuxedo bloody and shredded, face and hands a mass of scratches and caked-on dirt, glasses missing one lens and hanging from either side of my nose by a shred of Sven's adhesive tape. If I was an ornament, it was the one the cat smacked off the tree.

There was only one other guest in the room, drinking quietly.

The back of his buzz-cut head twitched as if sensing me through that hard skull. He turned, and regarded me sourly.

"Christ on a bicycle, you're a mess," said Cobb. "You stick your nose in somebody *else's* business?"

"Guess I did at that," I conceded.

"Hey, George," called Cobb to a black waiter who looked to be off-duty. "Another glass." George (almost certainly not his name) hopped to it, perhaps having heard of Cobb's method of rewarding substandard service, and set down a glass for me.

"Normally, I'm a little choosier about my company," I explained, "but I've had one freaking lousy day." Again, I may have used a stronger adverb. I sank into the chair, exhausted. Cobb poured me a bourbon from his nickel-plated hip flask.

"Quit bellyaching," he advised. "In just the last year, I got beat up by my own team, had my tonsils hacked off by a quack with no ether...and my daddy was shot dead by my mother."

I threw back the bourbon. My throat now hurt as bad as the rest of me, but I wasn't about to show Cobb. I just grinned at him.

"I can beat that."

An hour later, the bartender whose name was not George had locked up and left. Cobb and I sat at the only table with chairs still on the floor. I enunciated around the bourbon as clearly as possible, trying to introduce him to a classic concept in quantum physics.

"Schrödinger's cat is in a box with a uranium atom. If the atom doesn't decay, the cat lives. If it decays, it's g'bye Puff."

"Good," growled Cobb. "I hate cats."

"You do?" I pondered the insight this afforded into Cobb's character. "You really *are* an asswipe." Cobb, well in his cups, mulled that over but the term was probably unfamiliar to him, so he let it slide. I wished I'd been able to have this conversation with Einstein, or Ben Franklin, or even Orson Welles, but I'd denied myself that pleasure. That was back when I thought history could still be salvaged.

"Anyway," I continued, "It's a thought experiment. Not a real cat. Quantum physics says, till an observer opens the box and observes, Puff's both dead an' alive."

"What the hell you talking about, boy? How can it be dead *and* alive?"

"Trust me, it can. We're the cat. Caught between two potential universes. The time traveler is the observer. Whatever he sees, is how history turns out. Any minute, any hour now, we—you, me, everyone we know—could all go *pffft*! Or maybe, just one of us. Or maybe we become just a little different, an' we'd never know what hit us."

"Horseshit," opined Cobb.

"I agree. And who cares? She *likes* bad boys. Prob'ly forgot me already. She thinks her ol' boyfriend's a hottie. An' you know what I am?"

"An egghead."

"Nope. I'm a primitive."

Cobb snorted. "You coulda fooled me."

"An' history? For her, it's just one big vacation."

"Women," fulminated Cobb. "Who needs the faithless bitches?" He stared off darkly. I wondered what female in his life had sent him stalking off to his lonely destiny. Mom "accidentally" shooting Dad?

Cobb peered at me. "If you were really from the future, you could tell me what happens to me."

Thanks to Andy, indeed I could.

"You become the greatest ballplayer in history. You die with literally a million bucks in your suitcase...and not a friend in the world."

Cobb's eyes widened. "A million bucks, huh?" He seemed to find nothing discouraging in my prediction. "You know why people hate me?"

"Yup. You're a racist, catcher-spiking asshole."

Cobb shook his head. "'Cause I want to win more than anybody else. Just like that fella who got your gal."

"He's also got a time machine."

"Excuses, excuses. You said you had a gun on him, but you didn't kill him when you had the chance. If you wanted her enough, you'd have done it. You'da done anything to keep her."

I thought about that for a long while. Then I got up, shoved my hand in my pocket, and was surprised to feel the heavy coin there. Damn, I'd meant to put that back. Luckily, I'd forgotten. I looked at Cobb.

"You're buying," I told him.

I walked out of the room. I could hear Cobb chuckling mordantly.

Well, let him laugh. I waited out in the lobby. He stumbled up to his room half an hour later, so drunk he couldn't find his key. I found it for him, led him over to the bed, and laid him down on the floor. I did give him a pillow. He was out like a light.

Then I used his private bath to soak away the blood and the dirt. Drying off, I saw that I wasn't quite the wreck I thought I was. I took Cobb's bed, making sure to wind the alarm clock and set it for six. I needed rest and there was no point setting out any earlier. My plan required full daylight and a large pool of laborers.

When the clock rang I silenced it quickly. While Cobb snored on, I took a change of clothes from his suitcase—including his brand-new pair of Levi Strauss blue jeans—and transferred the contents of my pockets. I burned the tux in his fireplace. I kept my smashed up plastic-framed glasses, but only for disposal in a more modern era. I wasn't going to be doing much reading for a while.

Meanwhile, I had a hearty breakfast sent up, charged it to the room and signed his name for a bigger tip than I bet Cobb gave over the next fifty years put together. My only regret was I couldn't get cash out of Cobb's money belt without waking the paranoid bastard. On my way out, I searched through the armoire and found his loaded revolver. I took that.

I rode the morning's first trolley over to the Great Incline. I was happy to see they had already gotten the spare funicular out of the car barn and had it in operation.

I descended to the base of the hill, this time at a sane rate of speed, and posted my handwritten notices at the Pacific Electric car barn, and also down the line at the Mountain Junction stop at Lake Avenue and Calaveras Street. Word spread, and by mid-morning much of the population of Altadena, including a number of boys and girls who should have been in school, were lined up at the car barn in Rubio Canyon to hear my offer.

"I hold here in my hand a genuine gold English guinea, worth at least a five-dollar gold piece, and undoubtedly more as a collector's item. It is dated 1776, with a portrait of George the Third, and I know for a fact that it once belonged to Thomas Jefferson. I shall award it to the person or persons who find my late mother's pendant, a large aquamarine with a hole in its center, lost off the incline car during yesterday's terrible accident."

My mother is alive and well, thank you, but she does love aquamarines, and I could hardly tell anyone what I was actually looking for.

Even with the mountainside crawling with eager would-be prospectors, I tried to keep my expectations low. For all I knew, the time limit was already up and the object of my search had automatically returned to 2109. My hopes rose when one ginger and sunburned lad of twelve came running up, all excited. He held out a big hunk of rose quartz.

"No, no, it's a cut stone, like a diamond," I informed him. "And it has a hole through the middle."

Vexed, the boy mopped his brow with this sleeve. "Aw, gee willikers." He scrambled back up the incline, poking through the scrub brush.

An hour later, a heavily whiskered old man with one glass eye—if not a real prospector then perfect casting for one—offered me an odd pistol of unknown manufacture, with a seven-sided barrel. It was bent like a pretzel.

"Close, but no cigar," I told him. But to prevent any brother archaeologists from wracking their brains over this conundrum, I swapped him Cobb's hip flask of bourbon for it.

It was early afternoon when I was approached by a little Chicana girl—well, she would have just called herself *Mexicana*, though I expect she was born American. She couldn't have been more than nine. Holding her Papa's hand, she came up to me and shyly showed me Ariyl's Crystal. I could tell she really preferred to keep the beautiful gem, but Papa told Rosita in Spanish that she may not keep that which was not hers. She dutifully handed it over and accepted the gold coin as her reward.

The Crystal glowed, full of charge. But would it allow anyone but Ariyl to use it...and even if it did, was I right about where Ludlo took her?

28

MEANWHILE, BACK IN ATLANTIS

The thing about that golden Minotaur is, no matter how many times you lose it, it kind of grows on you. Like me, Ludlo regretted letting it go. So his destination was Thera, two weeks before the eruption.

Ariyl was no idiot. Stranded back in the Bronze Age with no Time Crystal of her own, she set to work making up with Ludlo. She tearfully apologized for her impulsive behavior at Echo Mountain, and for having given him the impression that a crude pre-Change knuckle-dragger like me could ever have meant anything to her.

She worked her considerable wiles on Ludlo, but he was in no mood for romance or sex, until he located the Minotaur. He did appreciate its artistic and historic qualities, but for him, it also symbolized his biggest mistake—letting Ariyl meet me.

So Ariyl and he spent many precious hours retreating in time to locate the Minotaur before the eruption, entering the temple on May 1st, then back on April 14th, then April 1st...

By the time they were back to February, Ludlo realized the shaman had hidden it in the hills many months before the final eruption.

Impatient, Ludlo planned to choke the shaman into revealing its location, or the day when he had removed it, but Ariyl pointed out that the man might be more afraid of his gods than death...and if Ludlo tried to get rough, he might never retrieve it. So he reluctantly decided he would let his earlier self bury the Minotaur by the temple steps on May 10th, and avoid earlier-Ariyl by retrieving it after the eruption of Thera. He told Ariyl they had to find it before May 13th, which was when the collapse of the caldera would flood the entire area.

During the eruption of May 11th, 1628 B.C., the blistering pyroclastic cloud had dissipated before reaching the Temple of the Dolphins. Choking ash had fallen everywhere, but the Minoan—that is, Atlantean—soldiers who stayed behind were dead anyway. Hydrogen sulfide gas had permeated the village and suffocated the three of them, including my old jailer Sorehead, who had stayed behind to loot while his wiser comrades put to sea.

Ludlo was immortal in most ways, but he had no gene-tooled resistance to poison gas. It was Ariyl's suggestion that they jump ahead to May 12th, the day after the eruption, and the day before the submersion of Atlantis. The sea breezes had had time to clear the air, and it was safe for them to dig up the Minotaur.

Ludlo offered to do it on his own, while she waited later in history. That way he would erase her memory of David Preston.

Ariyl assured him that it wasn't necessary, there was nothing to erase. She and Ludlo were the gods of this world. Why would a goddess care about a mere mortal? No, she would help him search.

So they jumped ahead to dawn on May 12th.

The island was covered in steaming ash. The mountain to the west was gone, leaving only a vast, hollow caldera. The pressure on the magma pool which lay beneath the peak had been relieved by the blast.

Where once a clear mountain stream had run past the temple to the ocean, glowing orange lava now hemorrhaged from a new vent, five miles east of the caldera. It flowed past the flattened, incinerated forest and village, to coagulate as basalt in the steaming sea.

Soon debris and sand would encase the temple ruins, in what would eventually become the Cave of the Dolphins. But for now, the shattered temple was covered only by a blanket of ash. As were Sorehead and his fellow looters, lying where they had dropped, their mildly puzzled expressions a testament to how quickly death had come.

It took only an hour or two of tossing away debris and poking around with the sword of one of the dead soldiers for Ludlo to locate the corner of the steps and dig until he found the leather sack he had buried on May 10th. He reached for the sack.

"Wait," pleaded Ariyl. She was no longer blandly supportive. Her tone was now anxious.

"Why?" demanded Ludlo, instantly suspicious. "Because your precious David is downtime from us! Right? Because when I pull this out, it means he will never meet you?"

Ariyl shook her head, but a tear ran down her cheek, betraying her.

Ludlo seized her head between his palms.

"I was wrong before. I admit, I did plan to erase you. But you're too beautiful to kill! My problem is that contact with that Cro-Magnon has infected you. So I have to kill the part of you that lies to me!"

"I'd do worse than lie to you—you pathetic psycho!" she spat back.

"I'm no psychopath," he breathed, squeezing her face in his powerful fingers.

"If you say so," she winced.

Ludlo nodded, with a manic grin.

"I'm so different from what I was forty-eight hours ago, Ariyl. Before, I was just the impotent product of N-Tec's dead-end world. But I have something to offer you now. This journey has made me realize what I truly am. What I was born to be. I'm not a tourist, not a collector, not a thief. I'm an artist. The greatest one in history. My clay is Time. When I dig out an item here, a person there...I can sculpt history into whatever I choose."

"Artist?" Ariyl stared at him, appalled. "You're a *loon!* You're crazy with power. But you'll never make me forget David, no matter what you do!"

Ludlo laughed. This is what he'd been waiting for.

"You stupid cunt. I don't need *you.* I just go back to Dodger Stadium in the first hour of our trip, to the you who never met Preston. And now, never will. But first, I get rid of the ungrateful bitch he turned you into!"

He threw her down, grabbed the Minotaur and raised it to bash out her brains.

That's when I shot Ludlo in the face. He went down like a sparrow hitting a picture window.

The honorable thing would have been to give him a warning, or at least a Schwarzenegger one-liner before I fired. But fuck him, he needed to die and I was taking no more chances.

Besides, I'd only arrived from 1908 a second earlier. I had no idea what they'd been saying, so any quip would be a lame non sequitur. I just aimed and fired.

"Jesus, it's about time you showed up!" yelled Ariyl, yanking Ludlo's Time Crystal off his bleeding head, and putting it over hers.

"Move! I'm putting five more into that asshole!"

That was when Ludlo leaped to his feet and threw his arm around Ariyl's throat, using her as a shield.

His ruined right eye was gushing blood, but the bullet had exited from his right temple, hitting no brain tissue. The speedy bastard must have moved at the last second. Damn, I *knew* I should've aimed for his heart.

I didn't dare target his arm around her neck—I'm not that good a shot. I might kill her.

Ludlo was the lean, wiry type, and didn't protrude much from behind Ariyl's silhouette. But his shoulders were wider, and my second shot nicked his left one. He yelped in pain, but he held on and the wound began healing almost immediately. Then Ariyl lurched to one side and drove her elbow into Ludlo's solar plexus. That seemed to hurt him more than my bullet.

"Bitch!" roared Ludlo, throwing Ariyl at me with enough force that we both flew ten feet back. The wind was knocked out of me so hard I didn't think I would ever inhale again. The force of our landing knocked Cobb's revolver from my hand. It skittered across the rocks and dropped into the lava flow. I heard the bangs of the cartridges exploding, as the gun softened and sank into the molten rock.

"David, are you okay?" gasped Ariyl.

Ludlo felt his throat, and realized his Time Crystal was gone. In two leaps, he closed the twenty feet between us, shoved me aside and tried to rip his Crystal off Ariyl's neck. She couldn't reach me. She twisted free of Ludlo and in a panic, scrambled back from him, up the pile of stones that had been the temple. At the top of the pile, the precariously perched roof stones gave way beneath her, and she fell headfirst into the darkness with a scream.

I finally got my wind back. I raced up to the top of the rubble pile. Sunlight sifted down through the broken walls. Ariyl had fallen all the way through to the stone floor of the dungeon, two stories down. She lay unmoving, blood pooling under her face. I tried to get closer, but another block gave way beneath my feet and fell in beside her. I leaped back. I wouldn't let myself believe she was dead, but she sure looked it.

"Ariyl! Ariyl!" I cried. She didn't stir. Ludlo stared down at her, impassive.

"You piece of shit!" I yelled, punching him as hard as I could. My hand would have broken, if it hadn't slipped along his sweaty jaw. Ludlo just smirked, then backhanded me. I tumbled painfully down the side of the ruins and landed on my back, staring up.

One glancing blow from this monster, and my head swam like a goldfish in a spin-dry cycle. Whatever I did, I couldn't let him hit me again. Ludlo strode down the shattered stone blocks, his eyes glittering. Well, actually just the one eye. The other merely oozed and looked disgusting. That pleased me. With any luck, his major organs wouldn't self-repair.

Ludlo stopped to pick up a chunk of marble the size of an oil drum. He raised it over his head, and descended the steps toward me.

"Too bad Ariyl isn't around to watch me squash her new boyfriend like a bug." His next step would be onto a large brick near me. I kicked it aside and his shoe landed four inches below where he thought it would. He stumbled, overbalanced and fell.

Before he could get up, I leaped on him with a stone in my fist. I smashed him in the face with it three times, damaging him a lot less than I'd hoped. Suddenly, his foot was on my chest and the next second he sent me airborne. I was getting used to these long falls, and this time I managed to tuck and roll as I landed.

I wound up near the hole that Ludlo had dug in the ash. The Minotaur lay where he'd dropped it. More importantly, so did the bronze sword he'd used. I scrambled to the hole and grabbed it.

Ludlo leaped off the ruins and landed two yards from me. By his feet was the body of Sorehead, clutching his sword with rigor mortis resolve. Ludlo snapped the weapon free, sending dead fingers flying.

He came at me, swinging amazingly fast for a novice, but without skill. I parried half a dozen of his blows—he looked truly surprised at that—and gave him better than I got, driving him backwards.

His last parry was off and on my next blow I swung at his throat for all I was worth. The blade, still remarkably sharp, sliced halfway through his neck, but he had backed up to the broken temple wall and my sword tip hit the stone behind him, stopping my blow before it could sever his spine.

Ludlo jerked away. Blood geysered from his neck. He swore and clamped his hand to the wound, backing away from me.

I should have followed up instantly, but I still wasn't used to this gene-spliced healing. It took me two seconds to realize he wasn't going to keel over dead. Then I swung again but it was too late.

Ludlo parried so forcefully that he knocked the sword from my hand.

I dashed to retrieve it, and by the time I did, Ludlo's bleeding was under control. He kept holding his hand to his neck, but in a few minutes, he wouldn't even need to do that.

Oh, good, I thought. I've always wanted to meet the psycho ex-boyfriend who's also indestructible.

"Too bad you didn't cut my head off, caveboy. Anything less won't do."

"Thanks for the tip."

He came at me again. Damn, he was fast. Maybe not as fast as Ariyl now, but still scary fast. I'd been told clashing bronze blades don't give off sparks like steel ones do, but still I could've sworn I saw them.

As fast as he slashed his blade, he managed to keep up a line of chat.

"Ariyl said you were a fencer."

"Took the silver at London," I grinned, lying.

He sliced at my face. My forelock was suddenly an inch shorter. Intimidation was not working on him. But he kept trying it on me.

"You might have a snowball's chance in hell, if I wasn't ten times stronger and a whole lot faster."

He swung at me, but came up short. His eye remained a mess.

I forced a laugh. "How's your depth-perception, Cyclops?"

Furious, he swung so hard his blade jammed deep in one of the broken wooden columns. As he tugged at it I did my best to amputate his forearm. He yanked his sword free and all I sliced off was a strip of fabric and skin. But seeing him bleed even for a moment gave me satisfaction. Good. Getting him mad made him clumsier!

"Nobody steals my woman!" he snarled.

"You think you *own* her? God, no wonder she'd rather be dead than with you."

That did it. He came at me practically frothing at the mouth. I clambered up onto the ruins as he banged and clanged his sword at me, hitting every piece of rubble in his path. Stone chips flew in all directions. He was ruining his edge, but he swung with such force that I expected he would still be able to chop my head off.

"The stupid bitch deserved to die! She could've ruled all of history with me!"

I was tiring. I couldn't keep ahead of him. I fell at the top of the pile and Ludlo raised his sword for the kill.

"Hate to bum you, O King of the World," echoed Ariyl's voice from below, "but I'm alive!"

She leaped up from below, and grasped the stones at the rim of the chasm. Her forehead sported a bloodied and nasty purple bruise, but it was mending. Unfortunately, the stones she gripped fell into the chasm and she dropped back down.

Then came a rumbling sound, but not from falling stones. More like an entire falling mountainside.

"Okay, wrong tense," smiled our attacker. "But you will die, and soon. Feel that, Ariyl?"

The rumble was now palpable. The ruins shifted beneath our feet, and big chunks of stone went sliding off the pile. And I knew this earthquake would be only the precursor of something far worse.

Ludlo pointed to the volcano—or rather, to what was left of it. Having blown apart with unimaginable violence, the crater was now a huge hole with quadrillions of tons of seawater pressing on its unstable walls.

And now, clouds were rising from the far end of the crater, but this time, not an eruption. The crater's entire west side was crumbling in a monstrous landslide.

"You were so suddenly helpful, Ariyl, that I thought I might need an advantage. So I lied about the date that the caldera will collapse. That doesn't happen tomorrow. It happens today. Right now the sea is pouring into a cavity six miles across. In a few minutes, the sea will be here—in a tsunami a quarter-mile high!"

Plato wrote that Atlantis was destroyed and sank beneath the waves in a single day and night. We were just about at the twenty-four-hour mark. What a time for Plato to be right on the money.

I put my hand to the Time Crystal. It had been around my neck, inside my shirt, just a minute ago. It wasn't now. Of course, I had done a lot of tumbling and falling. I looked around madly.

Then I spotted where it had fallen. Five yards away, behind Ludlo. I couldn't try for it—he'd easily beat me to it. So I forced myself not to look.

I glanced instead at the distant, disintegrating mountainside, and the miles-long waterfall of seawater cascading into it. As water hit the rising magma in the bottom of the caldera, vast steam clouds exploded skyward, hiding the rest of the island from view. Lightning flashed. The wind rose to a screaming gale.

The sea raced away westward from the beach near the temple ruins, accompanied by a deafening roar of suction. I knew where the water was going, and I knew it would soon be back. And then some.

"It'll pound what's left of this island and drown you two like rats," shouted Ludlo over the din. "You have one chance, Ariyl—use your Crystal!"

"No!" she begged from under the ruins. "Jon, help me save him!"

"Sorry, Ariyl. I hate this guy too much to want him to live. Now, I could tell *you* the backdoor password, to move from down there to up here without losing a second," taunted Ludlo. "But see, that's kind of a family secret. I promised not to."

"Jon, please! I'll do anything you want!"

"Really? Good. Then leave him behind!"

"You bastard!" she shrieked.

Then I heard that sound I always associate with her, a wooden door being busted down. I figured she was trying to escape up the same stairs the Minoans brought me down. I heard her grunting, heaving stones and timbers out of her way.

She was never going to dig her way out in time.

"Ariyl, you have to get out of here!" I hollered. "If I can't stop him here, it's up to you!"

"I'm not leaving you!" she cried.

"Neither of you can stop me," said Ludlo. He raised his sword to decapitate me, but then peered at my throat, puzzled. It came to me: He still thought I had Ariyl's Crystal.

I leaped to my feet. I'd gotten my second wind, even if it was more like a faint breeze.

"Yeah, she's got your Crystal. So you need hers to escape, don't you?" I smiled, patting my (empty) pants pocket.

I had to keep him focused on me, keep him from finding out I didn't have the Crystal, keep him from looking behind him where I'd dropped it...keep him here until it was too late for either of us.

He came at me again.

As for Ariyl, she had to leave us both behind—history depended on her now.

Without binocular vision, Ludlo couldn't accurately gauge his blows. But I knew I couldn't beat Ludlo. He was too strong, too fast. Relentless, he forced me back. I was huffing and puffing; he wasn't even breathing hard. He was downright chatty:

"Come on, David, stop being selfish. If you really love her, don't let her throw her life away. Let me finish you now."

Clever. He made me hesitate, just a fraction of a second. He swung, slicing through my shirt. I felt a sting, and a warm trickle down my chest.

"Take a breather, caveboy. I make one quick stroke, and you can rest up for all eternity."

I kept jumping back. He swung three more times, getting closer each time. I was backing my way back down the debris pile, right toward the Crystal. My body was blocking his view, or he'd have seen it. It took all my will power not to look around at it.

"On the other hand, decapitation isn't painless," he taunted. "I saw Robespierre's head fall from the guillotine. The poor bastard still saw and felt and moved his mouth for several seconds. It's just, without lungs...he couldn't scream."

I ducked to avoid another swing, and saw more hair flying. My haircut was pretty much ruined.

"I'm not as strong as you," I said between gulps of air. "So it makes you wonder why she chose me, doesn't it?"

Ludlo lost it. He charged me in a rage, swinging like a berserker, striking chips off the fallen columns as I scrambled backwards down through the rubble of roof and walls.

Then my foot slipped, and wedged fast between two halves of a broken stone block. I was stuck.

Ludlo raised his sword. He couldn't resist one last mind game.

"Hand me the Crystal, and I might let her save you."

My eyes involuntarily flicked to the Crystal, lying fifteen feet from us. Just a fraction of a second, but Ludlo noticed, and turned to see it.

"You little prick!" he snarled, realizing all the extra work I'd put him to.

He drew back his sword.

I braced myself to see that final, tumbling ride that Robespierre's eyes had beheld. But then Ludlo rose into the air as if by magic, along with the timber he stood on. Ariyl stood on the last steps of the buried stairway, holding him over her head. Ludlo tumbled off backwards, hitting his head, and she tossed the timber at him.

"Miss me?" she panted.

I pointed. "Your Crystal!"

Ludlo saw it. He got to his feet and leaped across the rubble.

"Sword!" she said, reaching out.

I tossed it to her. "Don't cut yourself."

Ariyl launched herself after Ludlo, while I tried to dislodge my foot.

Ludlo reached the Crystal first, but half-blind, he fumbled the grab, and a second later Ariyl was there, hacking at him with the sword. She sliced deep into his left wrist. Too bad he was right-handed.

Now Ariyl and Ludlo went at it, their swords ringing with the power of their blows. Neither of them had great skill, but Ariyl was as strong as Ludlo, and a bit faster now. She had depth perception—while I guessed he would have to wait for a new clone-eye. And she was *pissed*. Inch by inch, she forced him back from the Time Crystal.

I frantically worked to unwedge my foot. I couldn't get my boot off. The knot was jammed against the stone. I needed something sharp to cut the lace.

And that's when I saw the horns of the goddamn Minotaur, lying at the base of the steps. Out of reach, as usual. And probably too soft to cut the lace, but I was desperate.

There was a long, charred tree branch nearby. I seized it, and stretched, trying my damnedest to hook the Minotaur with it.

Ariyl drove Ludlo back. The fallen Time Crystal was now a couple of yards behind her, and Ludlo couldn't get past her.

"Don't be a sucker, Ariyl!" he told her between parries and thrusts.

"You don't want our world back. (CLANG!) We can move through time, do anything we want! (CLANG!) We're immortal... we're gods! (CLANG!) Don't go back to being a nobody!"

Ariyl shot back, "*You're* the nobody, you selfish...(CLANG!)... lying...(CLANG!)...scumbag! (SWISH!)"

Ludlo had figured out her rhythm and jumped back. She swung so hard that without his parry, she overbalanced and stumbled. In a heartbeat, Ludlo stepped on her blade and jabbed his sword tip to her throat, drawing a little bead of blood.

The world darkened. The wind was a hurricane. Salt spray stung my eyes. All I could see on the western horizon was a wall of water, racing closer. If you've ever stared up at the Empire State Building, imagine a wave that could wash it away like a sand castle.

Ludlo still pressed his sword against her neck but also held out his empty hand, nearly healed from where she'd tried to hack it off. "Last chance, love!" he bellowed. "Forget this loser and come with me!"

"You go to hell!" she screamed. He grabbed the Time Crystal by the chain around her neck, and brought back his sword.

Andy, if you're up there, a little help, I prayed. Only fifteen feet, but the most important pitch of my life. I hurled the Minotaur end-over-end, like a tomahawk.

The bull's horn hit Ludlo in his good eye. He screamed and dropped his sword. Ariyl grabbed hers but didn't waste time on him.

The wave raced toward us, devouring the island. Four hundred yards. Three hundred yards. Two hundred.

With a leap Ariyl covered the distance between us. She heaved aside one of the stone blocks, and clutched my hand.

Ludlo was ten yards west of us, groping toward the other Time Crystal, as the wave rose above him.

I started for the Minotaur, right by his feet. I was sure I could get it. All I needed was a few seconds.

"Are you fucking kidding?" yelled Ariyl over the deafening noise. She grabbed me by the collar, pulling me up short. "Previous destination!"

I looked back. The last thing I glimpsed was Ludlo as the wave picked him up and smashed him on the temple stones like a fly against a windshield.

29

FEBRUARY 1, 1628 B.C.

Of course, we now had Ludlo's Crystal, and it was to his previous destination that we went: The Temple of the Dolphins, February 1st of that fatal year. We arrived literally the instant he and Ariyl had left, in an olive grove just northeast of the temple.

We just hugged for a few minutes. Then Ariyl attended to the cut on my chest, cleaning it with seawater. She ripped off the sleeves of the shirt I stole from Ty Cobb and bandaged it. We had a lot to talk over but my curiosity about Ludlo's Time Crystal was overwhelming.

I suggested an experiment: Ariyl left me there by the temple on February 1st, jumping ahead one day. I was mentally prepared to wait a day for her return. But she returned the next second. So we knew Ludlo had been bluffing about her needing a password: His Crystal's safeguards were already fully disabled. Of course, he outsmarted himself there: Since the Crystals were linked, there had been nothing to stop Ariyl's Crystal from responding to the commands of a stranger like me.

Ariyl and I caught each other up on what had happened since Ludlo kidnapped her from Echo Mountain. The only words of his I had understood as they'd vanished were "May first." Knowing his mania for that Minotaur, and his plan to erase me from her life...I'd gambled on 1628 B.C.

I had apparently missed Ariyl and Ludlo by minutes on May 1st, but I'd kept jumping ahead towards the eruption date, just as she'd hoped I would. And I'd skipped the actual eruption, of course, to arrive the next day, just in time to shoot Ludlo before he could brain Ariyl. She told me how she'd been buttering him up and stalling him at the temple, hoping I'd show.

And now here we stood, enjoying a pleasantly mild winter's day, thirteen weeks before this earthly paradise known as Atlantis would vanish beneath the waves.

For a long while, we just sat in silence, looking at the slopes of the slumbering volcano, the idyllic pastures full of sheep and goats, the orchards, the whitewashed village, the magnificent temple. And everywhere, people living their lives.

Three-and-a-half months from now, they would be scattered, refugees at best, more likely slaves, and many of them drowned by the tsunamis that wiped out the coastal settlements of the Mediterranean world. Its central island and capital gone, along with most of their navy, the Minoans' failing civilization would circle the drain for another century and a half before vanishing from history.

Ariyl had tears in her eyes, but not for Ludlo.

"I can't believe I came back in time to watch all this be destroyed. Like it would be fun. What the hell's wrong with me?" she asked.

30

SANTORINI, 432 B.C.

WE WENT TO ATHENS FOR TAKE-OUT, IN THE SPRING OF 432 B.C. The height of Athenian glory under the rule of Pericles seemed a likely place to find great souvlaki. And not a trace of antibiotics or steroids. At least that's the reason I gave Ariyl. The truth was, I wanted to see the Parthenon. A ruin today, it nevertheless is, for me, the most beautiful building in history. I wanted to see it brand new.

When I beheld that stunning marble edifice—not white as we know it, but colorfully painted—standing atop Acropolis Hill, I choked up. More than a millennium had passed since Atlantis died, but Western civilization had been reborn.

"It's nice. It's no Disney Hall," opined Ariyl.

"Definitely not," I nodded.

Ariyl, as usual, was in a hurry to eat. We traded our now-antique bronze sword (in superb condition, of course) for food, blankets, a suitable tunic for me, and wine.

Then we returned to Santorini. At dusk, we sat on a homespun blanket, picnicking on the sand outside the Cave of the Dolphins. We finished the wine. I offered Ariyl the last spanakopita (well, its distant ancestor) but she shook her head.

"I'm full."

"Wow. Never thought I'd hear you say that."

She chucked a grape at me. "Don't mess with me, dude. I'll make you wish you'd never been born."

"Been there, done that."

Ariyl appraised me, sympathetic. "Why were you staring at that temple in Athens?"

"I had to make sure the Parthenon was still there."

"Why wouldn't it be? Ludlo's dead."

"Well, he's not getting any *older*. But he still exists throughout history. Especially, in 1908."

"But we know what he did after he left 1908. He went to Chavez Ravine...didn't he?"

I shook my head. "1908 is different now. This time he met me before we met at Dodger Stadium. Maybe that changed something. Changed him. Inspired him to make a side-trip."

My smart-ass joke to Ludlo about his pen was haunting me.

"You mean, he might have gone off and done something else?"

"It's possible."

Ariyl looked ill, as the import of this sank in. "And I was out of it in 1492, for...what, half a day? He could've gone to a lot of other times, jacked a lot of important stuff in that time."

"Or, maybe we get lucky, and he doesn't do anything different. But we can't rely on that."

She chewed her lip, thinking. "So what do we do? Start working our way forward in time, see if anything is wrong with history?"

"Yes," I said, impressed. "Very logical. The important thing is to stay behind him in time. At the first sign of a deviation in history, we figure out what Ludlo did, jump back to the day he arrived, and...you know...prevent him from changing anything."

"Without letting him know we're there. Or that he dies when Atlantis sinks."

"That would be optimal, yes." There was only one sure cure for Ludlo, but did I dare tell Ariyl? I'd better save that for last.

"Eventually," I added, "we'll reach my era, and make sure it's on track. And then finally, fix whatever he did to ruin yours."

"Hey...do you think Jon's first change might've been to kill Marcus, before he designed the N-Tec software? Maybe that's where he went when he left me in Atlantis."

"If Ludlo killed his own grandfather, then there's a famous paradox that needs to be retired. But I don't think it's really a paradox now. As Sven pointed out, Ludlo wasn't changing his past. Or ours, since we were back in time as well. He was changing our future, and now we have to get it back."

"So it sounds like, if we find Ludlo, our best move is to sneak up behind him and put a bullet in his head."

Man. And I'd thought this was going to be a hard sell.

"I don't see any other way," I admitted. "He's too dangerous to leave behind in any era, or to take back to your N-Tec world. I suppose you could maroon him back in the Pliocene Era and hope the sabertooths get him."

"He's still immortal," pointed out Ariyl. "As long as he was careful, he could stay alive, waiting for us to evolve, just getting madder and madder all the time."

"And he's quite mad to start with. But what if we dumped him in *your* future? Say 2400 A.D. I mean, without a Time Crystal, what threat could he pose?"

"No can do. The Time Crystals aren't built to reach our future."

I didn't quite believe her, until we tried it. It wouldn't access anything beyond the day Ariyl jumped back in time.

By the way, Ariyl hadn't exaggerated about Ludlo's change to her era: The Los Angeles she'd last seen was still the kind of post-Apocalyptic horror show that gives dystopias a bad name. Something Ludlo did after 1945 was still mucking up her world. We couldn't get back to 432 B.C. fast enough.

"Isn't that interesting," I mused. "N-Tec considered changes to your history a containable risk...but your future is off-limits? I wonder why."

We pondered for a moment. Then Ariyl announced, "Okay. Ludlo has to die. We don't have a choice." Then she said what was already on my mind. "Look, if we're killing to save the world...why not kill Hitler, too?"

I nodded. "We could save six million people at a bare minimum. Two more assassinations, and seventy million deaths—an entire world war—might be prevented. We could save twelve million by taking out Joseph Stalin. We might save America a crapload of grief by shooting John Wilkes Booth and sparing Abe Lincoln. But if we do any of that, we don't get back to my world or yours.

"No," I concluded. "Ludlo was trying to play God, too. That way lies madness."

"Maybe you're right," she said quietly. Frankly, I could think of one possible reason to play God myself: I wasn't sure putting N-Tec back in charge of the twenty-second century was the smartest idea. But I sensed we were a long, long way from that, and there was no point bringing it up yet.

I found myself staring into the cave.

Ariyl followed my gaze. "Willya forget the freakin' Minotaur? It's not down there anymore! We totally lost it this time."

"It's not that," I said, shaking my head. "I'm thinking about the untold misery Ludlo caused, and it all began with a treasure hunt."

"Well, look at all the misery you went through to find your treasure. You know, you two are a lot alike."

I was ready to take offense, but then I caught the twinkle in her eyes. I chuckled sardonically. "Yeah, except I keep losing mine."

"Oh, God, I can't stand to see you so droopy." She assumed a dutiful air. "We'd better get started, so we can fix World War Four and make sure our side won."

"You mean World War Two." Wait, *what?* "There's a World War Four?"

"I'm not sure," she shrugged, helpless. "You know me and numbers. Which one had the death-ray robots?"

"Forget it! I don't want to know." I shifted, and something in Cobb's coat pocket poked me. I pulled it out.

"What's that?" asked Ariyl, surprised. "Oh, your gun that I bent!" She examined the warped steel. "I'm sorry I was being such a bitch."

"I was going to throw it in the ocean...but I decided to keep it. Call me sentimental."

Ariyl laughed that delightful laugh again. "You are so sweet."

But now I had to get serious.

"Ariyl...I know you had feelings for Ludlo. It must have been hard to see him killed. Are you sure you could look him in the eye and do it yourself? Because that's what we have to do now."

"Yes, I can do this," she said, locking eyes with me.

"Okay."

"I never hated anyone in my life, David," she continued. "But when he went after you...I *wanted* to kill him."

I waited a beat. "Well, I guess you had no choice. I'm your guidebook."

It was Ariyl's turn to look insulted. Then belatedly, she got the reference. "Yeah," she nodded, wryly. "That must have been it."

I stretched, and pushed my feet into the sand, and my toe hit something pointy. Something that now poked out of the sand. It glittered. I picked it up, and my jaw fell open.

"Aw, no. No. I do not believe it."

It was pure, soft gold, worn down by centuries of waves, until its body was a smooth stick figure and its bent horns look more like floppy ears. Miraculously, parts of the Linear-A inscription were still legible.

"The Minotaur?" gasped Ariyl.

"After a thousand years in the sea. Now he looks more like Goofy."

Ariyl took it and playfully made it hop around. "Uh-*huh!*

Gawrsh, Mickey!" She did a perfect impression of Pinto Colvig—the one and only, original Goofy.

I gaped at her in wonderment. "You know *Goofy?*"

"Sure. Where I come from, kids still watch cartoons."

I found that incredibly moving.

"Finally, something we have in common."

Ariyl's face was just close enough to mine that it was starting to go out of focus. If I'd had my glasses, they would have fogged up. There was an awkward pause. Ariyl seemed to be waiting for me to say more. What could I say? How about the truth?

"Ariyl, I didn't tell you everything before. I think you should know I have a fiancée."

"That's like a girlfriend, right?"

"We're engaged to be married."

"Wow. You mean she'd be your permanent girlfriend?"

"People don't get married much in your world, do they?"

"No. Forever is a long time. So, will she come on your digs?"

"God, no," I snorted. "She hates archaeology."

"You going to move where she is?"

"What would I do in Washington?"

"Washington? This is the one who was dumping you?"

"When did I say that? She was never dumping me!"

"Don't tell me, you're the one who described the relationship." Suddenly, she moved in close to me: "Quick—what's her name?" Ariyl's scent filled my nostrils, jamming my synapses. My tongue didn't work. Ariyl leaned closer, until she was pressing against me. "Don't think, just say it!"

"It's Myra. *Moira!*"

"Uh-huh." She sat back and appraised me. "So, what *are* you two going to do together? Have kids?"

"Eventually. I mean, we're both kind of busy right now, but naturally, when the time comes..." Suddenly, I was angry again, but not at Ariyl this time. At myself.

"Who am I kidding? We're not going to have kids. I don't want to marry her."

As insane as it was, as hopeless and doomed as a relationship had to be between mortal and immortal, human and superhuman...now there could be only one woman for me.

But how could I say that? I'd sound like an idiot.

After a pause, Ariyl stood up and brushed herself off.

"Well, I'm sorry about your Minotaur getting all effed up. I guess you're in a hurry to fix history. You know, get our worlds back. I mean, yours. And mine."

I took her hand, and gently tugged her back down, beside me on the blanket.

"Tomorrow. The world can wait."

"Really?" She lifted an eyebrow, dubious.

"We can make up for lost time."

"You're not mad at me about messing up your treasure?"

"Are you kidding?" I held up the Minotaur...and chucked it as far as I could, back into the sea. Then I gazed into those purple eyes. "Look what I found."

I kissed Ariyl. She looked at me for a long moment.

"You know, where I come from, the woman is really supposed to make the first move."

"So make it."

She kissed me back. And then some.

And if you skipped the previous thirty chapters to see how this book was going to end, you didn't miss a thing.

It was all about baseball.

ABOUT THE AUTHOR

DOUG MOLITOR is a TV comedy writer and novelist whose books include the Time Amazon series: *Memoirs of a Time Traveler, Confessions of a Time Traveler, Revelations of a Time Traveler* and *Chronicles of a Time Traveler*; and two Full Moon Fever novels, *Monster, He Wrote* and *Pure Silver*.

He wrote TV comedies like *Sledge Hammer!, Lohman & Barkley, You Can't Take It With You* and *Police Academy*, sci-fi/fantasy/adventure series like *Sliders, Mission: Genesis, Adventure Inc., Young Hercules, F/X* and the western spoof *Lucky Luke*.

In animation, he co-wrote the feature *SpacePOP*, and has been the writer for 200 episodes of such series as *X-Men, Bill & Ted's Excellent Adventures, The Future Is Wild, The Wizard of Oz, Happily Ever After, Sinbad, 1001 Nights, Where on Earth is Carmen Sandiego?* and *Sabrina*.

His 2008 election spoof, with Obama and Hillary singing "Anything You Can Do I Can Do Better" reached 2.5 million hits on YouTube. *Doug's Dozen* web series ran three years on FunnyOrDie with "12 Reasons the GOP Should Run Old Man Potter" rated #2 Political Video of All Time.

To be notified of Doug's next book, please send your email address to doug@dougsdozen.com

Connect with Doug Online:

Facebook: https://www.facebook.com/DougMolitorAuthor/

Twitter: http://www.twitter.com/DougMolitor

Webpage: dougsdozen.com/MemoirsofaTimeTraveler

ACKNOWLEDGMENTS

My gratitude for reading, notes, proofing, suggestions, kind words or invaluable advice: Larry Gelbart, Hal Kanter, Elayne Boosler, Ian Abrams, Jim Casaburi, Deirdre Molitor, Bob Elisberg, Graham Flashner, Gary Black, Phyllis Cannon, Michael Ray Brown, Courtney Flavin, Shelly Goldstein, Beth Szymkowski, Eric Heisserer, Lisa Kors, David Larmore, Mike Moberly, Dan Dobrin, Ron Zwang, Andrew Nordvall, Brenda Pontiff, Devon Schwartz, Robin Stein, Arthur Tiersky, Bob Sabaroff, Kelvin Wyles, Stel Pavlou, Jonathan Freund, Star Frohman, Lee Rose Emery, Phil Goldberg, Eric Estrin, Mel Sherer, Treva Silverman, Jacque Jones, Mae Woods, Bobby Logan, Peter Lefcourt.

Jonathan Prince, for the idea of the baseball. Erich Speckin, foremost forgery expert. Chris Patrich, advice on radiocarbon dating. Miriam Robbins Dexter and Xabier Mendiguren, for help with Euskara. Alexandre Brard, sommelier extraordinaire. David Kamp for his *Vogue* article on the possible fate of Orson Welles' workprint of *The Magnificent Ambersons*. Christiana Miller for advice in the e-book world. Book help from Larry Doyle, Elizabeth Cosin, Holly Sorensen and Alex Sokoloff.

Deepest thanks to Barry and Ellen, and Mickey Galef, and Mary and Richard Casaburi. Also Marty Rudoy, Glenn Camhi, Ian Abrams, Steve Chivers, Katherine Fugate, friends indeed.

And Sue and Deirdre, for enduring the journey to this book.

PREVIEW: CONFESSIONS OF A TIME TRAVELER

TIME AMAZON — BOOK 2

That night at Ford's Theater, I have every reason to believe that Ariyl Moro did not intend to kill John Wilkes Booth, much less unleash the insane events that followed. She was in a hurry, she doesn't quite know her own strength...and she definitely doesn't know history.

I had deliberately told the Time Crystal six A.M. on April 11th, to give myself a three-and-a-half-day head start on Ariyl. Suffice it to say, I did not anticipate spending almost all of that time in jail. My final successful escape attempt on the night of the fourteenth was a matter of pure luck, which was not the same as great luck.

As I ran down the dirt street, I saw a clock tower reading ten-fourteen. Thanks to the Crystal's default safeguards, I could not jump back to give myself more time or correct an error. I had to do this right on the first take.

A hundred yards up the dirt street, I spotted Ariyl at the arched entry of the big brick theater. I took off in her direction.

She was dressed like a western dancehall girl from some early Technicolor epic. It made her look vaguely of the period, but gaudy and wanton. She was pleading her case for entry with a tall, strapping

Army sergeant whose mustache grew right into his muttonchops, and who was blocking her way at the theater door.

The soldier had been born a century too soon to have seen the costuming in MGM musicals that her SmartFab outfit was apparently channeling. He plainly viewed as immodest those bared athletic arms and shoulders, and her eye-popping décolletage. That she had two inches on him also seemed to offend him.

Ariyl glanced to her left, and saw me running toward her. The soldier turned as guffaws erupted from the crowd within. Ariyl seized the opportunity—and the sergeant—lifting him into the air.

"Ariyl, no!" I yelled.

"Unhand me, you virago!" sputtered the sergeant.

That she did, flinging him backward across the lobby. He slammed against the far wall hard enough to split the paneling, and sank senseless to the floor. A big laugh erupted from inside the auditorium.

"Wait!" I called out, almost to the entrance.

Instead, Ariyl flew up the stairway, six steps at a time. I charged up those same stairs as rapidly as I could, but since she was far faster than me—or any other human before the twenty-second century—it was no surprise that she had vanished by the time I got to the second floor. I stuck my head inside the door to the balcony to get my bearings. I glimpsed an actress making her exit, leaving an actor alone onstage to deliver his comic monologue:

"Don't know the manners of good society, eh?" roared the player, to widespread chuckling. Then just above the right side of the stage, I saw the union flag draped as bunting across the fateful box—my eyes hadn't adjusted enough to the dark to see the president's shadowed face, but I knew it had to be him. I left the balcony and dashed down the right-hand corridor.

"Well, I guess I know enough to turn *you* inside out, old gal..." echoed the voice from the stage.

The door to the presidential box was ajar, and as I entered I realized Ariyl wasn't there—she must have gone to the wrong side of the theater. Standing to my left, so focused on his target that he didn't even notice me, was Civil War America's up-and-coming new stage star. Dark eyes shining in messianic victory, he was aiming his derringer at the base of the Great Emancipator's skull.

Read The Rest Of The Story In:
Confessions of a Time Traveler
Available Now

ALSO BY DOUG MOLITOR

Novels

Time Amazon Series

Memoirs of a Time Traveler

Confessions of a Time Traveler

Revelations of a Time Traveler

Chronicles of a Time Traveler

Full Moon Fever Series

Monster He Wrote

Pure Silver

Anthologies

Love and Other Distractions

Hell Comes to Hollywood II

To get information on new releases, sales or free books by Third Street Press authors, like Doug Molitor, sign up for our newsletter.

29585000R00173

Printed in Great Britain
by Amazon